W9-AZY-675

STEVEN SPIELBERG Presents

BACK TO THE FUTURE

A ROBERT ZEMECKIS Film

"BACK TO THE FUTURE"

Starring MICHAEL J. FOX   CHRISTOPHER LLOYD

LEA THOMPSON   CRISPIN GLOVER

Written by ROBERT ZEMECKIS & BOB GALE

Music by ALAN SILVESTRI

Produced by BOB GALE and NEIL CANTON

Executive Producers STEVEN SPIELBERG

KATHLEEN KENNEDY and

FRANK MARSHALL

Directed by ROBERT ZEMECKIS

 AMBLIN ENTERTAINMENT   Soundtrack on MCA Records and Cassettes   A UNIVERSAL Picture

© 1985 UNIVERSAL CITY STUDIOS, INC.

ATHENS REGIONAL LIBRARY
ATHENS, GEORGIA

PB485   92

A novel by George Gipe
Based on a screenplay by
Robert Zemeckis and Bob Gale

279122

ⒷⒶ®
BERKLEY BOOKS, NEW YORK

Athens Regional Library
Athens, Georgia

BACK TO THE FUTURE

A Berkley Book/published by arrangement with
MCA Publishing Rights, a Division of MCA, Inc.

PRINTING HISTORY
Berkley edition/July 1985

Copyright © 1985 by MCA Publishing Rights,
a Division of MCA, Inc.
All rights reserved.
This book may not be reproduced in whole or in part,
by mimeograph or any other means, without permission.
For information address: MCA Publishing Rights,
a Division of MCA, Inc.
100 Universal City Plaza,
Universal City, California 91608.

ISBN: 0-425-08205-9

A BERKLEY BOOK ® TM 757,375
Berkley Books are published by The Berkley Publishing Group,
200 Madison Avenue, New York, New York 10016.
The name "BERKLEY" and the stylized "B" with design are
trademarks belonging to Berkley Publishing Corporation.
PRINTED IN THE UNITED STATES OF AMERICA

BACK TO THE FUTURE

A Berkley Book / published by arrangement with
MCA Publishing Rights, a Division of MCA, Inc.

PRINTING HISTORY
Berkley edition / July 1985

Copyright © 1985 by MCA Publishing Rights,
a Division of MCA, Inc.
All rights reserved.
This book may not be reproduced in whole or in part,
by mimeograph or any other means, without permission.
For information address: MCA Publishing Rights,
a Division of MCA, Inc.
100 Universal City Plaza,
Universal City, California 91608

ISBN: 0-425-08205-X

A BERKLEY BOOK ® TM 757,375
Berkley Books are published by The Berkley Publishing Group,
200 Madison Avenue, New York, New York 10016
The name "BERKLEY" and the stylized "B" with design are
trademarks belonging to Berkley Publishing Corporation.
PRINTED IN THE UNITED STATES OF AMERICA.

•Chapter One•

Here, in the living room of a peaceful house in the suburbs, a typical family sits quietly. Dad reads the evening paper, unaware that disaster is about to strike. Mom cleans the dinner dishes, oblivious to the fact that in a few seconds their world will be reduced to a whirlwind of splinters and atomized debris. The children are in their rooms, doing their homework, little knowing that only a few moments of life are left to them, that they will never have to worry about homework again. The mightiest force ever created by man is about to be unleashed on them and there is nothing on earth they can do about it...

Five... four... three... two... one...

A second later, there was a flash of white and the unnamed family were enveloped in a surge of power that tore their tiny frames to pieces, bending them curiously out of shape before separating bodies from heads, arms from torsos, legs from abdomens. The solid-looking house simply

1

crumpled into thin shreds of pulp and instantly ignited into a raveling avalanche of flame. A wind-tunnel effect then whisked the body parts and wreckage of furniture and plaster into a horrible whirling mass that was sucked into the tortured atmosphere. A long silent moment followed, the noise of the blast diminishing to a soft echo evoking the end of life on the planet.

The class was not impressed by the violent display and aftermath. At least there were no visible signs of amazement, horror, or even acute involvement.

Nevertheless, the announcer—probably long since gone to his own last resting place—continued his narration of the film on atomic power, circa 1955.

You have just seen how this mighty force can utterly destroy a society unprepared for its use. For this reason, some have protested the utilization of any form of atomic power. But it is too late to go back now. The potential for good of this force outweighs its potential for evil. A vital source of energy that may someday replace that created by coal or even conventional electrical power . . .

Most of the class listened to the illustrated lecture with only one ear. It was late in the day, much too late to pay close attention, and they had all seen the film before. Some thought of other things: a few drew pictures on the covers of their books in the semidarkness.

One student, the most daring and enterprising of the class, listened to stereo rock music. His eyes were nearly closed and his limbs had to struggle to remain still rather than follow along with the beat, but he gladly accepted this limitation as his lips quietly formed the words of the song.

Got to have your love . . .

Scientists predict that by the year 2000, at least half the homes in America will be run by atomic power . . .

Got to have you in my arms . . . Need to hold you . . .

There'll be atomic cars with an engine the size of an

acorn. Ships with nuclear dynamos will be able to travel without refueling for indefinite periods, perhaps as long as a year. Finally, the idea that giant rocket ships powered by atomic fuel, going to the moon and even farther, will become a reality rather than science fiction.

Give me one more chance . . . Won't you please get up and dance?

This is our opportunity. The chance of a lifetime . . .

Give me one more chance . . .

Let us not fail . . .

Let's have one more dance . . .

The closing music of the film ended, followed by popping noises from the projector and then a soft solo baritone voice.

"Let's have one more dance . . ."

Twenty heads swiveled in the direction of the singer. Unfortunately, one of them was that of Mr. Arky, the social studies teacher. His sense of direction told him immediately that the singer was Marty McFly, but his decided myopia veiled certain specifics. For one thing, he didn't see Marty deftly remove the headphones from his ears and return them to the hollow book, which also contained a tiny but powerful Walkman cassette player. Nor did Mr. Arky see the sly smile Marty exchanged with Jennifer Parker, the attractive 17-year-old who sat next to him.

"What was that, McFly?" Mr. Arky challenged.

"Nothing, sir. I was just saying I hope we all have one more dance."

"Indeed."

For a long moment, Mr. Arky surveyed the young man, scanning his features for signs of arrogance or rebellion that he could convert to a reason for punishment. Singing in class was technically sufficient, but even Mr. Arky felt that a single line could be excused. *If* that had been all. He fixed young McFly with his most intimidating gaze, hoping to panic him into either a confession or further punishable arrogance. Instead, the infuriatingly good-looking face framed by medium-length brown hair simply stared back. After a moment of indecision, Mr. Arky backed away from the confrontation as gracefully as he could.

"Now, as you all saw in that film," he intoned, "the attitudes about nuclear energy were quite a bit different in those days . . . You also—"

He was interrupted by the heavy rustling sound that always preceded an announcement over the school's antiquated public address system.

"Marty McFly, please come to the office," the PA voice mumbled, barely above the threshold of intelligibility. "You have an emergency telephone call. Marty McFly."

"Must be my agent," Marty murmured to Jennifer and the others within earshot.

He was wise enough to remain in his seat until a reluctant motion of Mr. Arky's hand released him. Then, gathering up his books, he walked quickly out of the room.

In the nearly deserted hallway between classes, his mood vacillated from the joy of being dismissed early from Arky's postfilm debriefing and concern that there really was an "emergency." What could it be? An accident or death in the family? At 17, his life so far had been serene; he therefore had no premonition of disaster. In addition, being a genial and optimistic person, he was not disposed to consider life darkly. Then, nearing the office, his mind clutched at the worst possible calamity this particular day could offer— cancellation of his band's audition!

"No," he said aloud. "Don't let it be that!"

Suddenly he found that his steps had taken on a new urgency, that he was nearly running.

The band was everything. At least for the moment it was his chance to be somebody different from everyone else. It was his opportunity to excell, impress, win friends and influence people. He knew he had talent, that the possibility existed of his becoming a rock star. Yet there was something deeper than that, a feeling of freedom when he was jamming with the group. At those times when they were really going well, he experienced the excitement of doing something new, of courting disaster and somehow coming away not only unscathed but also glorified. It was an out-of-body experience, bringing with it a sense of weightlessness, a feeling that no world existed outside the sphere reached by his music.

Jennifer was terrific, of course. He was quite taken by her, even felt that he "loved" her in the most adult sense. She was beautiful and fun to be around and she loved his music. Yet somehow she was not quite as important to Marty as the musical experience. Perhaps in time she would grow to be vastly more valuable to him, but for the moment Jennifer was of this world and his music was of the next.

The school office was quiet, populated only by the usual mousy staff and one student who sat hunched in a corner of the waiting room. Nevertheless, the secretaries went about their business very slowly and deliberately for more than a minute before one of them looked up enough for Marty to get her attention.

"Emergency call for me," he said.

The chubby woman in her fifties, whose name he had never learned, motioned for Marty to come into the office area and use the phone on her desk. Then with studied politeness she moved to a faraway desk so that he could speak and listen with greater privacy.

Such was not the case with Gerald Strickland, the school disciplinarian who took his job as seriously as any prison warden. Five minutes ago, he had taken the so-called "emergency" call himself. Phony, he had thought at the time. The breathlessness and urgency were there in the man's voice on the other end of the line but there was something that struck him as decidedly fake. Strickland considered himself a student of human nature, a master of detecting the deceitful maneuver. Though over sixty and nearing the end of his long career in education, he relished each day's mental combat with the selfish young men and women who regarded him as nothing but an evil obstacle to their willfulness. Strickland knew they laughed at him behind his back, chuckled at his wearing a bow tie every day, and considered him a tyrant. But, by God, they didn't laugh when he was looking at them. No smart remarks emanated from their lips when he interrogated them. They knew he had the power to make their lives temporarily miserable and they respected him for this.

Now, timing his motions with Marty McFly, whom he could see across the room through his half-open door, Strickland picked up the receiver of his telephone at the same time as the young man.

"Hello," he heard Marty say a bit nervously.

"Marty, it's me," the other voice said.

"Doc!"

Strickland experienced a momentary pang of doubt. Doc? Was it possible the caller was actually a physician about to inform McFly of some genuine emergency? If such was the case, he would not only be deprived of the opportunity to confront and punish the young man; it would be a severe setback to his own confidence in his ability to combat deceitfulness. The pulse of anxiety passed as quickly as it came, however, the relaxation caused by the casualness in McFly's tone. How many teenagers call bona fide adult physicians "Doc"? No, it was too familiar. Doc, whoever he was, was a personal friend. Strickland, the moral bloodhound, was on the right track after all.

"I told you never to call me here," Marty continued. "I'm in school."

"I know," the man called Doc replied. "I had to get in touch with you."

"Why? What's so important?"

"You'll see. Listen, can you meet me at Peabody's Farm around 1:15?"

"Peabody's Farm? Where's that?"

"I'm sorry," Doc amended. "I mean Twin Pines Mall. I still think of it as Peabody's Farm, but I guess that was before your time."

Marty looked up at the large clock on the wall.

"But it's after 1:15 already," he replied.

"I mean 1:15 in the morning."

"Tomorrow morning? About ten hours from now?"

"Yeah."

Gerald Strickland smiled. Whatever the "emergency," it was obviously something that could have waited until the young man was out of class, school, and had arrived home. He had seen through the sham after all and he experienced a surge of pride in his continuing ability to outwit those nearly fifty years younger.

"Let me get this straight," Marty said into the phone. "You want me to meet you at Twin Pines Mall at 1:15 tomorrow morning?"

"Right. I've made a major breakthrough and I'll need your assistance."

"Can't you tell me now?" Marty asked.

Gerald Strickland found himself nodding in response. Yes, he thought, do explain more. Whatever it was sounded definitely shady and perhaps illegal. Most students are notoriously lazy, not at all likely to be awake at such an early hour. What could they be engaged in? He licked his lips, fascinated at the possibilities in this telephone call. It had made his otherwise dreary day.

But the one known as Doc was obviously a cagey customer.

Refusing to yield more information, either to McFly or Strickland, he said simply: "Look, I'll give you all the details at the appropriate time."

"O.K.," Marty replied.

"Oh, and Marty," Doc continued. "Good luck on your gig this afternoon."

"How did you know about that?" Marty asked.

But there was only a click and silence at the end of the wire.

Gig, Strickland repeated inwardly. He had heard the word used before, of course. It usually referred to something musical, but he had heard it used less definitely. Perhaps whatever Marty McFly was involved in was shady enough to be mentioned elliptically. But no matter. The gig, innocent or evil, would not be attended by McFly this afternoon.

With that, Gerald Strickland placed his receiver down and started out of the office. He reached Marty just as he was about to push through the swinging door separating the inner office from the waiting area.

"Just a minute," Strickland said.

Marty stopped, looked at the older man with a blank expression.

"Are you finished with your emergency call?" Strickland asked, a slight smile playing at the ends of his thin lips.

"Yessir."

"And is everyone in your family well?"

Marty nodded.

"Then may I ask what the emergency was?"

"It's too complicated to explain," Marty began, trying to dredge up some confidence.

"I have time," Strickland replied curtly.

Marty swallowed and then plunged ahead. "There's an aunt in Wisconsin," he said. "And an uncle. They're both crippled. They were in a car accident about ten years. Anyway, she's going into the hospital tomorrow for another operation and they asked me—"

"Bull droppings," Strickland interrupted.

"Sir?"

"I said, bull droppings. There's no crippled aunt and uncle in Wisconsin. That was a personal call, McFly. You know students are to use the school phone only for emergencies."

"Well, this was an emergency," Marty shrugged. "Sort of."

"I don't think so, McFly."

"Well, maybe not to me, but it was an emergency to the person who called me."

"It's all the same. It's study hall for you."

"But why?" Marty challenged. "How can I help it if somebody says it's an emergency and it's not? Maybe you should send them to study hall. Anyway, how do you know it wasn't an emergency?"

"Because I was on the extension in my office and heard the entire conversation."

Marty felt his ears starting to burn. "But that's wiretapping," he said angrily. "That's against the law."

"For your information, McFly," Strickland returned. "It's not wiretapping. It's eavesdropping. But it wouldn't matter. You're in school, and here I'm the law. Whoever called you with a nonemergency call did you a great disservice. When you've come out of study hall, you can tell *Doc* he's no friend."

Marty stared. Inspired by the confrontation, Strickland had a sudden flash of intuition.

"That wouldn't be Doc Brown, would it?" he asked.

McFly's silence told him he had successfully identified the caller—Doc Brown, the town eccentric, a man who in Strickland's estimation was simply no good, a child who never grew up.

"Let me give you a nickel's worth of free advice," he said. "That Doc Brown is trouble. A real nut case. Perhaps even dangerous."

"To you, maybe," Marty replied loyally. "I don't see it that way."

"Then you're not only dim-witted, McFly. You've got a severe attitude problem. You're a slacker. You've got aptitude but you don't apply yourself." Realizing that he hadn't quite gotten to the young man, Strickland then applied the crusher. "As a matter of fact," he rasped, "in a lot of ways you remind me of your father. He was a slacker, too."

Marty blanched, for Strickland had struck the one nerve he was unable to protect. He simply did not enjoy being compared to his father, especially when the person doing so put them in the same category. If Strickland had been a contemporary, Marty would have thrown back an angry retort. That, of course, was impossible under the present circumstances, so he merely looked away.

"Excuse me," he said. "I'm late for class."

He started to take a step toward the door, but Strickland's hand shot out quickly.

"I didn't excuse you, McFly," he said sharply, grabbing Marty's elbow.

The sudden motion caused Marty to lose control of his books, two of which started to slide down his leg. Raising his knee, Marty succeeded only in knocking the others loose. A split second later, everything hit the floor, including the hollowed-out book containing his Walkman stereo. As luck would have it, the illicit unit slid tantalizingly across the waxed tile in slow motion, coming to rest in the far corner of the waiting area.

Strickland regarded it with narrowed eyes. Too late, Marty started gathering up his books, quickly placing his body between Strickland and the Walkman.

"You know the rules," the older man smiled. "No radios in school. That means detention for one week."

Marty gulped. He started to protest, then accepted the inevitable. "Yessir," he muttered.

"Starting today," Strickland continued.

"Today?" Marty gasped. "But I can't! Me and my band have an audition for the YMCA dance, Mr. Strickland. I have to be there at four o'clock."

One might as well have tried begging a shark to seek food elsewhere. Through rheumy eyes spiked with malicious glee, Strickland stared unflinchingly at his victim. Then, with a curt wave of his hand, he began to turn away.

"An audition, huh?" he said. "Well, McFly, it looks like you just blew it."

The clock read 3:42.

Marty was beginning to wonder if he had somehow offended a local deity governing the fates of Hill Valley high school students. It was all too pat to be impersonal—the calculated eavesdropping of Mr. Strickland, bad luck in dropping the Walkman stereo, and now this. After careful consideration, he had decided to skip detention, pleading tomorrow that there had been a misunderstanding as to when the week's punishment was to begin. That, however, was before he peeked into the classroom to see what teacher had charge of the detention session.

It was none other than Mr. Strickland himself.

"Damn!" Marty hissed.

There was no way of convincing *him* that a misunderstanding existed. He didn't even have time to debate the pros and cons of simply splitting and taking the consequences. No sooner had he spotted Strickland than the piercing eyes honed in on him like enemy radar.

"Come in, McFly," Strickland ordered.

Head down, Marty walked into the room. It was a typical classroom in the school which had been built at the end of the Great Depression. Green blackboards had replaced the old black types and the walls, desks and ceiling had been repainted. A new sprinkler system had been added, too, but the place still had a dreariness that Marty found almost terminally depressing. The expressions on the faces of the ten other students enduring punishment indicated that they regarded the place with equal misery. All stared glumly ahead or down at the desk top in front of them. One of the victims, a thin-faced kid named Weeze, had a skateboard tucked beneath his books, almost as if he expected Mr. Strickland to confiscate or destroy it.

His fear, if he harbored it, was not mere fancy. At the front of the room stood Strickland, ten Walkman units lined neatly on the desk next to him. Those who had been through it before knew what was about to happen next, a fact which did not make it much easier.

"Now . . ." Strickland smiled sadistically, "we are going to see how we deal with those who violate our 'no Walkman' rule."

Gently, almost reverentially, he lifted one of the units and placed it in the jaws of a woodworking vise mounted on the corner of the desk. He then began tightening the jaws until the set broke in half, the sound approximating that of bones breaking. As bits of plastic and mangled parts trickled to the floor, one student winced as if the pain were being inflicted on his own body. Strickland, well aware of which unit belonged to each student, smiled wickedly at the horrified young man.

"Now then, Stevenson," he said. "You may come up here and claim your stereo."

Stevenson got up and knelt down to pick up the shattered remains of his set.

With gleeful deliberation, Strickland continued the crunching orgy. Marty's set was fourth in line for execution but he was more concerned about the passing time than the fate of his Walkman. He could still make it to the audition if Strickland released them early.

Fat chance, he thought. Then, after a moment of black despair, he forced his mind to think. There must be a way out, a scheme clever enough to create panic or some legitimate emergency. His eyes scanned the room. Only a sprinkler system offered possibilities, but he couldn't formulate a workable plan of attack.

"This is yours, isn't it, McFly?" Strickland interrupted Marty's thoughts. "Number three?"

"Four," Marty said evenly. He was determined not to let the creep see how much he hated to lose his Walkman.

With a brisk smile, Strickland dispatched the next set and then reached for Marty's stereo with something like renewed passion. The jaws of the vise pressed in, causing a low scraping sound, almost as if the set were crying out in pain. Then, with a particularly loud snap, the Walkman's splintered remains shot out of the vise in all directions. Momentary panic crossed Strickland's features as shards of plastic flew past his eyes and head.

"It's all yours, McFly," Strickland said, quickly regaining his composure.

Marty got up to collect the broken pieces of his set. As he did so, the hint of a smile played around his lips, for he had conceived a daring plan that was at least worth a shot. He switched the shattered bits of plastic to one hand, then made a detour on the way back to his seat. Passing by the Carousel slide projector on a side table, he paused long enough to reach out and surreptitiously slide the lens into his pocket. Busily involved in the execution of the next Walkman, Strickland did not notice Marty's quick movement.

Returning to his seat, Marty reached into the pencil pouch of his loose-leaf binder, withdrawing a rubber band and book of matches. He then reached into his pocket, unwrapped a stick of gum and began to chew. His chewing, however, was not that of a person seeking pleasure; rather, it resembled a chore that had to be accomplished as quickly as possible.

A minute later, taking the gum from his mouth, he opened the matchbook cover and spread the soft sticky gum on the back side like a tiny pancake. Next he "loaded" the cover into the rubber band and waited. He had always been a deft shot with rubber band–launched objects but never had so much depended on his accuracy as the shot he planned now. Above him, perhaps a dozen feet away, was the smoke detector connected with the sprinkling system. It was small, hardly an inviting target, but Marty knew he had to try. If he was successful, phase one of his two-part plan would be accomplished. If he missed . . . well, at least he had made an effort. If Strickland saw him, he could probably expect to remain in detention until well past Easter vacation.

The heck with it, he thought. I've gotta gamble.

He waited patiently until Strickland put the screws to the tenth and final Walkman. Just as it shattered, Marty aimed at the valve, pulled the rubber band back as far as it would go, and let fly.

Like a rocket, the matchbook raced up to the ceiling and hung there, the gum making a tenuous connection.

A miracle, Marty thought.

Phase Two was rather less dramatic but nevertheless contained a great potential for being caught. Withdrawing the Carousel projector lens from his pocket, Marty adjusted it so that the bright slanting rays of the afternoon sun struck it and were refracted onto the matchbook stuck to the ceiling. Glancing upward even as he pretended to study from the book on his desk, he was amazed at how well the plan had worked so far. A sharp pin prick of white was focused on the matchbook. If only the sun would hurry up and do its thing!

The clock now read 3:52. He would be late for the audition but by only a few minutes. His hand was getting tired, holding the lens in an unmoving position, but he dared not rest even a second. Did he see a wisp of smoke? He squinted, decided it was his imagination.

Then he saw something that definitely was not imaginary. Getting up, Mr. Strickland strode to the back of the room and began pulling down the blinds.

"No!" Marty nearly shouted.

He twisted his head almost completely around, noting that the three rear rows of the room were now in semidarkness as a result of Strickland's action. As he watched, the next three rows fell beneath the dark cloud.

But now there was definitely a wisp of smoke slinking downward from the matchbook.

"Come on, come on," Marty whispered. "Burn, you sucker, burn."

A couple boys near him had already discovered what was going on. They watched in awe and amusement as the smoke grew more violent, a half circle of red crawling up the edge of the matchbook cover toward the double row of matches.

With a snap, Strickland released the next-to-last set of blinds.

"Poof!"

Just as the last strip of bright sunlight disappeared from the classroom, a mini-explosion of flame from the matchbook started a chain reaction. Smoke curling around the ceiling detector immediately triggered the sirens and sprinkler system. Panic, or something very close to it, followed.

"Fire!" somebody yelled.

"Let's get outa here!"

"Stop! Wait!" Mr. Strickland's voice shouted above the din. "We must file out in an orderly fashion!"

He raced toward the front of the classroom as fast as he could, arms raised above his head. But heavier shoulders and faster, more muscular bodies rushed past, sending him spinning sideways against the wall.

"Wait!" he shouted again, just as a sprinkler valve went into action directly above his head, dousing him with cold water. The rest of his words were indistinguishable.

Marty, more prepared for the confusion than anyone else, was halfway down the hall by that time. As soon as the alarm sounded and the rain began to fall, he leaped to his feet and grabbed the skateboard belonging to Weeze.

"Let me borrow this," he shouted back over his shoulder at the bewildered student. "I'll bring it back tomorrow."

Less than a minute later, he was skateboarding down the front steps of the high school, gliding in a wide arc onto the main drag of wide sidewalk bounding Town Square. Glancing nervously to his right, he passed the Hill Valley Bank's time and temperature board just as it changed from 3:57 to 3:58. A man making a transaction at the Versateller leaped to avoid the oncoming figure, tripping himself and falling backwards in the process. Then it was Marty's turn to gasp, a car bearing down on him so rapidly he had to pirouette like a ballerina to maintain his balance. For a half block after that, he raced out of control, his arms flailing and body tipping to 45-degree angles until he slowly managed to right himself.

Just ahead, the YMCA building beckoned. Leaning forward to gain even more speed, Marty pivoted at the steps, grabbed the skateboard and ran into the building.

His group, known as the Pinheads, was already set up. Nearby, Jennifer also waited, nervously checking her watch. As he raced onto the stage, she let out a noisy sigh of relief and Marty winked at her.

A fat man, also glancing meaningfully at his watch, stared intently at Marty.

"Are you ready?" he asked coldly.

Marty nodded. His guitar, amp and microphone were already set up for him. Sitting quickly, Marty took a deep breath and tuned up in the shortest amount of time possible. Then, grasping the microphone, he looked toward the dance committee and spoke with a voice that rang with confidence.

"All right," he said. "We're the Pinheads, and we're gonna rock 'n' roll!"

The band kicked into a hot number, Marty's fingers dancing across the strings and frets in a complicated lead line. Keyboard, bass and drums followed, embellished his thematic figures, hit the rhythm harder, preparing for the transition into Marty's first variation.

"Fine," a metallic voice called out. "That's enough. Thank you."

Marty could hardly believe his ears. In fact, he continued to play even as the rest of the Pinhead sound dribbled off into confused silence.

"Thank you," the fat man repeated. "May we hear the next group, please?"

Marty came down off the stage in a daze. Had he gone through an afternoon of hell for *this?*

"What happened?" he asked Jennifer.

"I don't know," she muttered. "You sounded great. Maybe they're looking for something else. Something more like Lawrence Welk."

Ten minutes later, as they walked home, he was still in a state of shock. Jennifer put her hand on his arm. "Marty," she said comfortingly. "One rejection isn't the end of the world. You're good and you'll succeed one day."

"I don't know," he murmured. "Maybe I'm just not cut out for music."

"Sure you are," she persisted. "You're really good and so are the rest of the guys. The audition tape you made is really great."

She handed him the cassette he had lent her a few days before. "Promise me you'll send it to the record company before you decide to quit."

"But what if they hate it?" Marty sighed. "What if they say, 'Get outa here, kid, you got no future'? Why should I put myself through all that anxiety?"

Jennifer didn't answer.

"Jeez," Marty said finally. "I'm starting to sound like my old man now."

Jennifer looked at him quizzically.

"He's kind of a pushover," Marty explained. "No guts. People are always using him."

"Well, they say all our emotional anxieties come directly from our parents," she smiled. The words coming out of her mouth sounded a bit strange even to her. Where had she heard the phrase? Sociology class? *People* magazine? She wasn't sure, but it sounded plausible.

"In that case, you can kiss me off right now," Marty muttered.

"I'll just kiss you instead," she said, reaching up to peck his cheek.

They walked hand-in-hand for a while. "Is your father really that bad?" Jennifer asked finally.

Marty shrugged. "I think deep down inside he means well," he said. "But the man just can't get it together."

They had reached Town Square, and the presence of the big Toyota dealership, with its gleaming recessed windows and spotless showroom, made Jennifer think of happier things. "Well, at least your dad's letting you borrow the car tomorrow night," she smiled. "That's a major step in the direction of getting it together."

Marty nodded.

They stopped at the edge of the glass and looked inside at the salesmen circling potential customers like lions readying their attack on smaller beasts. "How come there are no used car saleswomen?" Marty asked. "I've never seen a woman selling cars, have you?"

Jennifer shook her head. "Maybe women can't lie as well as men," she offered.

Marty laughed, turned his gaze to a tricked-out four-by-four pickup truck in the showroom.

"Hey, check out that four-by-four," he said. "Wouldn't it be great to take that up to the lake tomorrow night? We could put our sleeping bags in the back . . . make out under the stars."

"Mmmm," Jennifer replied.

"Someday, Jennifer, someday," Marty said.

Looking at her smooth profile and even white teeth was starting to make him feel better. Perhaps music wasn't everything after all.

"What about your mother?" Jennifer asked as they turned away from the window and continued walking. "Does she know you and I are—"

"Are you kidding? She thinks I'm going camping with the guys."

"Would she mind if she knew the truth?"

"Yeah," Marty replied. "If she found out I was going camping with you, she'd freak."

"I'm that bad, huh?"

"It's not you. It's a moral thing. She'd give me the standard lecture about how she never behaved that way when she was in high school. She must have been a real goody-two-shoes, I'll bet."

"Most people then were, weren't they? I mean, that was way back in the 1950s, before the pill or rock 'n' roll or a lot of things that were really good."

Marty nodded. "Yeah, I guess it wasn't easy, growing up in those primitive days."

They were opposite the former Courthouse Building of Town Square, which had seen better days. The 1950s, in fact, had been the heyday of this part of town. Then people gathered at Town Square to socialize, do business, simply pass the time of day or evening. There had been a Texaco station here then, a soda shop, florist, the Essex movie house, a record store, a realtor's office, women's dress shop, Studebaker dealer, barber's, an Ask Mr. Foster travel agency, stationery store, Western Auto appliance center and numerous other small businesses. Now nearly all were gone, victims of progress and lack of adequate parking. Many of the building facades were boarded up, covered with peeling notices and signs. One set of election posters read: RE-ELECT MAYOR "GOLDIE" WILSON. HONESTY, DECENCY, INTEGRITY. The picture beneath the inspiring words showed the face of a black man, about fifty years old with a gold front tooth.

"This was where Mom used to hang out," Marty said. "There used to be a soda shop here."

"I guess you couldn't get in trouble there," Jennifer smiled. "Anyway, maybe she's just trying to keep you respectable."

"She's not doing a very good job, is she?" Marty laughed, sliding his arm behind her back.

"Terrible . . ."

"Wonderful . . ."

They were standing with their hips touching, about to kiss . . .

"Save the clock tower!" a grating voice suddenly ordered, causing them to jerk apart.

Simultaneously, a donation can was placed between the two teenagers. It rattled hollowly, as if there were only two or three lonely coins inside.

"Save the clock tower!" the voice repeated.

Jennifer and Marty turned to look at the person who had interrupted them. She was a middle-aged church-type woman with prematurely blue hair. Her upper lip, Marty noted with just a touch of revulsion, was covered with nearly enough fine hair to provide an aspiring young man with a decent mustache. Under her arm were dozens of printed flyers.

"Please make a donation to save the clock tower," the woman said, rattling the can again.

"Lady, can't you see I'm busy here?" Marty asked. Ordinarily, he would have been pleasant to the interloper, but the events of the day had worn his nerves to a frazzle.

The woman was not put off by his lack of interest, however. Stepping between the two youngsters, she addressed them with swiveling head.

"Mayor Wilson is sponsoring an initiative to save or repair that clock," she intoned, pointing to the stopped clock mounted high on the old courthouse tower. "We at the Hill Valley Preservation Society think it should be preserved exactly the way it is, as part of our history and heritage. Thirty years ago, lightning struck that clock tower and the clock hasn't run since. We at the Society feel it's a landmark of scientific importance, attesting to the power of the Almighty."

Marty took a deep breath, preparatory to interrupting her spiel, but apparently that was it. They had heard the complete speech.

"All right, lady," Marty said, relieved that they didn't have to listen to even more. "Here's all I have at the moment. A quarter. Is that O.K.?"

"We're delighted with anything," the woman smiled, revealing badly stained dentures. "A good cause can get by with nickels and dimes because it has the backing of the people. A bad cause, even if funded by millions from evil sources, is nevertheless bound to fail."

Marty nodded, started to leave with Jennifer.

"Don't forget to take a flyer," the woman urged. "It tells the whole story of the clock tower."

Marty took the flyer from her hand.

"And here's something for your friend," the woman continued, thrusting yet another flyer at him.

Something nearly snapped in Marty then. For a long

moment, he considered not only taking the proffered flyer but as many as he could carry, telling the woman he would distribute them at school. Then he would look for the nearest trash can and dump them. At the last moment, fortunately, he realized that the woman, though irritating, really meant no harm.

"Thanks," Marty said, taking the flyer and handing it to Jennifer.

With a curt smile, he grabbed his girlfriend's arm and guided her away from the crusader as fast as he could move without breaking into a run. A few moments later, they were safely around the corner.

"Now . . . where were we?" he said.

Jennifer snuggled closer to him, looked both ways and then turned her face upward toward his.

"Right about here . . ." she murmured.

They moved closer. Marty could smell her skin, feel her breath against his chin. Slowly he put his hand on her neck, just below the ear and bent to kiss her . . .

A car horn shattered the magic moment. Jennifer looked away from him and Marty saw annoyance in her eyes.

"That's my dad," she said.

"How did he find you here?" Marty asked.

"Just luck."

"The kind of luck I've been having all day."

"Nothing lasts forever, not even bad luck."

The horn honked again.

"I'll call you tonight," Marty promised.

"I'll be at my grandma's," she said.

"What's the number?"

"243-8480."

Marty repeated the number, got two numbers transposed.

"You should have saved one of those flyers," Jennifer said. Then, looking at her hand, she saw that it still clutched one of the propaganda pieces. Waving to her father to wait, she took out a pen and wrote something on the back of the paper and thrust it at Marty. Then she hopped in the car and left. Marty waved and watched her until the car was out of sight.

Only then did he look at the paper. On it was written the telephone number and the simple phrase: "I love you."

Marty smiled.

Folding the paper, he put it in his pocket and skateboarded down the street toward home.

•Chapter Two•

"If only I don't die of a heart attack or a stroke first," Dr. Emmett Brown muttered aloud.

He was close to seeing his dream become a reality. No doubt about that. One by one the scientific and physical obstacles had been eliminated. Was this to be "the day"?

"Don't count on it," he replied to himself. There was no use getting too high, he reasoned.

At sixty-five, he was one of the nation's most talented and most unheralded inventors. In fact, no one except Marty McFly even knew of his accomplishments, but that didn't matter. Soon all that would change. His lifetime of struggle, of being the recipient of ridicule, would suddenly turn golden.

He looked around his workshop, which was nothing more than a garage filled with the detritus and equipment that had been accumulated over a forty-year period. Some of that gear included a jet engine, piles of circuit boards, enough automobile parts to build at least two cars, a short-wave radio, Seeburg jukebox, workbench with welding equipment, the remnants of a robot, a working refrigerator, and dozens of clocks. Clocks were Doc Brown's favorite collector's item. He had everything from cuckoo clocks to digital models—and every one was in dead sync with the others.

The presence of so many timepieces was not accidental. Time was Doc Brown's latest, and perhaps final, dominating interest. During the 1950s, he had tried to uncover the secrets of the human mind via a variety of mind-reading devices. None had worked. A half-decade earlier, he had been smitten with the theory that all mammals spoke a common language. Some other schemes included the notion that gold could be mined by superheating the earth's surface, that each person's age was predetermined and could be revealed by studying the composition of their fingernails, and he published a paper which claimed that the sex of babies could be predicted before they were conceived. The fact that all of Doc Brown's work yielded nothing should have discouraged him but did not. Through the '50s, '60s, '70s, and into the '80s, he continued to experiment, earning perennial scorn as the crazy scientist of Hill Valley.

Now, on October 25, 1985, he was ready for fulfillment. He had worked out every element of his time-travel theory until it was perfect. By the end of the century, scientists and historians would be using his device to explore the future and past, and through this exploration, work to improve the present. His view of time as a dimension was summed up in the simple explanation he once gave to the editor of the Hill Valley newspaper. "I think of time as spherical and unending," he said. "Like the skin of an orange. A change in the texture at any point will be felt over the entire skin. The future affects the past and present, just as the past and present affect the future."

"But the past is over and done with," the editor replied. "How can it be affected?"

"That's just my point," Doc Brown had retorted. "The past isn't over and done with. It's still there. And once we can find a way to penetrate it, we'll be able to change things that may happen tomorrow."

The editor didn't buy it but he printed the interview anyway. Residents of Hill Valley either ignored the article or complained that valuable space had been wasted printing the ravings of a madman.

Such unfavorable publicity once hurt, but now that was all behind him. "If all goes well..." he murmured as he began to prepare for the evening's work.

The sentence remained unfinished. Whistling softly, he dressed slowly in a white radiation suit, slipped the hood over his head to test its feel, then took it off, pressing it flat against his back. Checking his image in a mirror, he ruffled his wild white hair even more, perhaps perversely adding to his own reputation as a wild eccentric. He then walked to the front of the garage, opened the rear doors of the oversized step-van on the side of which was lettered DR. E. BROWN ENTERPRISES—24-HOUR SCIENTIFIC SERVICE, and peered inside.

It was, of course, still there. Even in the sparse light of the garage, the sleek stainless steel DeLorean with its gull wings shone back at him like a giant Christmas tree ornament. How appropriate, he thought, that the vehicle which would propel mankind into the past and future should be such an extraordinarily beautiful piece of machinery. There was no doubt in his mind as he closed the doors.

"It will work," he said softly. "And I'll be famous."

All that remained was the final countdown check of minor items. Brown would handle that during the few hours before Marty arrived at the Twin Pines Mall and then, together, they would take a step as significant for mankind as the moon landing of 1969.

It was getting dark when Marty turned the last curve in front of his house, but he knew something was wrong long before that. Flashing lights are seldom harbingers of joy, except at Christmas, and that holiday was two months away. Through the trees blocking his home from view, he could see the flashers blinking yellow. Not the police, he thought. That would be blue and red. Yellow was the usual color of wreckers.

He was quite correct. Gliding onto the court, he could make out the tow truck poised like a giant praying mantis near the McFly driveway. In its jaws was the 1979 Plymouth Reliant, looking quite helpless with one set of wheels off the ground. As he drew closer, Marty saw that its front end was completely smashed, as if someone had driven it into a brick wall. Nearby stood Marty's father and Biff Tannen, watching in silence as the truck driver unhitched the damaged vehicle.

George McFly was forty-seven but seemed much older to Marty. An uninspired man who was generally afraid to take even the tiniest daring step, not having changed his haircut in over thirty years, he was dressed in an equally boring suit he had purchased four years before at Sears. The man standing next to him was a sharp contrast in both sartorial color and demeanor. Just a year older than George McFly, Biff Tannen stood with his potbelly leaning unashamedly over his trouser tops, an attitude that made his loud plaid suit, pinky rings and gold chains seem even more bizarre. Whereas George McFly was reticent, Biff was loud and obnoxious, the type of person who talks loudly in movie houses or yells epithets at players during sports events. He was, in short, an intimidating lout, and no one was more easily intimidated than his friend and associate George.

Now, as Marty approached on the skateboard, he heard the familiar tone of disgust in Biff's voice as he addressed his father.

"I can't believe you did this, McFly," Biff rasped. "I can't believe you loaned me your car without telling me it had a blind spot. I could have been killed."

Tell him good, Marty thought, tell him we'd all be better off if Biff Tannen was in traction.

George McFly, of course, could not stand up to Biff's assault. Instead he replied weakly: "Biff, I never noticed any blind spot before."

"What, are you blind, McFly? It's there! How else can you explain this?"

Tell him the driver was lousy, Marty thought. If only his father would stand up to him once!

George McFly looked at the ground and made no direct answer to the irrational question. "Can I assume that your insurance will pay for this?" he asked. It sounded more like begging.

"My insurance?" Biff returned hotly. "It's *your* car with *your* blind spot. Your insurance should pay for it. I want to know who's gonna pay for this."

He indicated his stained suit.

"I spilled beer all over it when that car hit me," Biff continued. "Who's gonna pay the cleaning bill? Tell me, that, McFly."

Marty couldn't stand it a minute longer. "Maybe the judge who hears you were drinking while driving will pay for it," he interjected.

Biff's eyes narrowed. "Tell your kid to keep outa this, McFly," he ordered.

George did not issue such an order but he might as well have done so. Pulling out his wallet, he extracted a twenty-dollar bill and handed it to Biff. "Will this cover it?" he asked meekly.

Biff snatched the bill out of George's fingers and cast a quick triumphant glare at Marty.

"It's a start," he said.

"It'll probably buy two of those suits," Marty shot back.

Biff flushed. "Shut up," he said.

Then, turning back to his primary target, he said to Marty's father: "Where are your reports?"

George McFly paled even more than his usual off-white fishy complexion. "Well, I haven't finished them yet," he apologized. "I figured that since they weren't really due till Monday . . ."

Biff stepped forward and tapped George's forehead with his fist, like someone rapping on a door. "Hello," he said. "Is anybody home in there? Think, McFly, think! I've gotta have time to get them retyped. If I turn in my reports in your handwriting, I'll get fired."

Marty was furious with his father. Tell him to do the reports himself, he thought.

Once again his father backed off. "O.K.," he said. "I'll finish them tonight and run them over first thing in the morning, if that's all right."

"Not too early," Biff muttered. "I sleep in on Saturdays."

Marty turned away. He honestly thought he was about to throw up. Not only was Biff's treatment of his father subhuman, but also he had just realized that, with the car wrecked, his date with Jennifer was out the window. It had been the worst of all possible days.

Biff Tannen wasn't through yet, however. As he turned to leave, he looked down at the ground.

"Oh, hey, McFly," he said matter-of-factly. "Your shoe's untied."

"Huh?" George said, falling for it by glancing down at his feet.

As he did so, Biff's hand flew up, hitting George in the

chin. A grating guffaw split the air, Biff Tannen having executed his idea of a terrific practical joke.

"Don't be so gullible, McFly!" he shouted. "Boy, you haven't learned a thing in thirty years."

George, pleading guilty to the charge with his silence, could only grin weakly.

Oblivious to the fact that Marty viewed him with disgust, Biff pointed to his sparkling new Cadillac nearby and winked. "Hiya, kid," he said, just as if there had been no bad words between them. "How do you like my new paint job?"

Marty shrugged.

A moment later, Biff and his newly painted car were heading down the road. George McFly started to walk into the house. Marty stepped in front of him.

Raising his hands, George stepped away. "I know what you're going to say, son, and you're right," he murmured. "You're absolutely right. But he happens to be my supervisor, and I'm afraid I'm just not very good at confrontations."

"Confrontations," Marty shot back, "you don't even practice self-defense."

George didn't answer.

"Dad, look at the car," Marty persisted. "Look what he did to the car. He nearly totaled it. And then he concocted some story about a blind spot. He blamed the wreck on you and you didn't say a thing!"

"Well, you can't argue with a person like that," George said feebly.

"Look at that car," Marty continued. "It's a mess. I was counting on using it tomorrow night. Do you have any idea how important this was to me, Dad? Do you have any idea at all?"

Not knowing that Marty was planning to take Jennifer away in the vehicle, it was not possible for George McFly to understand how much the trip truly meant to Marty.

"I'm sorry, son," he muttered. "All I can say is I'm very sorry."

For Marty that wasn't enough and the infuriating events of the day would not let him back off. "Dad, did it ever occur to you to say 'no' to people when they start pushing you around? Is that so hard?"

"Son, I know it's hard for you to understand," George said with maddening calmness, "but the fact is, I'm just not a fighter."

"Try it once, Dad," Marty challenged. "Just one time, say 'no.' N-O. 'No.' It won't hurt nearly as much as you think."

George shrugged.

I give up, Marty thought, I can't even get him to say "no" to the idea of saying "no."

George McFly turned away, finding it easier to look at the damaged front of his car than at Marty's accusing and disappointed eyes. He envied other men, macho types who taught their boys how to fight, encouraged them to be combative, stand up for their rights. These men invariably pushed their male offspring into organized sports, bragging when their boys won a big game, browbeating the lads when they took the final strike of the game with their bats on their shoulders. For his part, George McFly was secretly pleased when his sons Marty and Dave declined to take part in sports. At least he was off the emotional hook.

During his frequent moods of quiet self-analysis, George McFly managed to dissect his psyche, for he did worry about his own lack of grit. He thought it all went back to one occasion in grade school when he was accosted by the class bully. The bully had just punched his friend Billy Stockhausen and for a split second George was so angry he literally saw the red that everyone talks and writes about. Stepping up to the bully, he pulled his fist back—

And couldn't strike. The bully merely smirked and walked away. Since that moment thirty-five years ago, George had wondered what might have happened if he had followed through. His happiest fantasy was that his single punch would have sent the bully into oblivion. But even if the bully had hit back and he had learned the give-and-take of combat, might not that have been better than the cowardly limbo, never-take-a-chance attitude George had trapped himself in all these years?

He sighed. Why bother to relive that moment . . . Why bother to try explaining to Marty or anyone else why he was such a pushover? He could barely accept the most favorable rationalization himself.

Now, as if to underscore Marty's challenge of a moment before, a voice called to him from the window of the house next door. It was that of his neighbor Howard, a forty-year-old, potbellied, generally unpleasant character who, like Biff Tannen, spoke to George only when he needed something or wanted another person to berate.

His voice was less tinged with scorn at the moment, no doubt because he was looking for George's help.

"Hey, McFly!" he called down. "My kid's selling Girl Scout cookies. I told her you'd be good for a case."

"A case?" George replied. "What's a case?"

"What difference does it make?" Howard shot back belligerently. "Twelve. Twenty-four. Thirty-six. It's for a good cause, ain't it? Or do you want me to tell the kid you're a cheapskate?"

"It's just that—" George began, then hunched his shoulders helplessly. "Never mind. Sure. Tell her I'm good for a case, whatever it is."

Marty shook his head and went inside.

His sister, brother, and mother were already seated at the dinner table; none of them looked up when Marty entered and slumped into his chair. For once, Marty was glad they were so wrapped up in their own lives that they didn't think to ask how the musical audition had turned out. He didn't feel like explaining why he had lost or seeing their expressions of fake sympathy.

"Meat loaf again," he said flatly.

His criticism did not keep the jaws from working. Brother Dave, twenty-two, sat opposite him, wearing a Burger King uniform. He kept one eye on the clock and the other on his food, which he wolfed down in large sections, swallowing noisily like a half-starved animal. On Marty's left sat Linda, nineteen, who was cute in a kind of sleazy way, partly because she invariably wore too much eye shadow. Marty tried to remember when he had last seen her without either purple or green eyelids, and he finally gave up. On Marty's right was dear old Mom, who was once very attractive and bright. Now, at forty-seven, she was overweight, drank more than was good for her and had more food on her plate than anyone else. The fare, besides the inevitable meat loaf, included Kraft macaroni and cheese, Birds Eye mixed veggies, and French's instant mashed potatoes.

Dad, the last to be seated, turned the television to an old *Honeymooners* rerun and put papers instead of food in front of him. Marty noted angrily that he had already started doing the "homework" Biff Tannen had so ungraciously assigned him.

For a few minutes, Marty and Dave amused themselves and each other by reciting the *Honeymooners*' lines one beat ahead of the TV actors, a routine that finally got Mom's goat.

"All right," she said. "We know you've seen it a hundred times. But your father wants it on, O.K.? So let him enjoy it in peace."

Marty and Dave shrugged.

Silence reigned for a minute until Mom finally looked

at Marty, smiled, and said: "Well, Marty, how did the audition turn out?"

Marty exhaled wearily.

"We lost," he said simply.

Everyone tried to think of something to say, or at least everyone pretended to be thinking.

"It was probably fixed," Dave said at length, a superficial statement which surprisingly cheered Marty. That, in fact, was what he had been thinking since the sham contest was held.

"Could be," he shrugged.

"They probably knew going in who was gonna win," Dave nodded. "The rest was just window-dressing."

"Sour grapes," Linda said softly, not looking up from her dessert, which was Jell-O Instant chocolate pudding with a generic brand instant whipped topping.

"It's too bad," Mom sighed. "I think your group's very good. I just don't see how any other band could have been better."

Dad looked up from his homework. "Believe me, son," he dared to venture, "you're better off not having the aggravation of dealing with that YMCA dance."

"What aggravation?" Marty asked coldly.

"Well, you'd have to worry about getting all your equipment there—"

"We've done that lots of times already," Marty interjected. "It's no problem."

"You'd have to make contingency plans in case somebody got sick," his father continued.

"Nobody's ever been sick."

"All the more reason for somebody to be now," he went on. "Then you'd have to make sure you got your money, see that everybody got the right share, settling with the musicians' union . . ."

"Wow," Marty muttered. "You sure can find a lot of good reasons to do nothing."

It didn't slow down his father even a half-beat.

"What if you were so good other people wanted to hire you?" he continued. "Then you'd have to worry about scheduling your job around school."

"You're right, Dad. Maybe I'd better just take to my bed right away. The longer I stay alive, the more problems I'm going to have."

"Believe me, son, you're better off without all those headaches," his father concluded.

"He's right, Marty," Dave added sardonically, putting on his father. "If there's one thing you don't need, it's headaches."

Marty finally stopped arguing, even though quitting made him feel a little like his father.

Lorraine McFly turned her attention to Linda, who was finishing her pudding. "You didn't have to eat that, you know," she said. "We've got cake."

Linda raised her eyebrows. "What cake?" she asked.

Lorraine pointed to the three-layer cake on the kitchen counter. On the top was written WELCOME HOME UNCLE JOEY. Above the letters was a tiny black bird flying out of a barred window. It was hardly subtle, but Uncle Joey's situation wasn't a secret.

"It's looks like we'll have to eat this cake by ourselves again," Lorraine smiled grimly. "Uncle Joey didn't get a parole."

"Maybe we should just try putting a file in something," Dave suggested.

"It's a shame," Lorraine continued. "They practically assured him he'd get out this time. Then there was that shake-up in prison management. I guess that hurt him more than anything. Everybody has his own axe to grind."

"It's probably just as well," Marty said. "If he came out,

there'd be a lot of decisions to make. He'd have to find a job and fill out tax forms..."

"True," Dave chimed in. "He'd have to worry about getting from place to place, having enough change to make phone calls... It's probably better that he's gotta stay in the joint."

Lorraine frowned, looked at both of them angrily. George McFly did not look up from his homework.

"I wish you'd show a little more respect," Lorraine said. "He's my brother, you know."

"Well, I think it's a major embarrassment, having an uncle in prison," Linda murmured.

"We all make mistakes in life, children," Lorraine said philosophically.

"Yeah, but Uncle Joey made them consecutively," Dave smiled. "And while on parole. That's not only a mistake, that's plain dumb."

Lorraine didn't answer. Instead she took another helping of potatoes.

Looking once again at the clock, Dave wiped his mouth and pushed his chair back. "Damn," he said. "I'm gonna be late again."

"Please watch your language," his mother warned.

"Hell, yes," Dave said, getting up and starting for the front door. A moment later, they heard his car start up and roar off. Marty wished he owned his own car, even a heap like Dave's. At least he would be independent; if something went wrong with the car, he would have only himself to blame.

"By the way," Lorraine said. "That girl Jennifer called ... wants you to call her back."

Marty nodded.

"I think her last name was Parker."

"I know her last name, Mom."

"But it could have been another Jennifer, couldn't it?"

"Yes, but I don't know any other Jennifers right now."

"Sorry," his mother said, scooping up the remains of her potatoes with a crust of bread. "Anyway, I'm not sure I like her. Any girl who calls up a boy is looking for trouble."

Marty and Linda exchanged a meaningful glance. Had their mother lost her marbles?

"Oh, Mother," Linda muttered, "there's nothing wrong with calling a boy."

"Well, I think it's terrible," Lorraine persisted. "Girls chasing boys—whoever heard of such a thing? I never chased a boy when I was your age. I never called a boy, or asked a boy for a date or sat in a parked car with a boy . . ."

What a dull childhood, Marty thought.

"Because when you behave like that, boys won't respect you, Linda. They'll think you're cheap."

Linda rolled her eyes. She'd heard it several hundred times already, although it probably seemed like at least one million.

"Then how are you supposed to meet anybody?" she asked.

"It'll just happen," Lorraine smiled. "Like the way I met your father."

"But that was so stupid!" Linda whined. "Grandpa hit him with a car."

"It was meant to be."

"Maybe you should hang around the emergency wards," Marty suggested.

"That wouldn't do any good," Lorraine said, unaware of his sarcasm. "You see, you'll meet Mr. Wonderful in a certain way that you can't make happen. And you won't be able to avoid it either. It's just bound to happen, like the sun's supposed to come up tomorrow morning."

All the metaphysics did not impress Linda. "I still don't understand what Dad was doing in the middle of the street," she said.

Dad, oblivious to the entire conversation, did not look up from his work, so Mom raised her voice to get his attention. "What was it, George?" she asked. "What were you doing there—bird-watching?"

George shook his head like a person coming out of a coma. "Huh?" he muttered thickly. "Did you say something, Lorraine?"

"Never mind."

"He was probably just a very incompetent hitchhiker," Marty offered. He really wasn't interested in hearing how his parents had met.

Lorraine was interested in telling the story, however. "Anyway," she went on, "Grandpa hit him with the car and brought him into the house. He was completely unconscious..."

"Like now," Marty interrupted.

Lorraine shot a chiding glance at him. "He seemed so helpless...like a little lost puppy. And my heart just went out to him."

"Yeah, Mom," Linda smiled. "You've told us a million times. It was 'Florence Nightingale to the rescue.'"

Lorraine leaned back in her chair, her eyes dreamy with nostalgic thoughts and pictures. "The very next weekend," she continued, "we went on our first date. The 'Enchantment Under the Sea' School Dance."

"*Under* the sea?" Marty interrupted again. "You mean everybody came dressed as a clam or an oyster?"

His mother ignored him.

"I'll never forget it," she said. "It was the night of that terrible thunderstorm. Remember, George?"

"What's that, dear?" George McFly mumbled.

"The night of our first date."

"Mmm. It was raining."

"Worst thunderstorm before or since," Lorraine elaborated. "People still talk about it. Anyway, your father kissed

me for the first time on the dance floor . . . and that was
when I realized I was going to spend the rest of my life
with him."

"That really must have been some thunderstorm," Marty
smiled.

"I can't believe Dad actually got up enough nerve to kiss
you in public," Linda said.

Lorraine flushed. "Well," she said coyly. "I may have
encouraged him a little . . ."

"I'll bet you had to practically jump on his bones," Marty
offered.

With that, he finished eating, declining a piece of the
convict's nonhomecoming cake, wiped his mouth and stood
up.

Lorraine scarcely noticed, so lost was she in thought.
"Thinking back on it," she reminisced, "I did. I practically
had to—"

Not wishing to fall into contemporary "obscene talk," as
she called it, she let the rest of the sentence die in her throat.
It was an appropriate ending, anyway. Marty was halfway
out of the kitchen, Linda was looking out the window at
something happening next door and George was still lost in
his papers. Lorraine shrugged and reached for the nearest
knife. If no one was going to have a piece of Uncle Joey's
cake, she would give it a try.

Smiling in anticipation, she carved herself a four-inch
wedge, shoved it onto her coffee saucer, and began to attack
it. As the creamy icing melted in her mouth, so evaporated
any feelings that the past thirty years had been anything but
glorious.

•Chapter Three•

Doc Brown eased the venerable step-van onto the Twin Pines Mall parking lot shortly after midnight. There were more cars than he expected so he pulled to the far rim of the asphalt area and waited.

"Must be a long movie," he said to himself.

Einstein, the large dog curled on the passenger seat, hopped up as soon as the van stopped and poked his wet nose against the window.

"No, Einstein," Doc Brown murmured. "Not yet. We have a few minutes, so make yourself comfortable again."

Einstein yawned, curled his tongue back into his mouth and tried to scratch beneath the collar he was wearing. The battery-operated digital clock attached to it undulated in the moonlight, changed from 00:07 to 00:08, then came to rest as the dog either satisfied its itch or gave up trying to scratch where he couldn't reach.

A few minutes later, several dozen people emerged at

once from the mall's interior and moved to their cars. A series of starting engines, blinking lights and squealing rubber enlivened the vast treeless plain for a few minutes. Then all was silence again. The faint smell of gasoline fumes hung in the thick air as the tiny specks of light disappeared into the early morning darkness. In comparative solitude once again, Brown felt better. People made him feel vaguely insecure.

He was dreamily anticipating public reaction to his coming experiment when he suddenly realized he had forgotten one of the most important tools to be used.

"Damn," he muttered.

Fortunately, it was 1985 rather than the old days, when he would have been forced to find a public telephone booth somewhere in the mall. Reaching under the dashboard, he pulled out his telephone and began to dial.

Marty was not asleep, partly because he had every intention of meeting Doc Brown, and partly because his mind was filled with dark unsettling thoughts. As far as Jennifer was concerned, of course, the damage had been done. He had forgotten to call her. Looking at his watch, he decided it was too late to give her a buzz, especially since he didn't know if she was still at her grandmother's or had gone home. Possibly this was a rationalization for his being too lazy. In any event, he dropped his wrist down across his chest and closed his eyes once again.

In the light from the single lamp, it was possible to see that the room's occupant was heavily into rock music, cars and sound reproduction. Covering the walls were posters of rock stars and new cars, particularly Toyota four-by-fours. A tape recorder, portable home synthesizer and sizable stack of lead sheets were packed in one corner while a bass guitar and amp sprawled in another.

Although he was weary from all the running around,

Marty couldn't sleep. He continued to think of the shoddy treatment he had gotten at the hands of the section committee and began to wonder if he would ever get anywhere in the recording business. After twenty minutes, he got up and walked to the desk near his bed. He picked up the submissions form with R & G RECORDS on the letterhead, read it over, and put it in the accompanying envelope along with his demo cassette.

It's worth a try, he thought. Just send it.

And then another darker side of him hesitated. Send it for what? Another rejection? Spend postage just so he could live with hope for another few weeks before his bubble burst once more?

Shrugging, he dropped the cassette and letter into the waste basket and fell back into bed. His mind, occupied with depressing thoughts, eventually released him into a deep sleep that ended shortly after midnight.

Beep. Beep-beep.

Marty shook his head and reached for the cordless telephone next to his bed.

"Hello."

"You didn't fall asleep, did you?" Doc Brown asked on the other end.

"Uh, no. Course not."

"You sound like you just woke up."

"I was thinking," Marty said. "What's up? I don't have to leave for a while yet."

"Uh-huh," Brown replied. "I was just wondering. I forgot my video camera. Could you stop by my place and pick it up on your way to the mall?"

"No problem, Doc. Key still in the same place?"

"That's right. Under the potted plant."

"That's not a very good place," Marty said. "First spot a burglar would look."

"I haven't been robbed yet. Anyway, the place looks so

junky. Nobody'd ever suspect there's a billion dollars' worth of research in there."

"O.K., Doc. I'll see you in a half hour or so."

"Right."

Marty hung up, put his shoes back on, grabbed his jacket, the skateboard and his new Walkman, which he carried with him wherever he went. Then, retracing his steps to the bed, he shoved some extra pillows under the covers to make it seem as if a body were lying there, sound asleep. Even as he did it, he wondered why he bothered. This wasn't, after all, a prison. The guards didn't patrol every hour making a head count. But somehow it just seemed the thing to do when you were heading out of the house late at night.

Whistling softly, he closed the door quietly behind him and tiptoed down the stairs.

Letting himself out the front door, Marty walked a half block before putting down the skateboard and using it. He had discovered once, to his chagrin, how much noise they could make on a quiet evening. On that occasion, about two years ago, he had been sneaking out to meet the guys when his mother heard the sound and came after him in the car.

There was no such repetition tonight. Safely out of earshot, he whirred quickly along the back streets and around corners until he approached the dilapidated garage that was Doc Brown's place.

The key was in place. Marty grabbed it, let himself in and flipped on the overhead light.

He was halfway to the workbench where Doc kept his video equipment when a sudden cacophony caused him to jump in spite of himself. Set precisely, every clock with a way to announce the hour went off together—musical chimes, cuckoo sounds, digital beeps. For ten seconds, Marty stood still, listening until the last harbinger of the hour died away. A smile spread across his face, for he never tired of hearing this strange symphony arranged and orchestrated by the world's most fanatical timekeeper, Doc Brown.

"Must be one o'clock," Marty said softly. As indeed it was.

Moving quickly to the workbench, he located the video camera, put it in its carrying case, and skateboarded out of Doc Brown's garage. Ten minutes later, he neared the two pine trees in a row which marked the entrance to the mall. As he turned the corner, he picked out the familiar step-van and coasted toward it. The atmosphere, lit by sodium vapor lamps shrouded in fine mist, was appropriately eerie for a major scientific experiment.

"Doc," Marty said as he neared the truck.

There was no answer. Einstein, Doc's dog, peered out the passenger side window at him, his large dark eyes friendly but noninformative.

"Hiya, Einstein," Marty said anyway. "Where's the Doc? Where's the Doc, boy?"

A few seconds later, he heard an engine roar to life and rev quietly. It seemed to be coming from inside the van, but it didn't sound like the truck engine. It was too far back, for one thing, the sound emanating not from beneath the hood but somewhere midway of the vehicle.

Marty started to walk toward the back of the van.

Just as he arrived at the rear bumper, he heard a sharp grating sound, a slam, and saw the rear doors dramatically fly open. The drop-down gate lowered into position and a giant shining object swooped down onto the parking lot. It was the stainless steel DeLorean, modified with coils and some wicked-looking units on the rear engine.

Marty stared at it in amazement.

The DeLorean moved softly toward him and stopped. The gull-wing driver's door was raised to reveal the smiling face of Doc Brown.

Marty barely noticed his friend, however. He continued to stare at the DeLorean, which was unlike anything he had ever seen before. The front of the modernistic vehicle was a smooth slope from windshield to fender—beautiful but hardly startling. From the driver's compartment rearward, however, the car had been modified so that it resembled something you might see only in an atomic power plant. In place of the rear seat and hatchback door was a huge nuclear reactor, behind which jutted two large venting outlets, each with eight openings. Surrounding the vent and reactor was a six-inch coil which disappeared beneath the rear bumper only to emerge later and wrap itself around the top. A circular projection approximately eighteen inches in diameter, which Marty learned later was radar, hung over the passenger's compartment. Various heavy cables ran the length of the car from engine to front wheels, adding to its arcane look.

Doc Brown allowed his protégé to stare at the strange vehicle for a minute before speaking.

"Good evening, Marty," he said with smiling formality. "Welcome to my latest experiment. This is the big one— the one I've been working and waiting for all my life."

Marty was less interested in the experiment than the DeLorean. Walking in a circle around it, he took in every line and hidden seam. "It's a DeLorean," he said. "But what did you do to it?"

"Just a few modifications," Doc Brown smiled.

As he spoke, Brown got out of the vehicle, revealing himself in all his sci-fi splendor. He thought he must resemble Michael Rennie stepping onto Earth for the first time in *The Day the Earth Stood Still*.

"What's with the Devo suit?" Marty asked.

No respect, Doc Brown thought. He had gone to so much trouble preparing an appropriate outfit for the occasion and this young man called it a Devo suit.

."Bear with me, Marty," he replied. "All of your questions

will be answered in due time. Now if you'll roll the tape, we'll proceed."

Marty took the video camera from its case, set it on the tripod, and pointed it at Doc Brown. He raised his hand, then dropped it as he pushed the ON switch.

Rather formally, like the narrator of a documentary film, Brown began to speak. "Good evening," he intoned. "I'm Dr. Emmett Brown. I'm standing here on the parking lot at Twin Pines Mall. It's Saturday morning, October 26, 1985. It's 1:19 A.M. and this is temporal experiment number one."

Glancing down at Einstein, who had jumped out of the step-van and was padding nervously around the base of the DeLorean, Doc added: "Come on, Einstein. Get in, boy."

The dog obediently jumped into the car and sat down regally in the middle of the driver's seat. Doc Brown reached across and buckled him in with the shoulder harness. Then, turning to Marty, the camera and unseen audience, he continued the narration.

"Please note that Einstein's clock here is in precise synchronization with my control watch."

With that, he held his digital watch next to the clock on Einstein's collar. Marty, working the zoomar handle, moved in to a close-up of the two timepieces. Indeed, they were in dead sync.

"Now," Doc Brown said, "if we can show the entire car again, you will note that the dog is alone in the vehicle and that his clock reads the same as this one on my wrist. This first part of our experiment will involve the canine subject only. No risk is anticipated, but in the time-honored tradition of most breakthrough scientific experiments, we are allowing animals to go first."

Giving the dog a little pat on the head, he said, "Good luck, Einie," as he reached in and started the ignition. The DeLorean engine roared once again to life. Brown turned on the headlights and lowered the gull-wing door. Only the very top of Einstein's head could be seen above the window level.

Stepping backward several feet, Doc Brown continued the scientific narration. "I will now operate the vehicle with this remote control unit."

He tilted it toward the camera as Marty followed his movements. The remote control unit was similar to that used for a radio-controlled toy car. There were buttons labeled "Accelerator" and "Brake," as well as a joystick and an LED digital readout labeled "Miles Per Hour." It was simple-looking but quite sophisticated. Marty had no doubt Doc Brown could maneuver the DeLorean with the device, but at present he had no idea what the end result or product would be. Rather than try to puzzle it out, he decided to simply enjoy the spectacle as cameraman and audience member.

Brown switched the power button on and, using the accelerator button and joystick, sent the DeLorean roaring to the far end of the parking lot. There he brought it to a quick halt, turning it so that it was pointing toward them. Seeing the trail of rubber fumes rising as it turned, Marty hoped no policeman would happen along. It would be very embarrassing for him, as well as them, if he should be forced to arrest a reckless-driving dog.

For thirty seconds, the car sat, idling softly. To Marty it seemed to resemble a giant cat, readying itself to pounce on an unwary victim.

"We're now ready to continue," Doc Brown said. "If my calculations are correct, when the car hits eighty-eight miles an hour, you're gonna see some serious shit."

Suddenly aware that the video camera was still running, Doc shuddered at his own use of colloquial language. He added quickly and more conventionally: "When a speed of eighty-eight miles an hour is attained, unusual things should begin happening in this phase of temporal experiment number one."

He could, he reasoned, always edit in the more acceptable version later.

Taking a deep breath, he pushed the accelerator button. The Twin Pines Mall parking lot had been selected by him because of its extreme length—nearly one-third mile—but as the spanking new DeLorean began to roar away toward the far reaches of the black-topped strip, he wondered if even this was enough. Taking off like a racing car, its gears shifting automatically, the DeLorean's recorded speed whirled quickly past 30, then 40. By the time it reached 60, it seemed to be moving at a dangerously rapid speed. Marty followed it through the viewfinder, once or twice nearly allowing the vehicle to move out of the frame when a sudden burst of speed carried it forward.

"Sixty," Doc Brown announced. "Sixty-five . . . seventy . . . seventy-five . . ."

Marty wondered how Einstein felt, sitting there in his captive seat, watching the gauges and instrument lights flash against the black sky.

"Eighty."

Turning the vehicle in a huge arc, Doc Brown maneuvered it so that it was approaching them under full power. With nearly the entire length of the mall lot ahead of it on the return run, he now felt no compunction about leaning on the accelerator. The speedometer indicator leaped to 85, 86, 87, and finally 88, where it hung for a long second, the needle caressing the magic number as if to emphasize its importance.

Doc Brown waited. It should happen now, he thought, it should be happening at this very sec—

The thought was not completed, but instead was engulfed by a mind-numbing experience.

In the midst of its precipitous run down the center of the

parking lot, the DeLorean was suddenly swallowed up by a blinding white glow. For a split second, the silhouette of the car, surrounded by the corona of light, resembled an eclipse of the sun. Then a shock wave and explosion of sound hit Marty and Doc Brown just as the car disappeared in a huge trail of fire. The embers, large at first, gradually became smaller until only a pink fissure in the atmosphere remained. Then, a tiny, metallic sound, tinkly in quality, echoed across the lot. A shadow of something moving, something very small, could be seen. His fingers trembling, Marty zoomed in to the object.

It was the DeLorean's license plate, a vanity plate that read: OUTATIME.

"What did I tell you?" Doc Brown shouted, his voice elated. "Eighty-eight miles an hour! Just as I figured." He checked his watch. "Temporal displacement occurred at exactly 1:20 A.M. and zero seconds."

Marty shook his head in disbelief. "Christ Almighty!" he shouted. "You disintegrated Einstein!"

"No," Doc Brown said evenly.

"But the license plate's all that remains of the car and dog and everything!"

"Calm down, Marty. I didn't disintegrate anything. The molecular structure of both Einstein and the car are completely intact."

"Then where the hell are they?" Marty demanded.

Doc Brown looked at him with maddening serenity.

"Not where," he said. "When."

"I don't understand."

"The appropriate question," Doc Brown amended, "is not where are they, but where *the hell* are they? You see, Einstein has just become the world's first time traveler. I sent him into the future—one minute into the future, to be exact. And at exactly 1:21 A.M. and zero seconds, we shall catch up to him . . . and the time machine."

Marty still didn't get it.

"Are you recording this?" Doc Brown asked. "Because if you are, it might be appropriate to have the camera pointed at me or where the car was, rather than at the ground in front of you."

Marty shook his head, noting that he had allowed the video camera to drop downward during the interval of stress and excitement. Now he righted it, bringing Doc Brown into the frame.

"It's all right," Doc said, smiling indulgently. "We still have a few seconds."

"Few seconds until what?"

"You'll see."

"Are you trying to tell me you built a time machine out of that DeLorean?" Marty demanded.

Doc Brown smiled modestly. "The way I figure it," he replied, "if you're gonna build a time machine, why not do it with some style and imagination? Besides, there's a practical aspect. The stainless steel construction of the DeLorean made the flux dispersal—"

He stopped as his digital clock began to beep.

"Ten seconds," Doc Brown said. "Keep that tape rolling, Marty."

"It's never stopped."

"Five seconds. Brace yourself for a sudden displacement of air."

Marty held the camera tighter, aimed it at the spot where the DeLorean had disappeared.

"Four . . . three . . . two . . . one . . ." Doc Brown counted down, his voice filled with anticipation.

Exactly on schedule, a sharp blast of wind struck them, followed immediately by a deafening sonic boom, causing their hair to stand on end. No sooner had the shock registered

Athens Regional Library
Athens, Georgia   279122

than the DeLorean reappeared in the same spot it had last been seen. But it was not standing. It was moving at the same high speed as before.

"Eighty-eight miles an hour!" Doc Brown shouted above the surge of thunderous air.

Looking down at the remote control unit, he hit the brake button, causing the car to come to a screeching halt, smoke pouring from the body.

Doc Brown immediately started for the vehicle. Marty locked the camera in position and followed. He arrived at the DeLorean a few seconds after Brown, who pulled up to approach it cautiously. Indicating that Marty should wait until he examined it, he gently touched the door handle. To Marty and Doc's surprise, he recoiled with a shout of pain.

"Is it hot?" Marty asked.

"No. It's cold. Damned cold," Brown said, shaking his fingers back and forth.

He waited a few seconds, then raised the door on the driver's side. Einstein peeked out at them, his tail wagging against the back of the seat. Marty was relieved to see that no apparent harm had come to him. Doc was also pleased that his pet was in good condition, although his attitude was more clinical. Instead of petting the dog, he reached down to turn the collar so that he could read the digital clock inset into the surface of it.

The clock read 1:20:10. Doc Brown looked at it and smiled. His own watch read 1:21:10.

"There's exactly one minute difference," he said triumphantly. "And Einstein's clock is still clicking. It didn't stop."

"Is he all right?" Marty asked.

"He looks fine to me."

Brown unbuckled the shoulder harness. Einstein bounded out of the car, playful and happy. Doc Brown reached into his pocket and gave him a milk bone as a reward. "A small price to pay for such invaluable research," he said.

"You're sure he's O.K.?"

"Yes," Brown replied. "And he's completely unaware that anything happened. As far as he's concerned, the trip was instantaneous. That's why his watch is a minute behind mine. He 'skipped over' that minute to instantly arrive at this minute in time..."

Seeing Marty's frown, Doc Brown indicated that he should move closer to the DeLorean. "Come here, let me show you how it works," he offered, sticking his own head into the cockpit of the car.

Marty edged closer, looked inside at the still-blinking array of dials and gadgets.

Like a kid showing off a new toy, Doc Brown began to flip switches and talk at the same time. "First you turn the time circuits on," he said. A colorful battery of indicator lights went on inside as he pushed a button.

"This readout tells you where you're going, this one tells you where you are, and this one tells you where you were," he continued.

Marty looked at the readouts closely. They were labeled DESTINATION TIME, PRESENT TIME, and LAST TIME DEPARTED.

Without waiting to find out if Marty had any questions, Brown went on at a rapid pace. "You imput your destination time on this keyboard," he said. "Want to see the signing of the Declaration of Independence?"

Marty stared blankly, his mind abuzz. Was he kidding? Could this machine, however sophisticated, perform such miracles?

Again without waiting for an answer, Doc Brown punched up a date on the destination time board: 7-4-1776. "Then all we have to do is head for Philadelphia. Or perhaps you'd care to witness the birth of Christ."

With that, he changed the dial to read 12-25-0.

"Of course," he added didactically, "there's some dispute about that date. Some scholars say Christ was born in the year 4 B.C. and that somebody made a mistake in what year it was during the Dark Ages. But assuming 12-25-0 is correct, all we'd have to do is find our way to Bethlehem."

"No sweat," Marty said.

Now quite caught up in describing the mechanics of his system, Doc Brown changed the DESTINATION TIME to 11-5-1955. "Now here's another red-letter date in the history of science and progress," he went on. "November 5, 1955. I believe it was a Saturday. Yes, now that I think about it, I'm sure it was. The weather was kind of grey."

"What happened then?" Marty asked. That was more than a decade before he had been born, so he could only speculate. "Was that the Salk vaccine or something like that?" he asked, remembering from science class that the polio cure went back to about that time.

"No," Doc Brown went on. "It's a red-letter date in science that nobody knows about—yet. Nobody except me, that is. You see, that was the day I invented time travel—"

"Then what's today?" Marty interrupted.

"Today is the carrying-out, the execution," Brown smiled. "November 5, 1955 was the conception, the moment when it all came together as a theory that I knew could work." He leaned against the shiny frame of the DeLorean, his eyes misted in happy nostalgia. "I remember it vividly," he said. "I was standing on the edge of my toilet, hanging a clock. The porcelain was wet. I slipped and hit my head on the sink to my left. And when I came to, I had a revelation—a vision that was absolutely perfect—a picture in my head of everything I needed to do and how I could do it."

He gestured to the car. "Believe it or not, I saw this," he continued. "My dream or hallucination or whatever it was contained a picture of this."

"Amazing," Marty said, his eyes wide with sincerity. He

knew the feeling. Once he had awakened during the middle of the night with the lyrics and melody of a new song literally playing inside his head. All that he had to do was find paper and take dictation. That was small potatoes compared to a scientific breakthrough such as the invention of time travel, but the emotional impact was similar.

Leaning inside the DeLorean, Doc Brown pointed to a particular centerpiece unit. "Get a picture of this on tape," he said.

Marty pointed the camera at the strange-looking object. Moving his head next to it so that he could be on camera and describe its workings at the same time, Doc Brown continued in his professional tone. "This is what makes time travel possible—the flux capacitor."

"Flux capacitor, huh?" Marty repeated. "Is that its real title or something you made up?"

"It's a logical title applied by me when I decided to describe its function in one or two words. Any brilliant scientist would have arrived at approximately the same title if given the chance."

Marty chuckled inwardly at the man's lack of humility. He did not dislike him for it, however. As a matter of fact, he found it charmingly refreshing.

"It's taken me almost thirty years and my entire family fortune to fulfill the vision of that day when I fell off the toilet . . . My God, has it been that long? I've been working on this for exactly . . ."

He reached into his inside coat pocket to withdraw a small calculator. Punching buttons quickly, he said presently: "I've been working on this for twenty-nine years, eleven months, and 355 days. Excluding vacations, of course, and a few weeks off for petty illnesses. Think of it. Almost thirty years. It's amazing. Things have certainly changed during that time. This all used to be farmland here, as far as the eye could see . . ."

He looked off toward the horizon, dominated now by the huge department stores of the mall and sodium vapor lamps lining the periphery of their vision like ugly ornaments. "I can hardly believe it's gone," he murmured.

"What?"

"The farm . . . the years . . ."

He suddenly looked very sad.

Marty tried to shake him out of the mood. Slapping the side of the DeLorean, he said, "This is heavy duty, Doc. I'm really impressed."

The compliment caused a shift in Doc Brown's attitude. His eyes turned to the present, unclouding and becoming instantly brighter, sharper.

"Yes, I'm proud of it," he smiled.

"And it runs on, like, regular unleaded gasoline?" Marty asked.

Doc shook his head and grinned. "Unfortunately, no," he replied. "I tried that in the beginning. That was a dream that just wouldn't come true—to have this device run cheaply and simply. That may happen in the future, but for the moment, it requires something with a little more kick."

"You mean, atomic power?" Marty guessed.

Nodding, Doc Brown pointed to a container with purple radioactivity signs painted on it.

"Plutonium? You mean this sucker's nuclear?"

"Electrical, basically," Doc Brown replied. "But I need a nuclear reaction to generate the 1.21 gigawatts of electricity I need. The flux capacitor stores it, then discharges it all at once, like a gigantic bolt of lightning. It's really quite efficient."

"Hold the phone, Doc," Marty said. "Plutonium's illegal. Did you rip it off?"

"Of course. How else does an ordinary citizen latch onto plutonium?"

"You out and out stole it?"

"In a manner of speaking. That is, I had someone else steal it. No, that's not quite accurate. Someone else who had already stolen it gave it to me."

"Gave it to you?" Marty challenged. "You mean to tell me somebody just donated it?"

"What are you, a federal agent?" Doc Brown smiled. "Look, I don't want you to know too much. It might be bad for you. All I can say is that someone had this plutonium and they gave it to me for another project. I deemed that project not only less important than mine but actually harmful to the future of society. So I killed two birds with one stone by switching the plutonium from their evil project to my progressive and kindly project."

"You're not screwing around with our space program, are you?"

"Nothing like that," Doc replied sanctimoniously. "I consider the conquest of space a beneficial scheme. Perhaps scheme isn't the best word, but rest assured I'm all for it. Now please don't press me further. It's for your own good that you should know no more details."

"All right," Marty murmured.

"Now, before we proceed further, we must protect you," Doc said.

He strode to the step-van and removed a yellow radiation suit. "Put this on," he said.

Marty locked the video camera and stepped into the suit. The night had become chilly and it felt good to add the extra layer of material. With the hood pulled up, he felt totally divorced from the rest of the world, like a deep-sea diver on the floor of the ocean.

Working slowly, Doc Brown took a four-inch cylinder from the step-van, handling it with great delicacy. Marty knew that within the capsule must be a plutonium rod, surrounded by water, the new source of power for the time vehicle. Inching the DeLorean closer to the truck so that the plutonium would not have to be moved far, Marty returned to the video camera and started it again as Doc Brown stepped to the rear of the car and placed the plutonium cylinder into the loading hopper. He then sealed the hopper shut and tossed back the hood of his radiation suit.

"It's safe now," he smiled. "Everything is lead-lined."

Marty took off his own hood and waited for Doc Brown's next instructions.

"Just be sure you get my send-off," Doc Brown smiled. "It'd be a shame if everything came out on tape but that."

"Where are you headed?"

"The future."

"How far?"

"Whoops," Brown muttered, snapping his fingers. "Almost forgot my luggage."

He jogged back to the step-van, grabbed a suitcase and returned to the DeLorean. "Who knows if they'll have cotton underwear in the future?" he said. "I'm allergic to all synthetics. It would be rather unpleasant to find myself in the future with a terrible rash."

"Are you sure it's safe?" Marty asked.

"My machine works," Doc Brown retorted. "You just saw it, didn't you?"

"I meant, are you sure the future's safe? Suppose you run smack into the bomb? Or it's a society of robots that take you prisoner. At least you know the past is safe. Nobody there has better equipment than you. But the future—"

Doc Brown smiled, touched by the young man's interest in his safety. "What you say makes a lot of sense," he admitted. "I gave it a lot of thought when I was considering where I should go first. But I've always dreamed of seeing the future a lot more than rehashing the past. I'd like to see where mankind's headed, up or down. And besides," he added with a sly chuckle, "if I head down the road a quarter century, I'll be able to find out who won the next twenty-five World Series and Super Bowls. Won't that be a nice piece of information to have for my old age?"

Marty nodded. "Well, be sure to look me up when you get there and I'll fill you in on the details of what's been happening," he said.

"Indeed I will."

Clearing his throat, Doc once again assumed a more serious attitude as he addressed the camera.

"I, Dr. Emmett Brown," he began, "am about to embark on a historic journey—"

Einstein started barking furiously.

Brown halted in mid-phrase. What was it—a mall security guard, a cat, or something worse?

He heard the sound of the engine before he saw the lights. Then a sudden turn of the vehicle threw the lights directly at them, the twin glares rising and falling as the car fairly leaped over the speed bumps leading into the mall nearly a half mile down the road. It could have been joyriding teenagers, but something in the vehicle's headlong desperation and purpose told Doc Brown that the worst had happened.

Marty stopped working the camera, looked out of the viewfinder at Doc Brown. The man's face was ashen, his mouth open; his breath came in shallow gasps. Indeed, he exhibited every symptom of shock except a tendency to faint and that might be imminent. Locking the camera, Marty came around to the front, prepared to help Doc Brown any way he could.

"What is it?" he whispered.

Doc seemed not to hear him. His piercing eyes continued to follow the progress of the vehicle moving generally in their direction. A slight sideways turn revealed presently that it wasn't an ordinary car or even a police cruiser. Square except for the long sloping hood, it was an ominous van, dark in color, with windows that seemed to have been blacked either by painting or the installation of dark curtains.

"You're right, Einie..." Doc Brown finally said, stroking his dog's head. "It's them."

"Who?" Marty asked.

Doc Brown seemed not to have heard him. "They found me," he muttered. "I don't know how, but they found me."

•Chapter Four•

Shortly after three o'clock on the afternoon of October 26, 1985, the swarthy man who was known only as Sam received the coded message from his superior officer. As he read it, his anger grew, until his dark moody eyes flashed vengefully.

"We've been taken in," he said simply to the four men and one young woman who sat in the dingy motel room, awaiting instructions.

As he spoke, he slammed back the bolt of his AK 47 submachine gun, put the weapon on the table next to him and began searching in his brief case.

"We're always being taken in," said the young woman. "We're not ruthless enough. If the world knew we killed those who oppose us instead of negotiating and weaseling, we'd be unstoppable. Instead, we're looked upon as clowns with guns."

Sam had heard it before. His own career as an international terrorist dated back nearly thirty years and there had always been one member of the organization who wanted nothing but more killing. Sometimes it was the youngest member, anxious to show the others how tough he was; now, it was Uranda, a twenty-five-year-old ex-fashion model from Damascus who got her kicks by pumping bullets into other people's bodies.

"Don't worry," Sam rasped. "We won't be weasels tonight. There'll be only one dead body, but it will be very very dead by the time we're through."

He pulled the pages from his briefcase. The folder showed a color head shot of Doc Brown along with a ten-page, single-spaced résumé of his past activities and habits, a map of his home and work area. Sam had received the folder a week before, when it appeared that Brown might not be as reliable as the organization hoped. Confirmation of Doc Brown's duplicity came that morning, followed by the decision to eliminate him.

Sam put the color photo on the coffee table and indicated that the others should study it.

"What's he done?" Uranda asked. "Not that it matters. He looks Jewish."

"We hired him to build a nuclear bomb."

The young woman's eyes glistened with excitement.

"We stole plutonium and gave it to him. He delayed as long as possible and gave us the weapon only when we threatened him."

"Well?" another of the group asked.

"The bomb was nothing but a casing filled with used pinball-machine parts," Sam said.

Uranda rolled her eyes back, but a moment later, a look of happy anticipation engaged her features.

"We'll kill him tonight," Sam continued. "Headquarters has decided it's not worth it to bring him in for questioning.

You two tail him for the rest of the day. Chances are he'll end up at the garage he uses for an office or at Twin Pines Mall. He's been spending a lot of time there recently, usually late at night."

"Does he carry any weapons?"

"A handgun at most. An old .45-caliber revolver. It may not even work."

Now Marty watched as the black van hurtled toward them. His terror was complete, even though he had no idea who or what was heading their way. At that inopportune moment, something terribly perverse stirred in him—he was determined to know, if this was death unfolding, who was behind it.

"Who's in that car?" he shouted.

Doc Brown had no time for an elaborate explanation. Marty's hand gripped his sleeve so tightly he had to spin like a top to get away. As he did so, he yelled over his shoulder: "The Libyans I ripped off!"

Marty didn't understand but he did know that, to date, few Libyans he had heard of had been involved in anything but dark and dangerous business. The effect was of someone yelling "Fire!" in a crowded theater. Marty believed and acknowledged that there was trouble without further investigation. Hurling his body to one side, he looked for the nearest solid object that would provide cover. The only two choices were the step-van and the DeLorean.

Doc Brown was already heading for the step-van.

"Run for it, Marty!" he shouted. "I'll draw their fire!"

Simultaneously, he hustled into the truck and appeared a moment later with a revolver. By this time, the side door of the black van had slid open and a swarthy character resembling Yasser Arafat leaned out. He threw up an AK 47 submachine gun and opened fire.

Marty had never been shot at before, although he had once been beaned during a baseball game. The effect was vaguely similar. He seemed to move in slow motion, a helpless figure in an echo chamber of harsh reverberating sound. The horizon with its familiar objects—utility poles, lights, department stores—seemed to have disappeared, leaving him trapped in a globe of black fluid. The only two sounds—gunfire and his breathing—competed, each grossly and metallically augmented by panic.

He saw Doc Brown point the revolver at the van and squeeze the trigger. No sound or flash of fire emerged, however, as bullets splattered all around Doc at his feet and into the side of the van. Finally, dropping the revolver, Doc began to sprint for the safety of the mall, fully five hundred yards away.

The van screeched to a halt, backed up and started after Brown. Doc was no more than fifty yards closer to the nearest mall building when the black van started after him in low gear.

"No!" Marty shouted. "Doc! Wait!"

Even as he screamed the words, Marty knew it was poor advice. Were these desperate Libyans actually going to show mercy if Doc Brown suddenly surrendered and begged for his life? It was unlikely at best, but something in Marty forced him to cry for the impossible.

For one long moment, he stood still, his eyes darting from side to side, desperately searching for something that could help his friend. Then, even as he looked, a new barrage of machine-gun fire and a scream told him there was no use. He turned back in time to see Doc Brown clutch his chest, bend over sharply and pitch forward on his face.

"You bastards!" Marty heard himself yell. The voice almost seemed to come from behind him, sweeping past like a cold wind and echoing across the vast empty lot.

The black van made a U-turn, heading back toward Marty. Doc lay still, his left ankle turned at a strange angle. There was no doubt in Marty's mind that the man was dead.

He would be, too, if he didn't do something. For a moment, he thought of heading for the step-van. It was big and slow and cumbersome, but at least he knew how to drive it. His mind, working quickly now, rejected that as a suicidal recourse. He would never get to the edge of the mall in that pokey truck. Better to die, if such was his fate, in a burst of glory, or at least in an unmoving vehicle that had a great deal of class.

Grabbing the video camera—in case he needed evidence concerning Doc's death—Marty tossed it into the DeLorean, then leaped inside and lowered the gull-wing door. He looked around, dazed. Lights blinked on all around him, but the starting mechanism was nowhere to be seen. Meanwhile, as he hesitated, the black van roared up, passing to his right from a distance of no more than ten feet. Framed in the doorway was the dark Libyan with the machine gun. Marty thought he saw the ghost of a smile as he aimed the weapon at him and pulled the trigger.

No sound came. Marty, curled into the fetal position, blinked and looked out the window. The van was already twenty feet past and slowing down, the Libyan cursing and slamming his fist against the machine gun, which had obviously failed to fire. A tirade of angry gibberish, no doubt Libyan swear words, cascaded into the night.

"Start!" Marty yelled.

He looked at the array of switches and dials on the console with frightening bewilderment. What was the secret? A button? Something in the nature of a digital code? His eyes flew back and forth, trying to locate the solution to the mystery.

When he finally solved the problem, it was so simple he

almost laughed. There on the steering column, just like any other ordinary unsophisticated car, was an ignition switch and a key.

"I'll be damned!" Marty muttered.

As he spoke and reached for the key, he heard the squeal of tires that told him the black van was on its way back to him. Starting the DeLorean, Marty threw it into gear and floored it. The vehicle's response was even more than he'd hoped for. It seemed to surge forward as if it had been kicked from the rear. For a moment, he could see the Libyan van as a black mass in the left side of his vision, then it receded so rapidly he wondered if its presence had not been a mirage generated by his own fear.

In fact, had the Libyan driver not turned the wrong way in making his U-turn, Marty would have been an easy target for the machine gunner. But rather than turn right, the driver had swerved left, causing them to come nearly abreast of the DeLorean with the open door facing away from Marty. By the time the mistake had been rectified, the DeLorean was already in high gear and on the verge of rapidly out-distancing its pursuer.

Marty glanced out the rear-view mirror just as the machine gunner took aim. Swerving wildly, Marty saw the bullets churn up holes in the asphalt to his left and rear, but he had no time to congratulate himself. Ahead was the end of the mall lot, which he was approaching at seventy-five miles an hour. His lights struck the metal guard rail, warning him that in less than two or three seconds he would plunge through the barrier and over a steep abutment. Behind him, the bouncing lights of the black van dogged his every movement.

Marty grabbed the wheel tighter, faked a left turn and, downshifting quickly, spun the car hard to the right. The tires shrieked, kicked gravel into the guard rail and onto the windshield, but held, completing the turn and allowing Marty to roar away from the skidding van. As he did so, he floored the car again, saw the speedometer rise from 50 to 75 in one swift, almost spastic motion. But the Libyan driver was no slouch, either. Despite having less power and maneuverability, he managed to turn around quickly and accelerate to the point where he was barely twenty yards behind the sleek DeLorean.

"O.K.," Marty whispered. "From here on out, it's nothing but speed."

He glanced down at the speedometer as the DeLorean roared past Doc Brown's immobile body. It read 80. As he passed the step-van, it read 85 and the Libyans showed no sign of quitting.

"All right, you bastards," Marty hissed. "Let's see if you can do ninety!"

Behind him, machine-gun fire crackled, several bullets landing ahead of him, causing the road to ignite and bits of asphalt to clatter against the hood. Distracted, Marty looked to his right too late. For a split second, he had the ability to turn right, race through the entrance portals and perhaps outrun the van on the highway. That split second was now past. Ahead was the opposite end of the parking lot, another guard rail, and, he now noted, less area in which to turn.

Should he make his move now? That would give the Libyans a better angle on him, but it would also allow him to make a run for the entrance.

As he puzzled his dilemma, Marty looked at the speedometer.

It read: 88.

Behind his head, gauges and indicators began to light up, lines of digits formed and disappeared on the dashboard, and something like a siren sounded. What had he done? Blown a fuse? Driven the engine past its limits? Touched something he should have left alone?

His eyes quickly scanned the dashboard for some clue to the mystery. As he did so, he was suddenly conscious of a large object rising ahead of him, an object that had not been in his line of sight a moment before. Jerking his head up, he saw not the guard rail and arc lamps of the Twin Pines shopping mall—but the face of a scarecrow!

"What the hell—"

As abruptly as it appeared, the scarecrow disappeared, its crude head smashing against the windshield and falling away in a spray of straw. Then another object loomed—a large square building. Simultaneously, the car began to rock and pitch as if it had abruptly turned off smooth roadway onto cobblestones or a plowed field.

Thrown nearly into the passenger's seat, his head once striking the roof, Marty could do little but hold the wheel as tightly as possible. Meanwhile, the building ahead crowded out the lighter sky behind it until everything in front was variants of black and grey. Having an instant to maneuver, Marty aimed the DeLorean at the lighter square ahead, bracing himself for the crash which didn't come. Instead, as if falling down a well, he was enveloped by blackness on all sides. Jamming on the brakes, he felt the car decelerate until it smashed into something, causing Marty to fly against the dashboard. At the same time, something landed on the roof with a loud thump.

The air surrounding the immobile DeLorean was filled with floating saffron dust. Marty blinked, trying to orient himself with a new environment which seemed to have snapped him out of the air of the mall parking lot. Gradually objects began to take shape—vertical boards, bales of straw, a pitchfork. Everything was blinking on and off, which puzzled Marty until he realized that the hazard lights of the DeLorean had been knocked out. In the background, he heard a dog barking.

"Damn," Marty said slowly. "I'm in a barn. How did I end up in a barn?"

The evening had not been a pleasant one for Otis Peabody. At forty-five, he usually came in after a day's work on the farm dead tired and not at all ready for criticism and pleas from his wife and children. Mostly he just wanted to sit and relax after a good meal, read the morning paper and then drift off to sleep.

The first bad news to greet him when he walked in was that the car battery was dead.

"We can get it recharged," he said shortly, heading for the dinner table.

Elsie, his wife of seventeen years, shook her head. "Mart Petersen says it's shot," she replied. "Lord, it's been in there since we got the car six years ago, so it's about time it went."

"What's a new one cost?" Peabody said.

"Well, his are expensive," Elsie said, "but Sears has 'em on sale. A four-year battery is $14.95."

"Ridiculous," Peabody mumbled. "That's too much. I wonder what the ones not on sale go for."

"Well?" Elsie asked. "Will you be leaving the money tomorrow so I can get it?"

Peabody nodded, sighed, and prepared to sit.

Martha, his fourteen-year-old daughter, and eleven-year-old Sherman chose that moment to add their requests for the day. Actually, they had been bothering their father for nearly a month to buy a television set. Everyone else in the county had one but them, it seemed.

"Can you buy a TV?" Martha smiled. "Please, Daddy. We'll be going to Sears for the battery anyway."

"No," Peabody said bluntly.

The kids were prepared for a negative reaction. Instead of backing down, they launched into a litany of wonderful programs that could be seen—Ed Sullivan, The Mickey Mouse Club, Colgate Variety Hour, The Cisco Kid, Ozzie and Harriet, an endless list.

"They're all pap," their father said.

"It's not fair," Martha cried. "Some of our teachers are assigning television-watching as homework."

Peabody looked at her skeptically.

"It's true. Peggy Ann McVey just took notes from the news about President Eisenhower's heart attack and turned it in as a complete report. She got an A."

"You can use the newspapers. Same difference," Peabody replied.

"No," Martha persisted. "Teachers can tell when you copied from the newspaper but not from TV. Anyway, when the teacher suggests that you watch Edward R. Murrow, how are you gonna see that in the newspaper?"

"We'll get a television when we can afford it and not a day before."

"I want to see the football games," Sherman added, pouting.

Peabody started filling his plate, choosing to ignore the children until they stopped bothering him. The meal was largely a silent and sullen one, at the end of which everyone moved to different parts of the house and went to bed.

Several hours later, the object struck the barn.

Sherman, curled up in his bed reading the latest issue of *Tales From Space* comics, saw the rapidly moving vehicle first. He knew immediately by the shape and flashing lights that this was no ordinary earth machine. True, he had just finished reading a story entitled "Space Zombies from Pluto," which dealt with aliens in radiation suits who enslaved human females and traveled around in a modernistic car with gull-wing doors. That may have made him more susceptible than usual, but Sherman was extraterrestrial all the time.

Space was his hobby and now his hobby seemed to be coming true. Grabbing the comic book, he rushed down the stairs.

His mother, father and sister were already at the back door, staring out toward the barn. In the dim light, they could see where the roof had caved in, but that wasn't the most frightening thing. The stainless steel DeLorean faced them head-on, headlight beams shining through the dust and drifting straw fragments. With its wheels buried in the debris and amber hazard lights blinking, it looked exactly like the flying saucers they had been hearing about for nearly ten years.

"What is it, Pa?" Mrs. Peabody asked.

"Looks like an airplane . . . without wings," Peabody said cautiously.

"Airplane?" Sherman whispered. "It's a flying saucer, Pa. From outer space!"

The four Peabodys looked at each other, awe-stricken. Although it was illogical, they walked slowly toward the object. In Pa Peabody's hand was a baseball bat, which he had grabbed from the basement closet moments after the vehicle plowed into the barn. Led by him, the rest of the family crossed the lawn and crusher-run driveway to the barn. A closer view provided no new clues as to the identity of their visitor.

Finally Sherman spoke. "In the movies and comics," he said, "Earth people always try to act peacefully to the aliens. But it doesn't usually work."

"Quiet," Peabody ordered.

His eyes were fixed on the gull-wing door, which had opened a crack and was starting to move upward. The family watched expectantly, uneasily, with expressions of curiosity mixed with fear.

"Something's coming out," Martha whispered.

"Don't panic," Sherman warned, noticing her feet which were doing a little dance. "Sudden movements may set them off."

Inside the stalled DeLorean, Marty was unaware that he was being watched. He had his own problems, chief among them being a total disorientation as to his whereabouts. Had he blacked out during the chase? If so, how had he managed to get from the mall parking lot into a barn that was obviously nowhere near Hill Valley? If he had not blacked out, what had happened to the guard rail? Where were the Libyans? Was some weapon pointed at him this very moment, about to finish him off?

He shook his head. Despite the risks, it seemed best to go outside and see where the devil he was.

Reaching for the handle, he finally discovered how to open the strange door and pushed his way out. A light rain of dust fell on the shoulders and hood of his radiation suit as his upper body started to move out of the car.

"It's an alien," Sherman Peabody whispered.

Indeed, the emerging figure seemed to be just that. Pa Peabody stared at it, transfixed, the baseball bat still in his hands. Using such a flimsy weapon against an alien was out of the question. Logic and morality both dictated that, but his primary motivation was fear. Poor Pa Peabody's mind had turned to jelly and all he could think of was self-preservation.

"Run, children!" he yelled. "Run for your lives!"

He then proceeded to show them exactly what he meant, streaking for the safety of the house. He had remembered the shotgun which he kept hidden under the bed in case he discovered a burglar in the middle of the night. This emergency qualified as sufficiently life-threatening for it to be used.

Sherman, seeing his father disappear into the house, realized that as the temporary male leader on the premises, it was up to him to find a way of preventing disaster. Having read up on human behavior when confronted by space creatures, he was not sanguine about being able to deal with the alien, either via force or kindness. In the comics and movies, neither method seemed to pay off very well. He remembered most poignantly the scene in *War of the Worlds* when the clergyman walked gently toward the Martian space vehicle, only to be zapped into nothingness for his troubles.

Nevertheless, a quick evaluation of the situation suggested strongly that the humane approach rather than the belligerent one would be better. He possessed no weapon with which to threaten or attack the alien; fear probably showed in his eyes, if not on his entire face. Thus it seemed preferable to throw himself on the creature's mercy.

He extended his hand gingerly.

"Peace," he murmured.

The alien was nearly all the way out of the space vehicle now. It was a biped, with arms and general body lines that resembled man's configurations. Sherman wondered what it looked like under the hood, whether it could utter sounds that were at all comprehensible.

"Hey," the alien said in perfect English. "Hello. Where am I?"

It took several steps toward them. Sherman, Martha, and his mother slowly retreated before it.

"Excuse me," the creature said. "Who are you? Where am I? Is this Hill Valley?"

Pa Peabody's footsteps sounded on the porch steps. Still clad in his red flannel underwear, he raced toward them with the shotgun held at near shoulder height.

Sherman, regarding the creature closely, made an instant decision based on analysis of alien behavior in comic books and movies. "Shoot it, Pa!" he yelled. "It's already mutated into human form! Shoot it!"

Although nervous and unsteady, Pa raised the weapon to his shoulder and took aim.

Marty, his vision blocked by the hood's limited field, walked toward the three people directly ahead of him, oblivious to Pa Peabody. As he moved forward, he reached up to take off the hood.

"Look out, Pa!" Sherman shouted. "He's going for something!"

"Take this, you mutated son of a bitch!" Pa yelled, squeezing the trigger of the shotgun.

A spray of buckshot whizzed past Marty's ear, cracking into the barn wall behind him.

Undeterred but still quite nervous, Pa squeezed off a second shot. It kicked up dirt in front of the creature, missing clearly, but caused it to turn and race back into the barn.

Comforted by the fact that the alien experienced fear, Pa broke the shotgun and started reloading. Moving cautiously forward, he looked into the barn.

"Careful, Pa," Sherman warned. "Don't get too close or he'll take over your brain."

"What the hell are you talking about, boy?"

Sherman still had the comic book in his hand, opened to the story about space zombies from Pluto. "It's all in here, Pa," he said. "Read it."

"Who's got time for reading now?" his father asked, not without logic.

Meanwhile, Marty had raced back to the DeLorean and hurled himself inside.

"Damn crazy farmer!" he gasped, reaching for the starter. The engine roared to life and he kicked the car backward, not bothering to see if anyone was behind him. Straw flew everywhere, but he could see well enough to spin around and head out through the barn door. As he did so, the four people scattered before him like bowling pins. He had too much speed, however, and was unable to swerve and avoid hitting the white picket fence surrounding two newly planted pine trees. The DeLorean tore through one of the pines before Marty guided it onto the dirt access road.

"You space bastard!" Pa Peabody yelled after him. "You killed one of my pines!"

Jerking the shotgun to his shoulder, he squeezed off both barrels at the departing vehicle. The shots went wide, striking the Peabody mailbox and blowing it to shreds.

"Whew!" Marty breathed, looking back at the tiny figures, one of whom was still waving an angry fist.

He had survived but still had no idea where he was. At least the people spoke English . . . but there was something about their clothes that seemed different. Replaying the scene in his mind, Marty concentrated on their outfits. The women's dresses looked old-fashioned. Perhaps they were very old hand-me-downs. Then there were the hair styles. Something seemed different about them, too, but Marty couldn't say exactly what it was. He had seen these people before—or types just like them. They seemed to be out of an old black-and-white movie.

"It's probably my imagination," he mused, realizing that he was frightened and disoriented. His brush with the Libyans had upset him more than he cared to admit.

Cruising along the dirt road, he made a conscious effort to regain his composure. "O.K., Marty, get ahold of yourself," he said aloud. "There's gotta be an explanation for this. It's probably all a dream, one very intense dream. It's all gonna resolve itself . . ."

As he rounded a corner, his headlights fell on an object that caused his jaw to drop.

"Holy shit!" he whispered.

Bringing the DeLorean to a sharp, almost spinning, halt,

he backed up so that the headlights would fall on the house again. Blinking, he studied it, trying to find one aspect that was different, one minor detail that would restore his sanity.

But the house was the same. It was *his* house . . . the home presently occupied by the McFly family. It was sitting out in the middle of nowhere and it looked newer than Marty had ever seen it, but it was definitely the identical structure.

The pieces of the puzzle slowly formed themselves into a cohesive picture. In front of his house was a sign that read MODEL HOME . . . pennants flapped limply in the soft night breeze . . . and next to the building was a large sign with an artist's rendering of an idyllic home nestled between magnificent oak trees with a typical American family of four standing next to a Cadillac . . . A very old shiny Cadillac . . . Below the picture, in huge block letters, was the promise of a dream fulfilled: LIVE IN THE HOME OF TOMORROW . . . TODAY! LYON ESTATES. SCHEDULED COMPLETION, THIS WINTER.

"It's my house, only brand new," Marty whispered.

Sitting in the middle of the dark countryside, he slowly glanced down at the dashboard of the DeLorean.

The DESTINATION TIME read 11-5-1955.

The PRESENT TIME read 11-5-1955.

"Nineteen fifty-five!" he shouted. "I can't believe it!"

But the evidence was all around him in addition to being on the dashboard. This was how the neighborhood must have looked while it was under construction. The roll of the land was the same and in the background were several familiar objects. Somehow he had entered a world that would not hear of him for another thirteen years.

"What a trip . . ." he murmured.

His eyes fell on the dashboard readouts once again. One in particular caught his eye. It was located directly below the Plutonium Chamber, a flashing light that blinked EMPTY over and over.

Shifting into gear and moving ahead, Marty realized that did not mean he was unable to move. It simply meant—

"Good God!" he said. "What *does* that mean? That I won't be able to go back?"

Having nowhere else to go, he backed into the driveway of his new home and sat, thinking, for quite some time. Idly, out of habit, he turned on the radio. Although it was nearly morning, there were still a few stations on the air, but they were all playing absolutely terrible music. One featured someone named Eddie Fisher singing the songs of Jerome Kern, another played numbers by Mitch Miller's orchestra and a bland singer named Guy Mitchell, and the announcers were all so tired-sounding.

"Is this what it was like?" Marty grimaced, turning the dial.

He stopped at a newscast. "President Eisenhower predicted that 1955 would see an increase in housing starts," the man intoned.

"Eisenhower?" Marty repeated. "Yeah, sure. We studied him in history. A nice enough guy who didn't do much except give Nixon his chance."

The news continued, much of it sounding exactly like news of 1985. "Big Four envoys gave up on disarmament talks," the announcer said. "The Russians rejected a United States plan that would have banned nuclear weapons... Officials at the First Smog Conference in Los Angeles said that smog may keep industry away from cities affected by this form of air pollution... Census watchers, meanwhile, predict that Los Angeles will be the second largest metropolitan area in the United States in a few years, passing Chicago... In the troubled Middle East, the United States laid down new rules to Egypt and Israel..."

As the newscast continued, there were many strange-sounding items and some that were slightly familiar. "In college football, quarterback John Brodie of Stanford continued to lead..." (The same middle-aged gentleman who occasionally turns up as color man on football broadcasts?) "U.C.L.A.'s ace placekicker Jim Decker..." (Jim Who?) "Texas Christian's sensational quarterback Jim Swink..." (Swink? Is he kidding?)

Marty turned up the radio, leaned back against the DeLorean's plush interior. He rather enjoyed this trip through his own personal time tunnel. Now the announcer was reading a few items dealing with gossip and entertainment. "Actress Joan Crawford and new husband, soft-drink executive Alfred Steele, celebrated their first half-year of marriage ...Jack Webb and actress-wife Dorothy Towne are reportedly having marital troubles... Back after this word from Northwest Ford..."

A different announcer launched into a sales pitch that Marty found not only irresistible but humorous. "You can get a new Ford pickup truck for just $1454," he said. "That's right—$1454 for a 1956 Ford. That's because we deal in volume..."

Recognizing the outline of a police cruiser, Marty quickly killed the lights and turned off the radio. It would not do, of course, for him to be picked up by the police. Even forgetting the fact that he had just arrived from a different time period, he would have enormous difficulty explaining the DeLorean, plus he did not have the necessary registration papers for it or a 1955 driver's license. He wondered what the officers would say if he showed them his 1985 license!

"Low profile," he murmured. "That's the best thing to keep for right now."

Sliding down in the seat, he watched as the patrol car passed quietly by. Then he got out, walked to the garage door and tried to open it. It was locked.

"Damn," he muttered.

On a whim, he reached into his pants pocket and took out his key ring. Thirty years was a long time for a lock to remain operative, but it was worth a try...

He whistled softly as the key slid into the lock and turned.

"That's better," he said. "I was beginning to think this wasn't my day."

Opening the garage door, he got into the DeLorean and backed it onto the pristine concrete slab. A moment later, in his normal street clothes, he walked out of his house and down the road toward Hill Valley.

Somewhere in the town below him was the key to getting back to 1985. Wherever it was, he had to find it.

• Chapter
Five •

Although most of the streets around his 1955 home were not yet constructed, it was comparatively easy for Marty to find his way from his house into Hill Valley. His sense of direction was good, and there were enough benchmarks for him to find his way through woods and across lots that later became streets and housing developments. Keeping his eyes fixed on the courthouse made it simple, of course, and as he drew closer to the center of town, the streets and buildings had changed less over the years.

At least it looked that way from a distance. As he moved closer, Marty realized that practically every building would undergo a change of identity from 1955 to 1985. Overall, the area seemed cleaner now, more vibrant, bustling with activity and excitement. The people who moved about appeared to know each other and be friendlier. But if this was true, it also worked against a stranger such as Marty. Several times he noted people watching him, staring at his clothes in a suspicious manner. He could almost hear them asking themselves—who is that young man? Why is he wearing green shoes? Is he some kind of pseudo-sophisticated show-off from New York?

The attitude bothered Marty but only briefly. As he neared the Town Square, he found himself quite caught up in seeing, live and in living color, genuine history. Even more fascinating was the fact that no one here could possibly share his feelings of amazement. To them it was humdrum, perhaps boring. The passing parade of subjects and styles was something they saw every day and took for granted. To Marty it was a museum that was one hundred percent accurate and throbbing with life.

The first object to greet his eye was the large sign at the corner of the square, at 2nd and Main streets. WELCOME TO HILL VALLEY, it read. A NICE PLACE TO LIVE, PLEASE DRIVE CAREFULLY. Symbols for the Jaycees, Optimists, and Future Farmers of America decorated the sign like medals on an old soldier's chest.

Turning right on Main, Marty strolled past Lou's Cafe, the "soda shop" he associated with his mother and father's growing-up years. Painted a sickly light green, the shop was largely empty now, probably because it was still quite early in the morning. Marty could imagine the place teeming with young people, though, ordering Cokes and malts, sundaes and burgers just as his mother had described the scene. Now the store was occupied only by a counterman and one or two coffee-drinking customers.

Turning away from the soda shop, Marty continued walking past Roy's Records, another hangout for Hill Valley teens. Out front was a sandwich-board poster which announced: JUST ARRIVED—THE BALLAD OF DAVY CROCKETT, 16 TONS, MANY MORE . . . Color posters in the window showed four women singers who called themselves The Chordettes; others promoted "Patti Page in the land of Hi Fi," "Eydie in Dixie Land," and "Unforgettable Songs by Nat 'King' Cole." There did not seem to be the slightest hint that rock 'n' roll existed or was on its way.

Next to Roy's was a Texaco filling station with a large hand-printed sign that proclaimed: PRICE WAR 19½¢ GAL-LON. Chuckling to himself, Marty walked close to the two pumps. One, green and silver, contained Sky Chief "super" gasoline for 21.9 cents; the red pump offered regular gas for just 19.9 cents per gallon. A cigarette machine against the front of the building advertised cigarettes for "20¢ a pack all brands," while a soft-drink machine offered Pepsi Cola for a dime.

Continuing to the end of the block, Marty found himself in front of the Essex Theater, a movie house which he had never seen before but felt he knew intimately. According to his mother and father—especially when a few drinks loosened their lips—the Essex was the local petting parlor on Saturday nights during the early and mid-1950s. There, in the balcony or deep recesses of the back rows, many warm and wonderful relationships were spawned. Occasionally, people even went there to see a movie, although oldtimers like Mom and Dad never reminisced about what was on the screen. Now it advertised in large red letters: CATTLE QUEEN OF MONTANA, starring Barbara Stanwyck and Ronald Reagan. Beneath the marquee floated a banner that read AIR CONDITIONED.

Looking across the grass plot of the square, Marty noted that the clock atop the beige courthouse building was actually running. When had it been struck by lightning and permanently immobilized? He tried to recall what the lady with the pamphlets had said earlier that day...

Earlier that day? More like thirty years in the future, Marty thought. At any rate, he remembered that the clock had stopped sometime in 1955. "Right about now," he mused. "Maybe I arrived here just in time."

He smiled. The great historical events of other cities were battles or memorable natural disasters; Hill Valley's claim to fame was nothing more exciting than a clock stopping. Well, at least he would be able to tell his grandchildren, assuming they didn't question him too carefully about how he happened to be here on the memorable occasion thirteen years before his birth.

Walking across the edge of the square, he turned right on 2nd Street, which was the confluence of routes 395 West and 295 East. Next to the Bank of America—one of the few businesses still operating in 1985 that was also here now—was the Ask Mr. Foster travel agency. It advertised "fabulous 10-day vacations in Cuba." Once again Marty chuckled. He rather liked sharing history's little secrets of what was to come.

Adjoining the travel agency was J.D. Armstrong's realty office, in the window of which was a color ad for Lyon Estates, his past and present home. A total price of $17,500 brought you a three-bedroom, two-car garage house complete with "totally electric kitchen." Another advertisement offered bomb shelters at equally reasonable prices.

He continued past Zale's Jewelers, the Hill Valley Stationery Shop, a barber offering haircuts for seventy-five cents, the Bluebird Motel with its room for five dollars ("and up," of course), a Western Auto store that sold nearly everything from Daisy air rifles to "the world's smallest radio," which was about a foot long. Past Ruth's Frock Shop and its dresses from Paris for $40 was the future Toyota dealership space, now known as Statler Motors Studebaker.

This was the most interesting historical oddity in Hill Valley, at least in Marty's opinion. He liked cars, new and old, and the Studebaker held a special place in his heart because, like the Edsel, it thrived and became extinct more or less during Marty's lifetime.

He looked in the showroom for a few moments, then

studied the used cars in an adjoining lot.

"These would be worth a lot in 1985," he murmured, "even the clunker on the right."

The four used cars on display ranged from $950 to a bargain-basement $395. All were clean-looking and had a brief bit of praise written in white on the windshield: "Sharp, Clean," "Low Mileage," "A steal at $450," and "Runs Good" for the clunker. Marty felt the urge to give them a spin, but he knew no salesman would allow a teenager to do so, especially in this day and age.

Continuing past the Studebaker lot, he stopped in front of the Town Theatre, a marvelously typical piece of art deco from the 1930s. A basic tan-colored tower rose above its green marquee and red tile entrance, which was lined with display shots of its current attractions, *The Atomic Kid,* starring Mickey Rooney and Robert Strauss.

He didn't know what *The Atomic Kid* was about, but it struck Marty that he could apply that title to himself. Using a small amount of plutonium, he had managed to travel back in time, something no one else had done. The knowledge pleased him, but at the same time he was visited by another thought.

"What next?" he asked aloud. "How long does this go on? How do I get back?"

For the first time, it occurred to him that the time-travel process might not be reversible. The circumstances under which the transformation took place, for example, were hardly scientific, with the scientist being killed and the time traveler literally pursued into the experiment. Now it seemed there was only enough plutonium for a one-way trip. Perhaps this is it, Marty mused darkly.

Who could help him? Who could answer his questions? Certainly no one in 1955, an era which was only tinkering with space travel. Unless—

"Sure!" Marty said, snapping his fingers. "Doc Brown

must be somewhere around here."

He walked briskly back toward the soda shop, which he was sure must have a telephone booth. It being Saturday, the place was largely deserted now. A nerdy-looking kid sat at the counter, eating Rice Krispies and reading a comic book. He did not look up as Marty entered. Behind the counter were signs reading "Hamburger—25 cents," "Ham and Cheese—30 cents," "Chocolate Sundae—15 cents." The prices fascinated Marty so completely that he must have stared at them long enough to convince the counterman that he was undesirable.

"Whatever you're selling, kid, we don't want any," he said abruptly.

"I'm not selling anything," Marty replied. "I just want to use the telephone."

Marty nodded and started for the booth at the back of the store. Grabbing the directory, he flipped through the pages until he came to the familiar name. "Brown, Emmett L." Immediately following was the word, "Scientist," then Brown's address and telephone number.

Marty smiled and withdrew a nickel from his pocket.

The phone rang and rang. No answer.

"Damn," Marty muttered, hanging up. "This just isn't my day."

He ripped the page out of the directory and sauntered back toward the counter.

"Can you tell me where 1640 Riverside Drive is?" he asked, when the counterman finally looked his way.

"You gonna order something, kid?"

Marty shrugged. Why not, he thought, if it would get him some information.

"Uh, sure," he said. "Gimme a Tab."

The counterman sighed loudly, looked at him askance.

"You'll get that later."

"What?"

"I can't give you the tab unless you order something," the counterman growled.

Marty didn't get it but just decided to roll with the punches. "Then let me have a Pepsi Free."

"Kid," the counterman said, making no attempt to hide his growing irritation, "if you want a Pepsi, you gotta pay for it."

Am I slow, Marty thought, realizing he had been trying to buy products which had not yet been invented.

The counterman continued to glare at him from beneath bushy eyebrows.

"Uh, well, just give me something to drink that doesn't have sugar in it."

The counterman shook his head, left, and returned a moment later with a glass of water and cup of black coffee. Marty did not enjoy black coffee.

"Have you got any Sweet 'n' Low?" he asked, then quickly added. "Or something like it?"

"Tell me what Sweet 'n' Low is," the counterman said, forcing patience into his voice.

"It's an artificial sugar substitute with no calories," Marty said.

"We don't have anything like that."

The Middle Ages, Marty thought.

"Maybe you better pay for this right now," the counterman said, eyeing Marty suspiciously.

"Sure."

He reached into his pocket and found only a couple of nickels and a dime. Surely not enough. The smallest thing in his wallet was a twenty-dollar bill. He took it out and handed it to the man.

"A twenty?" he said in horror. "What do you think this is, a bank? I can't break a twenty for a nickel cup of coffee, kid."

"Oh, it's only a nickel?" Marty smiled, relieved. "I'm

sorry. I thought it'd be a lot more."

"How much more?"

"Well, at least fifty cents."

"Thank God things ain't come to that," replied the counterman, taking the nickel. Then his eyes narrowed. "Say, what's a kid your age doing with a twenty-dollar bill, anyway?"

There were only two possibilities, and since one of them involved illegal activities, Marty decided to plead guilty to the second. "I'm a spoiled rich kid," he said. "New in town."

It satisfied the counterman. "Tell your old man it would be a lot better if you got a job and learned the value of money instead of his just givin' you everything," he said scornfully.

"Thanks. I'll tell him."

The counterman walked away.

Marty raised the cup of coffee, took a sip, grimaced and put it down.

"Hey, McFly!" a voice suddenly called.

Marty nearly knocked the cup over. Spinning around on his stool, he looked toward the direction of the voice.

Four young fellows of about seventeen were moving from the entrance of the shop toward the nerdy boy several stools away. The face of the leader looked vaguely familiar. The beady eyes, lips curled into a sneer and beefy jaw presented tantalizing clues but Marty couldn't solve the puzzle. The other three gave him problems, being nondescript types of the period. One chewed a wooden matchstick and obviously thought it made him appear either cool or tough or both; the second wore his hair in a crewcut that was just this side of being bald; the third peered out at the world through red-green 3-D glasses.

"Answer me when I talk, McFly," the leader said.

The superior tone in his voice provided the last piece of the puzzle for Marty. Of course! The punk was simply a

young version of the biggest punk of them all, Biff Tannen.
And the nerdy kid—

Marty looked at him closely. There was no doubt that
the nerdy kid was George McFly, his father. The same
terrorized look was in his eyes as Biff Tannen approached,
the same nervous mannerisms and body language that told
you he wanted to be anywhere else but around his tormentor.
Unfortunately, there was also the same cowardice which
kept him rooted to the spot like a helpless slave.

"Hi, Biff, how's it going?" young George McFly asked,
trying to sound casual but not carrying it off very well. His
voice had a distinctly subservient tone.

"What d'you mean, it?" Biff shot back as his cohorts
laughed. "What's *it?*"

"Er . . . that's just an expression," George muttered. "I
. . . just wanted to make sure everything was all right with
you."

"Everything?" Biff repeated. "You're interested in *everything* about me? That's a lot. You mean, you're interested
in what I had for breakfast, whether I burped afterward or
not—"

His pals howled as George forced a smile, then lapsed
into silence.

Still the same old punching bag, Marty thought, looking
at his future father.

"You got my homework finished, McFly?" Biff asked,
"you Irish bug?"

George's eyes avoided those of his nemesis. "Well, no,"
he muttered softly. "I figured that since it's not due till
Monday . . ."

Biff reached out with his fist and knocked three times
on George's head.

"Hello," he said loudly. "Anybody home?"

Once again his friends laughed automatically, emulating
Pavlov's dog perfectly.

"Think, McFly," Biff Tannen continued. "Think! I've gotta have time to copy it, right? Do you realize what would happen if I turned in *my* homework in *your* handwriting? I'd get kicked out of school."

"Yeah," George smiled. "I guess I didn't think of that. I'm sorry."

Marty sighed and shook his head. It was almost too painful to watch, this beginning of a thirty-year torture test which his father continued to fail.

"What are you looking at, butthead?"

Marty suddenly realized the words were directed at him, and not his father. But instead of looking away from the pitiful drama taking place in front of him, he continued to direct a gaze of disgust at both Tannen and George McFly. To his satisfaction, Biff looked away.

"So how about my homework, McFly?" he asked, continuing the badgering session.

George shrugged his shoulders, a gesture that was part resignation and part obeisance. "Uh, O.K., Biff," he said. "I'll do it tonight and bring it over first thing tomorrow morning."

Biff nodded coldly. "Not too early," he said. "I sleep in on Sundays. If you woke me up, I'd have to mess up your features a little."

His pals cackled once again, bringing a delighted smile to Biff's face. George sat tightly scrunched onto the stool, every twitch of his body indicating that he wanted nothing more than to see the last of Biff Tannen on this day.

His joy at Biff's leavetaking was to be delayed briefly, however. Turning as if to go, Biff suddenly whirled, looked down at George's feet and said: "Oh, hey, McFly—your shoe's untied."

"Huh?"

As George's glance dropped, Biff brought up his fist,

tapping him on the point of the chin. It was a blow that was more embarrassing than painful. "Fell for it again, didn't you, McFly?" Biff laughed. "Boy, if anybody wanted to coldcock you, they wouldn't have any trouble."

"I guess not," George murmured.

"Come on, guys, let's go," Biff announced, leading the way out of the shop.

George and Marty watched them go.

"I can't believe it," Marty said finally. "You're a young George McFly..."

His father-to-be looked at him, puzzled. "Of course I'm young," he said. "Do I know you from someplace? You don't look familiar."

"No," Marty replied. "But I know you."

"Not from school."

Marty shook his head.

"Then you couldn't know me," George said.

"Oh yes, I do... Your birthday's August 18th and your mother's name is Sylvia, right?"

George shook his head, not because the information was wrong but because he was amazed. Had the fellow gotten hold of school files or looked through his wallet? Was he a young cop or what?

"Well?" Marty continued. "Isn't that correct? Isn't it also true that your father enlisted in World War I as a sixteen-year-old, was sent to France before they found out, and shipped back without firing a shot?"

George nearly choked on his Pepsi. Someone could have gleaned the other information by looking at a questionnaire, but the story about his dad was inside-family material. How had this young man found out?

"Uh-huh," George replied. "That's all true. How did you find out and who are you?"

Having enjoyed amazing and confounding the young

George McFly, Marty suddenly realized he had no plausible answer to the question. He could not tell him the truth, of course. That was not only implausible but might bring on a new barrage of questions.

In reply, he smiled and tried to look enigmatic.

"Let's just say I'm your guardian angel," he said. "All that stuff about your family isn't really important, though. What's important is that you shouldn't let that creep Biff Tannen push you around."

"That's a fact, man."

The reply to Marty's charge, so rapid and direct, did not come from George McFly, but from Goldie Wilson, a black busboy who was sweeping up several feet away. George and Marty turned to look at him. Pausing in his work, Goldie returned their gazes with an intense, nearly mesmerizing, look of his own.

"Say, what do you let that boy push you around for?" he asked.

George blinked, taken aback by the usually quiet black man.

"This isn't the first time I saw him treat you like that," Goldie went on. "I clean up a lot of mess around here, but nothin' makes me sicker than seein' him practically spit on you. Why don't you stand up?"

"Well, uh, he's bigger than me," George stammered, his voice whiney and miserable-sounding.

"Everybody's bigger than you when you're on your knees," Goldie replied. "Listen, if you're gonna make it in this world, you gotta have some respect for yourself. You let people walk over you now, they'll be walkin' over you the rest of your life. You want to be a door mat, have people wipe their feet on you till you die?"

George shook his head. It wasn't a very decisive gesture.

"The man's right," Marty said. "And he's got a lot more

reason to curl up and die than you have."

"That's a fact!" Goldie nodded. "Look at me. Most people think I'm nothing, but I *know* I'm something. You think I'm gonna spend the rest of my life behind a broom in this slophouse?"

The counterman, attracted by the raised voices, had gravitated to the scene. Now he looked at Goldie with a curling lip. "Watch it, Goldie," he said meaningfully.

Goldie didn't flinch. "No sir!" he said to George. "I'm not gonna end up here. I'm gonna make something of myself! I'm going to night school. Every night of the week. I'm gonna be somebody!"

"Goldie," Marty interjected, something suddenly clicking in his mind. "Would that be Goldie Wilson, by any chance?"

Goldie nodded. "That's me," he said. "And you can just remember that name, because, like I said, it's gonna mean something one day."

The counterman chuckled.

"He's right," Marty said. "As a matter of fact, he's gonna be Mayor of Hill Valley someday."

Goldie looked at Marty closely, frowning, searching for the hint of sarcasm that would normally accompany such a remark made by a white man. There didn't seem to be any guile, however. This fellow was either sincere or the world's greatest actor. In either case, Goldie decided not to be put off by the comment but to accept it as a challenge.

"Mayor?" he said. "That's a good idea. I could show folks how to run this town. I wouldn't be a cheap politician on the take all the time. I'll be honest and efficient." Then, looking at Marty, he said: "You got a crystal ball or something? How do you know I'm gonna be mayor?"

"I just know, that's all."

"When's it gonna happen?"

Marty sighed. He had gotten himself in deep again with his knowledge of the future. "Do you really want to know?" he countered.

"Of course, man. Tell me. Why shouldn't I want to know when it's gonna happen?"

"Because it's a ways off. You might not want to wait that long."

"No, it's all right. Something like that's worth waitin' for. Besides, I'll know that nothing will happen to me between now and then, right?"

Marty nodded. "You'll be elected during the late '70s," he said.

"My seventies or the 1970s?" Goldie smiled.

"The 1970s."

"Heck, that's not too long to wait. My mother worked forty years and got nothing out of it. So I guess I can work another twenty or twenty-five for a payoff like that..."

As Goldie talked, the nervousness in George McFly began to grow nearly unbearable. It wasn't the situation or anything that Goldie said. Rather, it was this young man who professed to know everything. He seemed almost from another world, so assured, calm, different from all the other teenagers George knew. And he dressed strangely, wore his hair in an unusual way. George wasn't a religious person but he was superstitious. The occult, the unknown bothered him more than the concrete promises and strictures of formalized religion. Suppose this man could see the future? Others may have regarded that as a blessing, a way of becoming rich and avoiding life's pitfalls. Not so George McFly. He didn't want to know what lay ahead, for him or anyone else. Better to remain in the dark than be forced to think about some unavoidable tragedy or struggle. If this young man somehow knew everything past and future, George wanted to get away from him as soon as possible.

Having arrived at that decision, he took advantage of the

conversation between Goldie and Marty to edge his way toward the door. A few seconds later, he slipped around the corner and walked briskly for his bike.

Meanwhile, the counterman, who had listened to Goldie's speech with increasing frustration, finally managed to break in. "Mayor," he said. "Ha! A colored mayor of this town. That'll be the day!"

"You wait and see," Goldie returned. "Like this man here says, someday I'm gonna be mayor."

"I ain't impressed by this man here," the counterman retorted. "And as for you, just keep sweeping."

Goldie slid his hands up on the broom handle but didn't set to work immediately. "Mayor Goldie Wilson," he said softly. "I like the sound of that."

Marty smiled, rather pleased with himself for "inspiring" Goldie Wilson, or at least giving him hope. A moment later, the smile disappeared as he realized that George McFly was no longer in the store.

"Hey—" he called, catching a glance of George's back as he started to cycle away.

He raced out of the store, his arms waving. "George!" he called after the departing figure. "Hey, George! I want to talk to you!"

Either oblivious, out of earshot, or not wishing to prolong their conversation, George McFly moved ahead without so much as a glance over his shoulder. Marty started to run after him, then suddenly remembered that his father had grown up on Sycamore Street, near 2nd. He had driven past it with the family once and pointed it out. Sure that he could locate the house now, Marty slowed to a fast walk.

He wasn't certain exactly where he wanted his relationship with the young George McFly to go. The man, despite his failings, did survive the next thirty years. That was something. Nevertheless, Marty felt a compulsion to have at least one heart-to-heart talk with him. Perhaps, if nothing else, he could say something that would free George McFly of Biff Tannen's bullying for the next three decades.

"Wouldn't that be a wonderful present?" Marty said aloud as he walked. Playing it back, he was somewhat surprised that he had such kind feelings toward his father-to-be. Could it be because they had a certain kinship now? He had never thought of his father as a young man before. Yet here he was, the same age as Marty. It would be fun, of course, to see his father's reaction when he told him who he was, but that was impossible. It was also likely to drive George crazy, so Marty dispensed with the notion.

His sense of direction took him to Sycamore Street, which was decorated with solid homes built during the 1920s and '30s. White picket fences were everywhere, framing the neat lawns into meticulously edged walkways leading to the doors. It was a much nicer neighborhood than Marty remembered, having grown seedy by the early 1970s.

George's bike was leaning against a tree overhanging Sycamore Street but George himself was nowhere to be seen. Marty stood still a moment, debating whether or not to go into the house. In all likelihood, his grandmother would be there, no doubt looking younger than he had ever seen her. Marty wasn't sure he wanted to deal with that. Granny had been very close to him, and he felt this closeness would betray him. Somehow, even though Marty had not yet been born, he felt she would sense who he was and be terribly frightened by it.

His inner debate lasted only a minute. Looking upward through the limbs of the tree, Marty caught sight of George. He was nearly twenty feet up, perched precariously on a thick branch that jutted far over the street.

"I can't believe it," Marty breathed. "That's the most courageous thing I've ever seen him do."

He soon found out why George had taken such a risk. In his hands was a pair of binoculars, which the young man had trained on a second-story window of the house across the street. The profile of a woman's head and shoulders could be seen at street level. From the vantage point of twenty feet up, Marty could imagine what was visible.

"I'll be damned," he muttered, smiling. "Dad's a Peeping Tom."

Two things happened then in rapid succession. George, trying to gain an ever better vantage point, suddenly lost his balance. He slid sideways around the thick branch, grasped desperately for it, missed, then plunged downward toward the street. As he fell, his body struck several smaller branches, which served to lessen his rate of descent and perhaps spare him broken bones. Landing on his hip and receiving a minor blow to the head, he lay limp and dazed in the center of the road.

At that very moment, a car moving quickly around the corner headed directly at the young man's body.

Marty had no time to yell a warning. Instinctively, he threw himself toward George, delivering a neat cross-body block that sent him free of the car. Marty himself was not so fortunate. Hitting the brakes, the driver swerved to avoid the two youngsters but succeeded only in missing George. There was a loud bump as the car's fender struck Marty's shoulder and head.

"Crazy kids!" the driver yelled, not in anger but in horror. "They didn't give me a chance!"

He was nearly crying as he bent next to the young man who had saved the other's life. "Please, God," he prayed. "Let him be all right. I can't afford to be sued."

•Chapter
Six•

The next thing Marty saw after the shiny car bumper was a soft white lacy pattern, slightly out of focus, falling away from a table top. He blinked, looked around at the bedroom he had never seen before. Far away, a wall was decorated with unfamiliar pictures and pennants; to their right was a window, through which an outside street lamp poured sharp and painful light. He closed his eyes again.

His head was cold and felt the pressure of something resting on it.

"I think he's going to be all right," he heard a soft feminine voice say. It was a familiar sound.

"Mom? Is that you?" Marty whispered.

Gentle hands moved the cold object against his forehead, touched his cheeks.

"Shh. Everything's going to be all right."

It was his mother. Marty opened his eyes despite the pain

but all he could see was a silhouette. The voice had been unmistakable, though.

"God, what a terrible nightmare," he said. "I dreamt I went back in time . . ."

"In time for what?" the voice asked.

It was his mother, all right. Always so comfortingly literal. Marty started to sit up, but leaned back again when he experienced a slightly dizzy sensation.

"Take it easy, now," his mother said. "You've been asleep for almost nine hours. Better not hop right out of bed. Better to take it slowly."

"It was terrible," Marty continued. "It was a terrible place to be. The music was awful—they didn't have Huey Lewis. Our neighborhood hadn't even been built yet, except for our house. Everything was so weird looking and the people acted so strange."

"I see . . . You dreamed you went back to another time."

"Yeah."

"How far back?"

"Thirty years."

"All the way to the flapper days? That must have been interesting. But there's no need to worry. You're safe and sound, back where you belong, in good old 1955."

"Nineteen fifty-five!"

Forgetting the discomfort, he sat up and turned on the bedside lamp.

"Oh, my God!" he said.

The young woman was the same one George McFly had been spying on. But that was only part of it.

"What is it?" she asked, concerned.

"You're my . . . my m—" Marty began.

"Your what?"

"Nothing. Never mind."

His head fell back against the pillow.

"My name's Lorraine," the girl said. "Lorraine B—"

"Baines," Marty continued.

She smiled. "How did you know that?"

He shrugged. "I get around," he said cryptically.

Lorraine lifted the cold compress. "I'll get you some new ice," she said.

As she stood to leave, Marty released an involuntary gasp of surprise, causing her to eye him cautiously.

"Are you all right?"

"Yeah."

"What was that sound for?"

"It's just that you're so thin," Marty replied.

"Thanks, I guess," she said. "I've always been on the thin side." She patted her flat stomach. "You don't think I'm *too* thin, do you?"

"No. It looks great," Marty said sincerely.

"Thank you, Calvin," she smiled.

"Calvin?"

"Yes. Isn't that your name?"

"No."

She frowned. "That's funny. I was sure it was. Your name isn't Calvin Klein?"

"No. It's Marty."

"Then why does your under—"

She blushed, looked away.

Marty suddenly became aware of his pants folded across the chair in the opposite corner. Reaching down beneath the covers, he realized he was clad only in his underwear.

"We took your pants and shirt off when we put you in bed," Lorraine said, a trifle embarrassed. "I've never seen purple underwear before, much less purple underwear with a man's name written on it."

"Oh," Marty replied. "That isn't my name. Calvin Klein is the name of the underwear manufacturer."

"And your name's Marty?" she asked.

"Yes."

"Well, I'm pleased to meet you, Marty," she said, sitting next to him on the bed. Her attitude seemed different now, much less motherly, more seductive.

"And what's your last name?" she smiled.

The word "McFly" formed on Marty's lips, but he managed to avoid saying it. That would have been hard to explain, McFly being a rather uncommon name. Instead of trying to deal with that, Marty winced as if a sudden rush of pain had just struck him.

"Oh, you poor boy," Lorraine whispered. She reached out to touch him but he moved away.

"Are you all right?"

"Yes," he said, exhaling softly as if the pain had passed. "Is it O.K. for me to sit here?"

Marty gulped. "Uh, sure," he replied. But even as he said it, he involuntarily moved as far away from her as he could without falling off the bed. He held the blanket tight around his waist, his eyes apprehensive. Lorraine continued to stare at him, fascinated, apparently oblivious of his nervousness.

"That's quite a bruise there," she said finally, reaching out to touch his forehead. Smiling weakly, he submitted, until she began running her fingers through his hair. When she started doing that, Marty found himself inching farther and farther away until—

Whump. Suddenly he was on the floor, stark naked except for his underwear. He reached for the blanket. Lorraine giggled naughtily.

"Lorraine! Are you up there?"

The voice was accompanied by the sound of heavy footsteps on the stairs outside the bedroom.

"Yes, mother," Lorraine said.

Grabbing Marty's pants off the chair back, she tossed them at him. Lying on his back, he struggled into them as the steps came closer.

"How's the patient?" Stella Baines asked as she entered the room. Then, looking around, she added: *"Where*'s the patient?"

Marty looked up over the edge of the bed. Stella Baines, forty, his grandmother-to-be, stared back at him. She was pregnant and looked terribly young. If Marty remembered correctly, she was carrying her last child, the one born after Uncle Joey the jailbird. She had the same pleasant eyes as when she was older, very pale blue and rather sad.

"Marty, this is my mother," Lorraine said, tossing him his shirt.

He put it on from a sitting position. "How do you do?" he smiled.

"Feel up to having something to eat?"

Marty nodded.

"Then come on downstairs."

Marty found his shoes, put them on and started out of the room after her. As they walked down the hall, Stella Baines regarded him with a half smile.

"So tell me, Marty, how long have you been with the circus?"

Marty could only stare. Lorraine made a sound that was half sigh, half snort of anger. "Mother," she said. "How could you?"

"The circus?" Marty murmured. "I'm not with the circus. What do you mean?"

"Your clothes seem so unusual," Stella remarked. "We thought perhaps you might be with a sideshow."

Marty smiled and shrugged. The green shoes and shirt with U.S. Patent Office facsimile probably did seem unusual to people of 1955. Rather than explain that these clothes were normal wearing apparel of the '80s, he said: "I guess I just like strange clothes, ma'am. Sorry."

"There's no need to apologize. We were just a little curious, that's all."

They entered the living room, where four children and Sam Baines, Marty's future grandfather, were relaxing. Sam, a gruff man of forty-five, stood next to the black-and-white television set, adjusting the rabbit ears. He didn't look their way until the picture locked in.

"Sam, here's the young man you hit with the car," Stella said matter-of-factly. "Thank God he's all right."

"What were you doing in the middle of the street, a kid your age?" Sam asked coldly.

"He'd fallen—" Marty began. Then he decided not to say that his father had fallen out of a tree. That could lead to embarrassing revelations or at the very least, suspicion. "He'd fallen . . . in the road," Marty continued. "There was this other kid. I rushed over to shove him out of the way. Didn't you see him, sir?"

"Pa never sees anything when he's driving," Lorraine said.

"What are you talking about?" her father snapped. "I'm a damn good driver. But there's nothing a good driver can do when kids jump out in front of him."

"Especially when you're going around the corner on two wheels," Lorraine added.

"By the way," Marty interjected. "What happened to that other boy?"

"He just got up and left," Sam said.

"I guess he didn't want to get involved," Marty murmured, thinking how much like George McFly that was.

"Anyways," Sam said, turning once again to the rabbit ears, "pedestrians got no right to be fooling around in the middle of the street. Any judge'll tell you that."

"Oh, don't mind him," Stella said. "He's just in one of his moods." She started to lead Marty toward the dining room, calling back to Sam over her shoulder. "Quit fiddling with that thing. It's time for dinner."

Sam, studiously ignoring her, continued adjusting the rabbit ears until the picture was completely unwatchable.

The dining room was already half-filled with people. Seated at the table, ready to pitch in, were Milton, twelve, who was wearing a Davy Crockett coonskin cap; Sally, six; Toby, four; and in the playpen on the floor, eleven-month-old Joey.

Stella made the introductions. Marty was utterly fascinated, seeing his aunt and uncles looking so different. Joey, about to take the first steps in a long unlucky life, was rattling the bars of his playpen and salivating wildly. Marty looked at him, shook his head. So you're my Uncle Joey, he thought; get used to those bars, kid.

"He seems to enjoy being there," he said to Stella. "It's like he belongs."

"Oh, yes," she replied, unaware that Marty was being mildly sarcastic. "Little Joey loves being in his pen. He actually cries when we take him out. So we leave him there most of the time. It seems to make him happy and certainly quiets him down."

He's become institutionalized already, Marty thought, laughing inwardly.

"I hope you like meat loaf, Marty," Stella said.

Some things never change, Marty thought.

"Oh, yes," he said.

"Sit here, Marty," Lorraine offered, pulling out the chair next to hers.

"Thanks."

Marty sat, noting that the plate in front of him was already filled with meat loaf, mashed potatoes, mixed vegetables, and macaroni and cheese. In fact, the dinner was an exact replica of the one he had eaten the night before in 1985.

Everybody pitched in, except Lorraine, who toyed with her food. Marty wondered when she had made the switch from finicky taster to eating machine.

As the family proceeded, Stella kept yelling instructions and criticism to everyone except Marty. "Milton, don't eat so fast! Lorraine, you're not eating enough. Have some mashed potatoes . . . Sally, don't hold your fork like that. You look like somebody who just got off the pickle boat . . . Don't push everything on the table, Toby . . . My Goodness . . . Sam, would you quit fiddling with that television set? Come in here and eat . . ."

Her husband had no intention of giving up television watching during dinner, however. Striding away from the living room set, he soon reappeared with a brand-new set on a plywood dolly.

"Look at this," he announced proudly. "I made the dolly myself so we can roll it in the dining room and watch Jackie Gleason while we eat."

"Oh, boy!" Milton exclaimed.

Mrs. Baines sighed wearily. About the only time she commanded attention was during dinner hour. Now Sam had found a way to take that away from her. But she was wise enough to know she couldn't fight it.

Sam fiddled with the rabbit ears of the new set, finally managing to bring in a rather muddy image of a cigarette commercial.

Marty watched, fascinated, as a surgeon stepped out of an operating room, lit up a cigarette, and began speaking to the audience. "After facing the tension of doing three lung operations in a row, I like to relax by lighting up a Sir Walter Randolph. I know its fine tobacco taste will soothe my nerves and improve my circulation . . ."

"That's incredible!" Marty said, in spite of himself. He had never seen a television commercial advertising cigarettes and couldn't quite comprehend the brazenness of it.

Sam Baines thought the young man was commenting on

his excellent job of fine tuning. He beamed as he said: "Yep. Look at that picture . . . It's crystal clear. You're right, boy, it's incredible all right."

"I meant the cigarette commercial," Marty replied.

"What's so incredible about that?" Lorraine asked.

"The way the doctor is advertising it. Cigarette smoking causes lung cancer. How can he do lung operations and then puff a cigarette? It's crazy!"

"Well," Sam muttered. "They ain't proved anything yet. Don't see why a doctor can't advertise cigarettes if he wants to."

"Because it's immoral."

"Don't be silly."

Sam's self-satisfied tone irritated Marty. "Well," he said, "it'll be outlawed someday. That's how silly it is."

The rest of the family, except those too young to comprehend, stared at Marty incredulously. To say that one day American television would be without cigarette commercials was like saying one day Christmas would be devoid of Santa Claus. Only Lorraine looked as if Marty's statement had any possible merit.

"Well," she said cautiously, "it may not happen, but I think it's a good idea. Too many young people see those ads on TV and think it's the smart thing to do."

Sam couldn't really argue with that so he decided to turn the topic in another direction. "Why would anybody want to go to the movies when you can see this in your own home—free?" he rhapsodized.

"Do you have a television set?" Lorraine asked, looking at Marty warmly.

"Yes," he replied. "Two."

"Wow! You must be rich!" Milton gushed.

"They're in color, too," Marty added, before realizing that was not too smart a thing to say to a 1955 family.

Milton's eyes widened.

"Bull," Sam Baines scoffed.

Stella smiled condescendingly. "He's teasing you, Milton," she said. "Nobody has two television sets . . . in color, yet."

She looked to Marty for confirmation.

"Yeah, that's right," he nodded. "I was just pulling your leg, Miltie."

The commercial break was over and *The Honeymooners* began. Marty recognized the segment immediately as the classic "Man from Space" episode. Almost without realizing he was doing it, he began saying the show's lines a split second before the actors said them. Everyone at the table regarded him with varying degrees of amazement. Lorraine laughed every time he did it; her father scowled.

"How come you know the lines?" Milton asked.

"Because I've seen this one before," he replied.

"What do you mean, you've seen it?" Milton asked. "It's brand new."

"I saw it on a rerun."

"What's a rerun?"

"You'll find out."

"O.K., smarty," Milton persisted. "Tell me what happens next."

"Sure," Marty said. "This is a good one. Ralph dresses up as a 'man from space.'"

"Quiet!" Sam ordered. "I want to see this!"

The family was silent for perhaps a minute. Then Stella looked at Marty closely. "You know, there's something very familiar about you," she said. "Do I know your mother?"

Marty couldn't help smiling. "Yeah, I think maybe you do," he replied, glancing sideways at Lorraine and smiling weakly.

"I'd like to give her a call," Stella said. "You know, to

let her know that you're all right."

"Well, you can't," Marty blurted.

"Why not?"

"Uh . . . She's not home yet. Nobody's home."

"She works?"

"Not exactly," Marty hedged. "Uh, both my folks are sort of away."

"I don't understand—"

"It's all right, Mrs. Baines," Marty assured her. "My Mom's used to my staying out late. She won't even miss me."

"You're sure?"

"Yes, ma'am. I could be away for the next thirteen years and she wouldn't notice."

The remark obviously tickled Milton, for he giggled hard enough to lose some of his food.

"Isn't anybody watching this show?" Sam muttered irritably.

Another minute of silence followed. Then, as a new series of commercials started, Marty remembered that he wanted to look up Doc Brown. "Uh, could anybody tell me where Riverside Drive is?" he asked.

"Riverside?" Sam replied. "Sure. It's on the east side of town, a block past Maple."

"A block past Maple?" Marty repeated, puzzled. "But that's JFK Drive . . ."

"J.F. what?"

"John F. Kennedy Drive."

"Who the hell is John F. Kennedy?" Sam demanded.

"Uh, never mind."

"Just keep heading east until you come to Maple," Sam said. "Then the block after is Riverside."

"Thank you."

"Mother," Lorraine said. "With Marty's parents away,

don't you think he should spend the night here? I'd hate for anything to happen to him with that bruise on his head. He could faint or something..."

She directed a slightly flirtatious smile at Marty, who smiled back weakly.

"Marty, maybe Lorraine is right. Maybe you'd better spend the night. After all, Dad ran into you. That means you're our responsibility..."

"Not legally," Sam interjected hotly.

"Maybe not, but morally he is," Stella retorted. She looked at Marty for a response.

"I don't know..." he temporized.

"You can sleep in my room," Lorraine suggested.

"Lorry's got a crush," Milton taunted. "Lorry's got a crush..."

Lorraine straightened up in her chair and glared imperiously at her little brother. "I'm just trying to be hospitable," she said.

No one really believed it, least of all Marty. He glanced at his watch, pushed his plate away. "Uh... if you'll excuse me, I really have to be going," he said.

"But there's pie—" Stella protested.

"I'm really sorry," Marty said. "I've got an appointment with this man..."

He got to his feet, nodded at Sam and the rest of the kids, all of whom continued eating. "Thank you for everything. I'll see you all later. Much later."

A moment later, he was gone.

Lorraine sighed. "I wonder what we said to make him act that way," she said.

"He's a very strange young man," Stella murmured. "He's pleasant enough most of the time, but other times he just seems to drift off into another world."

"He's an idiot," Sam Baines amended. "It comes from his upbringing. His parents are probably idiots, too, and maybe even his grandparents. I wouldn't be surprised if the whole family's nuts." He looked darkly at Lorraine. "If you ever have a kid who acts that way, I'll disown you. That goes for all of you."

Having restored his suzerainty in the household, he loaded his fork with a huge mouthful of instant potatoes and returned his attention to Jackie Gleason.

•Chapter Seven•

Doc Brown adjusted the instrument on his head, shuffled the deck of cards, and once again picked one. Placing it face down on the table, he twisted the series of dials which activated the contraption on his head. A crackling noise filled the room and a quick vision of a jack of spades passed before Brown's eyes.

"Excellent!" he cried.

He turned the card over. It was a three of diamonds.

"Damn," he muttered.

He tried once again, and once again failed to identify the correct card.

Leaving the latest of his inventions on his head, he got up and paced. Where had he gone wrong? Was it the machine or himself? A slight twinge of pain in his head reminded him that the fault could be in his own mind. That morning, while hanging a clock in the bathroom, he had fallen from the toilet and sustained a violent knock to the skull. The brain being a complicated mass of electrical impulses and energy, it was indeed possible that the blow had caused a short circuit powerful enough to make his tests invalid. But the day hadn't been a total loss. The fall generated something going in his mind which prompted him to write for several hours. When he was finished and reread the notes, he was sure a breakthrough had been scored in the realm of time travel. Excitement over that new project might also have interfered with his experiments in mind extension.

As he paced, he caught a picture of himself in the mirror. He was forced to smile. How outrageous he looked with this conglomeration of vacuum tubes, rheostats, gauges, wirings, and antennae on his head. It was, he was inclined to admit, the perfect stereotypical image of the mad scientist. But no matter. If the device proved practical in the area of mind reading, it wouldn't matter what it looked like.

While he studied himself, wondering whether or not to continue work for the day, Copernicus started barking. The dog, third in a line of pets named after famous scientists, raced from the kitchen into the living room, arriving there just as the rap sounded.

Without removing his headgear—it was so much trouble to hook it up—Doc Brown strode to the door and opened it. A young man of perhaps seventeen was there. His appearance caused Brown to almost clap his hands in sheer delight, for he was clad in a shirt that was illustrated with a blowup of a patent office entry. How this appealed to the heart of a frustrated and neglected and much maligned inventor can be easily imagined.

In this happy frame of mind, Doc Brown decided to continue his experiment. He turned the switch on, waited for it to warm up, pointed his finger at the young man, and said: "Don't say a word."

The young man obeyed, his mouth closing before he could get his first words out.

"I'm going to tell you your name," Doc Brown said. "Think of your name."

Marty did so. He was happy to note that Doc Brown seemed to be the same old guy, much younger looking to be sure, but with the same mannerisms and expressions. It was nice to see him again, even though they had been apart only a day.

"Peter Danforth," Doc Brown said.

"No."

"Evan Wentworth . . . Junior!"

"No, sir. I'm sorry."

"Melvin Petrucci."

Marty shook his head. "But my first name does begin with an *M*," he added encouragingly.

"That's not good enough," Doc Brown murmured. "Maybe it's not so good with proper names." Flipping another switch on his "Brain-wave Analyzer," he closed his eyes and cogitated once again.

"Let's see now," he said finally. "You've come from a great distance . . ."

"Yes!"

". . . because you . . . want me to buy a subscription to the *Saturday Evening Post*."

"No . . ."

"*Colliers* . . ."

"No. It's—"

"Don't tell me!" He threw back his head and thought for another moment. "Peanut brittle!" he fairly screamed. "That's it! You're selling peanut brittle for the Boy Scouts! How silly of me not to have said that right away!"

"No."

Doc Brown was crestfallen. Marty wished he could have given him better news, but lying wouldn't have been any benefit to his friend.

"Are you here because you want to use the bathroom?"

Brown asked, considerably subdued.

"No, Doc Brown," Marty answered. "But I am here for a reason that's very important to both of us."

"What *are* you selling?" Doc asked. "That's how all sales pitches begin."

"I'm not selling anything. Listen: I'm from the future. I came here in a time machine you invented—and now I need you to help me get back."

"Back to where?"

"Nineteen eighty-five."

"Incredible," Doc Brown breathed. "My God, do you know what this means?"

He paused dramatically, then began to remove the complicated contraption from his head.

"What does it mean?"

"It means this damned thing doesn't work at all!" he yelled, throwing the machine to the floor. It broke into several pieces, glass and plastic flying everywhere. "Six months labor for nothing! Where did I go wrong?"

"Please, Doc," Marty urged. "Forget the mind-reading machine. You're never gonna make it work."

"Who says so?"

"I do. Listen: Your big breakthrough will come with the time travel machine. Instead of fooling around with that other stuff, you should figure out how the time machine works . . . Because I need your help. You left me stuck here in 1955."

Doc Brown knit his brow and rubbed a bandage on his head.

"What are you talking about, time machine?" he demanded. "I haven't invented any time machine."

"No, but you will," Marty said. "And I'll be the first one to use it, except for your dog Einstein."

"My dog's name is Copernicus."

Marty nodded. "That figures. You name your pets after

great scientists. So isn't it logical that some future dog will be named Einstein?"

"Makes some sort of sense," Brown admitted. "But how do I know you're from the future? There's a lot of folks around here who think I'm a crank and a pest. Maybe they sent you as some kind of twisted joke."

"I'm not a joke," Marty replied. "And I can prove it to you."

He reached into his pocket, withdrew his wallet.

"Look," he said. "Here's my driver's license. Examine the dates on it."

He handed the card to Doc Brown.

"See that expiration date?" Marty said. "Nineteen eighty-seven. See my date of birth? Nineteen sixty-eight."

"You mean you haven't even been born yet?" Doc Brown asked. He turned the license over and over. "It sure looks authentic, all right," he muttered.

"It *is* authentic."

Searching deeper into his wallet, Marty withdrew a library card with a 1986 expiration date, a new piece of money, and a family picture. One by one he held them up for Doc Brown's examination.

"Look at this twenty-dollar bill," he said. "Series 1981 . . . And here's a picture of me, my sister, and my brother . . ."

"So?"

"So look at the girl's sweatshirt. Class of '84, it says, right?"

Doc Brown nodded, then shrugged. "Pretty mediocre photographic fakery," he said. "It looks like they cut off your brother's head."

Growing increasingly irritated, Marty thrust the picture back in his wallet without bothering to look at it. If Doc Brown didn't believe his story, who would? It was both ironic and annoying that the man behind his dilemma would not believe his own success.

"Please, Doc," Marty said passionately. "You've gotta believe me! I'm telling the truth."

Doc regarded him through narrowed eyes. "All right, future boy," he smiled. "Let me give you a little test. Who's going to win the 1956 World Series?"

Unfortunately, Marty had no encyclopedic knowledge of sports events, although he was as interested as most young men his age. "I don't know," he confessed. "That was almost thirty years ago."

"No, it's one year in the future," Doc Brown said quickly before realizing they were approaching the date from different perspectives. "All right," he continued. "I'm a Brooklyn fan. How many pennants and World Series do they win during the 1960s and '70s?"

"I don't think they win any," Marty replied. "Brooklyn's not even in the league."

Doc Brown laughed derisively. "No Bums?" he said, shaking his head. "No Brooklyn? I don't believe it."

"It's true."

"It's crazy. Who wins the pennants then?"

"The Miracle Mets won an exciting World Series in 1969," Marty said. "But I'm a San Diego Padre fan. I like the Chargers, too."

"Mets?" Doc repeated. "Who are the Miracle Mets? And San Diego? Are you kidding me?"

"No. Teams get changed around a lot."

"Yeah, but not that much," Doc muttered. "I haven't recognized a team you mentioned. Who are the big teams in football?"

"The L.A. Raiders . . . Miami Dolphins . . . Dallas Cowboys . . . San Francisco 49ers."

"Finally," Doc Brown said. "One team I recognize. This is incredible. How about this: Who's gonna be President of the United States in 1985?"

"Ronald Reagan."

"Ronald Reagan the actor?" Doc Brown asked, shaking his head.

Marty nodded somewhat ruefully. He wished Doc Brown had asked another question.

"Why, that's the most insane thing I've ever heard," Doc muttered. "Surely you could have made up a better answer than that."

Picking up his Brain-wave Analyzer, Brown started toward his garage. The joke was over as far as he was concerned. He had no idea what it had accomplished, but if someone had gotten a laugh at his expense, they were welcome to it. Marty followed him.

"Please leave me alone," Doc Brown said over his shoulder as he moved out of the room.

Marty, thinking furiously for the thing he could say that would convince the man, suddenly remembered what day it was: Saturday, November 5, 1955. Hadn't that been the day Doc had slipped off the toilet and—?

"Sure," Marty exclaimed. "He's even got the bruise to prove it."

Racing after Doc Brown, he began to speak in a rapid-fire patter. "Doctor Brown, listen to me!" he said. "That bruise on your head—I know how you got it! It happened this morning! You were hanging a clock and fell off your toilet and hit your head on the sink . . ."

Doc Brown whirled to look at him.

"What have you been doing—spying on me?" he demanded. "Haven't I even got privacy in the bathroom? When I sit down now, do I have to worry about some idiot with binoculars looking at me?"

"No," Marty assured him. "I didn't spy on you. In 1985, you told me about this morning. You said after the fall, you had a sort of vision about the flux capacitor, which is the heart of the time machine."

Doc Brown frowned. This was indeed a puzzler. How

could this young man know what went on in his mind unless he told him? While he was trying to figure it out, Marty spread his palms and voiced the same question.

"Doc, how else could I know that unless I was from the future?"

"You could be a mind reader."

"Yes, but I'm not. I'm just an ordinary guy you happened to confide in."

"Where is this time machine now?" Doc Brown asked. He was beginning to become intrigued.

"I've got it hidden," Marty replied. "I stashed it in a garage. It's so flashy-looking, I couldn't drive it around the streets without getting a lot of attention. Maybe the cops would even arrest me."

Doc Brown looked at the young man for a long moment. He wanted to believe him but there was something missing. It was just too fantastic. The kid was just a good actor who had somehow found out about his accident. Whatever motive was behind his story-telling wasn't important. He had other things to do.

"Good night, 'Future Boy,'" he said, closing the service door of the garage.

Marty stood silently for nearly a minute. Try as he might, he could think of no one else who could help him but Doc Brown. That meant only one thing: if Brown required more evidence to convince him, that evidence would have to be produced.

"But he probably won't let me in next time, if he knows it's me," he sighed.

He looked down, noting that the same potted plant, much smaller now, sat outside the door to Doc's garage.

"Is it possible . . . ?" he smiled.

Bending down, he lifted the pot and found the key. He put it in his pocket and walked away.

It was his plan to wait until dark when the DeLorean

would be less obtrusive. The machine itself would be sure to impress Doc Brown and contained several articles from 1985 that would serve as evidence. Walking slowly, Marty went back to the Town Square, bought himself a burger and Pepsi, and watched the hands on the courthouse tower clock slowly move toward four o'clock. Finally, growing bored with people-watching, he decided to take in a movie.

He strolled toward the Essex, but after only a few paces turned left in the direction of the Town. Westerns had never been his favorite type of movie and Ronald Reagan was far from his favorite actor. At least *The Atomic Kid* was a picture he'd never seen on television.

He paid his fifty cents admission cheerfully, bought an Almond Joy for a dime and went inside. The movie was pretty lame and Marty actually found himself yearning for television commercials as a way of relieving the tedium. Ninety minutes later, having suffered through the story of a prospector who becomes immune to atomic radiation and tracks down Communist spies, he went outside, noting with satisfaction that it was considerably darker.

By the time he returned home, it was quite dark. Marty opened the garage, got into the DeLorean, dropped the seat into a reclining position and closed his eyes. He had decided to wait until at least midnight so that few people would be around to see his car from another world.

Eventually he dropped into a fitful sleep, a succession of dreams reminding him that he was in a serious situation . . . He saw himself pursued by professional gamblers eager to pick his brain for future knowledge that could be turned into money . . . Police and government officials, meanwhile, wanted to silence him in order to prevent panic . . . Lorraine was after his body . . . He had no way of returning to 1985, to Jennifer, his friends . . . Awakening with a start, he looked at the digital clock on the DeLorean dashboard. It was after midnight.

Bringing the car to life, he rolled softly out of the garage and returned to Doc Brown's house on Riverside Drive. True to its image, Hill Valley had rolled up its sidewalks early and only a few cars were on the roads.

Arriving at Doc's garage, Marty opened the door with the key he'd appropriated and pulled the DeLorean inside. Doc Brown was asleep, snoring loudly, at his workbench. Beneath his slumped figure were blueprints of the Brainwave Analyzer and a note pad with scribbled memoranda.

Marty touched Doc gently on the shoulder.

"Doc . . . Wake up," he whispered.

Brown's eyes fluttered open. "Huh?" he muttered thickly, his expression vacant.

"It's me," Marty said.

A twinge of anger came into Doc Brown's eyes. "What the hell are you doing here?" he demanded. "How the hell did you get in?"

"I borrowed the key . . ."

"You got a lot of nerve—"

As he spoke, Doc Brown's eyes fell on the DeLorean and the words died in his throat.

"Good Lord," he muttered.

"This is your time machine, Doc," Marty smiled. "I brought it over."

Doc Brown started to move toward it, his eyes wide with wonder, his mouth open. Marty thought he was about to start salivating.

"Now will you believe me?"

Doc Brown didn't answer. Very deliberately, he walked in a complete circle around the machine. Then he withdrew a folded piece of paper from his pocket and handed it to Marty.

"After I fell off the toilet," he said, "I drew this. Does it look familiar?"

Marty unfolded the sheet and immediately recognized a

crude but accurate sketch of the flux capacitor.

"You bet," he answered.

He opened the car door and pulled out the real thing. When he saw it, Doc Brown's eyes lit up. Hopping in place, he began to shout, emitting words between the yipping sounds of happiness.

"Ha! It works . . . it works!" he wheezed. "I finally invented something that works!"

Suddenly he reached out to hug Marty and give him a kiss on the cheek.

"This is great!" he exuded. "This is wonderful! I can't believe it!"

But he obviously did believe it, for the next thing he did was stand very formally, as if addressing an audience of very learned people.

"Ladies and gentlemen," he said in a deep and sonorous voice, "and members of the Nobel committee . . . It is a great honor for me to accept the Nobel Prize for the year nineteen—"

He paused, turned to Marty. "What year do I get the Nobel Prize?" he asked.

Then, before Marty could speak, he waved his hands and continued. "No—wait, don't tell me. I don't want to know. Let it be a wonderful surprise. No man should know too much about his own destiny."

He seemed about to address the imaginary audience again when a look of sudden realization gripped his features. "Hold it!" he said. "Wait a minute! It's starting to come back to me now. You mentioned something about being my first guinea pig, except a dog."

"That's right."

"And you also said I left you stuck here in 1955 . . ."

Marty nodded.

"Why would I do that?" Doc Brown demanded haughtily. "I'm a responsible scientist. Every test I've performed has been absolutely safe. I would never send a kid back in time and just leave him there."

"You didn't do it on purpose," Marty explained. "It was an accident. Some other people intervened. Things got pretty heavy, really . . ."

"Heavy?" Doc said. "What does weight have to do with this problem?"

"I'm sorry. That's just an expression. What I mean is, well, what happened after the first—"

"Wait, don't tell me," Brown interrupted. "My knowing too much about the future . . . in fact, your simply being here . . . could be very dangerous. We might accidentally alter the course of history—"

"I don't think so," Marty said. "I'm just an ordinary person—"

"You don't understand. One molecule, one atom out of place could destroy the entire fabric of the space-time continuum . . . So we must be careful that we don't do anything significant."

Marty shrugged.

"Show me how this thing works," Doc Brown said. "We've got to send you back—back to the future."

"That's fine with me," Marty replied. "But I'm not an expert. You gave me a couple minutes' instruction time in 1985 and that was it."

"Why so little?" Doc Brown demanded. "If you were to be my subject, why didn't I explain everything fully and completely? That's irresponsible, to send a boy thirty years into the past with improper instruction."

Marty smiled. It sounded as if he were criticizing someone else when he was actually commenting on the activities of his future self.

"No, Doc," Marty explained. "It wasn't a matter of being irresponsible. You see, we were attack—"

He paused. Should he tell Doc Brown the manner in which he had been killed? It hardly seemed appropriate and certainly not kind.

"Quite right, my boy," Brown nodded. "Let's not go into details. I already know too much—"

"What, Doc?" Marty asked. "I haven't really told you anything important."

"Oh, no?" he shot back. "First, there's my matter of inventing a time machine. That's big news, not only to me but the entire scientific community. Then there's the Miracle Mets of 1969. And Ronald Reagan as President. You were kidding about that, weren't you?"

"Yes," Marty lied.

"Good."

An hour later, after figuring out how the DeLorean time machine worked, Doc Brown took out the suitcase containing his 1985 articles and began examining them one by one.

"What's this thing?" he asked.

"A hair dryer," Marty said.

"A hair dryer? Don't they have towels in the future?" He tossed it back in the suitcase. "Don't tell me I'll actually use that," he muttered.

He examined some of the clothing. "And these clothes," he said, "they're all made of cotton. I thought for sure we'd all be wearing disposable paper garments by 1985. Not much improvement there . . ."

A copy of *Playboy* was uncovered. Brown leafed through it, nearly dropping it when the centerfold fell out in all its glory.

"Hey!" he smiled. "Suddenly the future's looking a whole lot better." He turned the picture upside-down and then sideways. "This is kind of crazy," he laughed. "Here I am, ogling a woman who hasn't even been born yet."

"Yeah," Marty said. "If you want to blow your mind, take a look at this."

For the past few minutes he had busied himself setting up the video camera so that it could play back the tape he had taken on the Twin Pines Mall parking lot. Now he was ready to roll.

"Prepare yourself for a shock, Doc," he said as he hit the ON button.

A glitch was followed by the picture of Doc Brown's 1985 preamble to what he called temporal experiment number one.

"Who's that guy?" Doc Brown began. Then he gasped. "Why, that's me! Look at me! I'm an old man! But I don't look too bad for an old geezer. Thank God I've still got my hair—baldness runs in my family, you know. Even some of the women. But what on earth am I wearing?"

"A radiation suit."

"Of course, because of all the fallout from the atomic wars."

"No, Doc. There were several close—"

"Never mind. Don't tell me. Sorry I got out of line there. If I'm gonna avoid learning things about the future, I shouldn't make provocative statements like that. But this is truly amazing—it's a portable television studio. I never imagined that . . ."

"Watch this," Marty urged. "This is the most important part coming up."

Doc Brown of 1955 stood transfixed as Doc Brown of 1985 explained how the time machine was powered by plutonium. Marty McFly of 1985, looking exactly like the Marty of 1955, listened to Brown's comments, then spoke on tape: "Plutonium?" he said. "You mean this sucker's nuclear?"

"Electrical, basically," Brown replied. "But I need a nuclear reaction to generate the 1.21 gigawatts of electricity I need. The flux capacitor stores it, then discharges it all at once, like a gigantic bolt of lightning. It's really quite efficient."

"What did that old guy just say?" young Doc Brown demanded. "Let me see that again."

Marty rewound the tape and repeated the segment in question.

". . . 1.21 gigawatts of electricity I need. The flux capacitor—"

"Holy cow!" Doc Brown interjected, stepping on his own voice. "Did he say 1.21 gigawatts? Jumping Jehovah—1.21 gigawatts!"

With that, he turned and raced from the garage.

Marty stopped the tape and charged after him. "Doc!" he yelled. "Hey, Doc! What is it?"

By the time he caught up with him, Doc was already in a large room of his house which he used for painting. The walls were decorated with portraits of famous inventors and scientists such as Albert Einstein, Benjamin Franklin, Isaac Newton, and Thomas Edison. The centerpiece of the basically bare room was a large upright artist's easel on which a huge canvas was resting. Doc Brown stood next to the easel now, his features very agitated as he attacked the canvas with a paint brush, his arms whirling in great arcs like a malfunctioning windmill. Each time the brush struck the canvas a huge red streak appeared.

"One-point-two-one gigawatts," he mumbled over and over as he continued his nervous dance.

Marty stood and watched, certain that his friend had gone quite mad. A frightening thought struck him: suppose seeing himself on tape had been enough to send Doc Brown of 1955 over the edge? If the shock had been too great, might this not mean that all bets were off for the future? A 1955 Doc Brown gone insane would not be able to invent the time machine thirty years later. Would this leave Marty McFly stranded in 1955 or mean that the Marty of 1985 simply wouldn't meet Doc Brown?

He shook his head. The fact was he didn't really comprehend who or where he was. Was the real Marty McFly standing here at this point in time; or was this just a clone, as it were, thrown off from his later self? If something happened to him now, would he be reborn again in 1968? Was it even possible that there might be two Marty McFlys, separated by thirty years of age, who could meet in the future?

Doc Brown had stopped painting for a moment and was now looking up at the portrait of Thomas Edison.

"Tom!" he shouted. "How am I gonna generate that kind of power? It can't be done, can it?"

Abruptly, he dipped his brush on the palette and made another foray on the painting.

Marty stepped close to him. "Doc, what's wrong?" he asked. "What are you doing?"

"I'm painting! I always paint when I can't understand a problem."

Marty decided to humor him. "Well, use green," he suggested softly. "Green's your color."

"Is it? How did you know that?"

"I just know. Trust me."

Brown looked at him a moment, then swabbed a mass of green onto the palette and transferred several broad strokes of it onto the canvas.

He was almost immediately calmed.

"Why, yes . . . yes, you're right," he breathed. "That's much better."

Marty nodded. "I knew it would be," he said.

He waited a few moments before bringing up the problem again. The idea of sending Doc Brown into another tantrum was not appealing but Marty was desperate for information now.

"Is it possible for me to get back to 1985?" he demanded.

Doc Brown put his brush down and sighed. "Marty," he said, "I'm sorry this had to happen. But 1.21 gigawatts is just too much power. I can't get that kind of power. I'm afraid you're stuck here."

•Chapter Eight•

Marty looked for a chair. The statement by Doc Brown made his entire body feel so weak he actually thought there was a chance he might faint.

"No . . ." he murmured.

"I would like to help but I don't know how," Doc said. "It's outside the range of my capabilities."

"Plutonium, Doc," Marty said. "All we need is plutonium, right?"

Doc Brown laughed. "Archimedes said he could move the earth if he just had a place to stand," he replied. "That was a pretty safe statement. Ours is more or less the same. Yes, we can get you back if we have plutonium. If. It's not just a big if. It's a monumental one."

"Why?"

"Why? Because you don't know how tight things are in 1955, my boy. I'm sure that in 1985, plutonium is available at any corner drug store. But now it's hard to come by. In fact, just about impossible."

"How about through illegal channels?" Marty suggested. "Isn't there a black market for stuff like that?"

"Not that I know of."

"Damn . . . Damn . . ."

Doc Brown smiled and put his hand on Marty's shoulder. "It's not the end of the world," he said.

"It's the end of the world I've known."

"Sure, but look on the bright side. This isn't such a bad time to live. You could have gotten stuck back in the Dark Ages when you'd have to spend half your time dodging barbarians. Or you could have turned up during the Black Plague. Or even as recently as the early 19th century when there were no anesthetics, no television, movies. I mean, we're really pretty advanced. We've got 3-D movies, hi-fidelity music, Frank Sinatra, instant coffee . . ."

"Yeah, well, in 1985 we've got MTV, compact discs—"

"Wait," Doc Brown interjected. "I don't even know what you're talking about."

"—Burger King and birth control," Marty continued. "Don't you understand, Doc? I have a life in 1985. I like it and want to go back to it."

"But this time is so much safer. Here, you know there'll be a 1985. In 1985, do you know there'll be a 2015? Think about that."

Marty shook his head. "I'll have to chance that danger," he said. "My friends, my music, my girl's waiting for me. Look, here she is . . ."

He withdrew his wallet and showed Doc Brown the head shot of Jennifer.

"Say, she's not bad," he said.

"Not bad? She's great! And she's crazy about me!"

"Well, can't you find a nice girl here?"

"One who hums Pat Boone, you mean?" Marty shot back derisively. "No, thanks. None of them will ever measure up to Jennifer. See this? See what she wrote here? It's poetry!"

He pulled out the scrap of paper on which Jennifer had written: "I love you."

Doc Brown regarded it sympathetically but his shrug of helplessness was more significant.

"It's too bad..." he said.

"Please, Doc," Marty begged. "You've gotta help me get back to the future. You're my only hope! I know you can figure something out."

"How do you know that?"

"Because you've never let me down in the past."

"You mean, in the future."

"Right," Marty agreed. "You've always told me that if you put your mind to it, you can accomplish anything, solve any problem."

"I said that? How egotistical. But I must say it's pretty good advice."

"Doc, I know you can pull this off. Maybe now I believe in you more than you believe in yourself."

"Marty, I'm touched that you have so much confidence in me," Doc Brown smiled. "I really am. It means a lot to me. But it's going to take more than confidence to generate 1.21 gigawatts of power. Do you have any idea how much energy that is? The only power source capable of triggering that kind of energy is a bolt of lightning. And not a minor-league bolt, either. It would have to be a real wall-shaker, something big enough to stop a clock."

Marty snapped his fingers.

"Ah!" Doc Brown said. "You've had an idea, but you forgot to say 'Eureka!'"

"Maybe it's not a Eureka-type idea," Marty replied. "It just occurred to me that if we could use a lightning bolt for energy—"

"A reasonable thought," Brown interrupted, "and quite practical except for one thing. You never know when or where a bolt of lightning is going to strike. Of course, you've got a start by waiting for an electrical storm, but even then there's no assurance a bolt will even get close enough to use as a power source."

Marty waited patiently for him to finish, then smiled.

"Except that I know when and where a bolt of lightning is going to strike."

"You do?"

"I do indeed."

He turned over the piece of paper on which Jennifer had written her note. It was the flyer given them by the lady for the 1985 clock tower preservation campaign. At the very top of the sheet was a replica of the 1955 newspaper headline which read: CLOCK TOWER STRUCK BY LIGHTNING. CLOCK STOPPED AT 10:04.

Underneath was the date: Sunday, November 13, 1955.

Now it was Doc Brown's turn to snap his fingers.

"Eureka?" Marty asked.

"Eureka, yes," Doc Brown replied, nodding several times. "You're right! This is it! This is the answer! Since the newspaper came out on Sunday, it means that the clock tower will be struck next Saturday night. If we could some-how harness this lightning...channel it into the flux ca-pacitor...it just might work..."

Marty grinned. Now they were on the track! At least there seemed to be hope. All he wanted was a shot at getting back. If they tried and he failed, that would be unfortunate. But to remain here with absolutely no hope...It wasn't an alternative he cared to consider.

Doc Brown looked up at the portrait of Benjamin Franklin. "What do you think of that, Ben? Harness lightning? If you could do it, why can't I? It's brilliant."

He turned to look at Marty again. "You were right, Marty," he said. "I was right! We can accomplish anything if we put our minds to it. And we're gonna do it! Next Saturday night, we're sending you back to the future—with a bang! This calls for a toast."

He walked briskly to the water cooler and poured each of them a glassful. Then, raising his dramatically, he said: "To me! To you! To Ben Franklin! And to your girlfriend for writing this note."

"I'll drink to all of that," Marty agreed.

They drank silently.

"Yeah, Jennifer's really great," Marty smiled. "I can hardly wait to see her again and tell her about this. But I don't guess a week in 1955 will hurt me. As a matter of fact, it might be fun to check things out. You know, take in some of the local color, rub elbows with the natives, that sort of thing."

To Marty's surprise, Doc Brown frowned and began shaking his head.

"I'm sorry," he said. "That's completely out of the question."

"Why?"

"Because of the delicate nature of your being here. Apparently you still haven't accepted what a potential threat you are to this town, other people's lives, our whole society. No, I'm afraid you must stay in this house and not go outside. You can't see anybody or talk to anybody. Anything you do or say could have serious repercussions on future events. Do you understand?"

"Uh, sure," Marty replied. He didn't really accept Doc Brown's notion that he was such a "threat" to society. Especially now that he knew what could happen if he started talking a lot about the future. On the other hand, if he guarded what he said and just observed, what possible harm could he do? It was certainly better than hanging around Doc Brown's house and garage for a week.

"Marty, who else did you interact with today?" Doc Brown asked. "Besides me, that is."

"Well, I went to the movies. Do you think the fact that the Town took in an extra fifty cents today will change the course of history?"

"Don't be smart," Doc Brown replied. "That's a tiny item but even it could happen. Let's suppose the theater operator is looking at the balance sheet one day and thinking about selling. Maybe that extra fifty cents pushes the receipts from $999.75 to $1000.25. That is, it goes from three figures to four figures. That might be the psychological difference between keeping the theater or selling it. So, influenced by the extra fifty cents, he keeps it. Not long afterward, when the theater would be closed if he'd sold it, a fire starts and some people are trapped inside. One of them is a youngster who's destined to become President of the United States—except that now he's dead."

"And I did it," Marty muttered. "I killed him with my fifty cents."

"Not directly, but you get the point. History is a very fragile thing. A guy looks one way or coughs and one thing happens. He looks another way or doesn't cough and a different thing happens. It's scary. Didn't you see that movie, *It's a Wonderful Life?* That's a textbook on how our little lives influence everybody else's."

"Yeah," Marty said. "I get you now."

"Now who else did you interact with?"

"Lots of people. My grandparents, my mother and father. Biff Tannen . . ."

Doc Brown winced. "You looked up your parents?" he said. "How could you? That's totally irresponsible."

"I didn't look them up," Marty retorted. "I just bumped into them."

"Tell me what happened."

Marty recounted the events of the day. He considered them rather bland until he saw how deeply they affected Doc Brown.

"You say you saved your father from being hit by the car," Doc said.

"Yes, but I didn't save his life. If the car had hit him, he'd have lived."

"How do you know that?"

"Because it's a family joke about how Dad and Mom met for the first time when grandpa drove the car into him."

"Good Lord! You prevented your parents from having their initial meeting?"

"Yes, but they'll meet again. They go to the same school, you know . . ."

"No, no, no!" Doc Brown exclaimed. "You've done a terrible thing as far as your future life is concerned. Let me see that picture of your family again."

Marty withdrew the snaphot from his wallet and handed it to Brown. His expression became grim. "Just as I thought," he said.

"What's the big deal?" Marty asked.

"It's happened. This proves my theory. Look at your brother—what do you make of his head?"

He returned the picture to Marty. It was the same as he had always remembered it—except that Dave had no head. Looking closely at the photo, he saw that his brother's head hadn't been blotted out or torn off. Behind where his head should have been was a continuation of the rose bush which his body was blocking out. It was just as if Dave had no head when the snapshot was taken!

"Good God!" Marty whispered. "His head is gone . . . Like it's been erased . . ."

"Erased from existence," Doc Brown added significantly.

"I don't understand this," Marty said. "Or maybe I do but I don't want to."

Brown held up his finger. "Sssshh . . ." he said. "I'm developing a theory." After thinking a moment, he snapped his finger. "Kid, we gotta get you some clothes," he said. "You stay here and I'll do the shopping. Tell me what your sizes are."

An hour later, he returned from the local Sears, Roebuck with a shopping bag filled with a complete outfit. As he removed the labels from them and began to change, Marty discussed the situation with Doc Brown.

"Tell me about your theory," he said. "Are you sure it makes sense?"

"My theories always make sense," Brown replied. "It's a simple genetic-mathematical extrapolation."

"I don't get it."

"In plainer terms then: It was your father who was supposed to get hit by that car, not you. Thus, you interfered in your parents' first meeting. If they don't meet under those same circumstances, they may not fall in love. But that's water over the dam now. We've got to get them to meet somehow, because if they don't meet and fall in love, they won't get married. If they don't get married, they don't have kids. That's why your brother's disappearing from that photograph—he's the first since he's the oldest. Your sister will follow, and unless you can repair the damage, you'll be the next to fade away."

"So what can I do?"

"Go back to school."

"Why?"

"Because you're a kid. Kids go to school. Your parents

are kids. They go to school. You interfered in your parents' relationship. Therefore, you have to go to school to fix the damage you did."

"Can't I just hang round before and after classes? I mean, school was boring in 1985. When I think how dull 1955 will be, it blows my mind."

Doc Brown shook his head. "You can't afford to fool around now. There's less than a week we have to work with, right?"

Marty nodded.

"So you have to use every available minute to get them together. Otherwise, you won't exist in the future. It's as simple as that."

He stepped back to look at Marty's new outfit. "Not bad," he said. Reaching into the shopping bag, he pulled out a final purchase—a bottle of Vaseline hair tonic. As soon as he unscrewed the top, Marty curled his lip.

"Look, Doc," he murmured. "I'll admit that these threads are pretty cool. But you're not putting that greasy shit in my hair."

"Why not? A lot of the kids wear it."

"It looks terrible. And who knows what it contains? I mean, it might give me cancer."

"You need it for your disguise," Brown said. With that, he started combing some of it into Marty's hair. "Don't worry about it," he said. "This is supposed to very fashionable, for both kids and grown-ups."

"Well, then how come you don't use it?" Marty challenged.

"It's also very flammable," Doc replied.

"Great."

Doc Brown stopped combing Marty's hair, but seemed as if he wasn't quite finished. He looked sideways at the effect, not sure it was right.

"Allow me," Marty said, taking the comb.

Going to the mirror, he started combing the hair back along the sides and forced an errant curl to fall down across his forehead.

"If I'm gonna go through with this," he explained, "at least I'm gonna look like Elvis."

"Elvis? What's Elvis?" Doc Brown asked.

"You'll find out."

Having been built during the later years of the Great Depression, Hill Valley High wasn't new in 1955. Its worst days—the spray-can graffiti era of the late '60s and '70s—were still ahead, however, and it seemed clean and shiny to Marty as he drove up with Doc Brown on Monday morning. Dressed in his new outfit and with his hair slicked back, he barely resembled the young man from 1985, whom Stella Baines thought worked for the circus.

"Wow, they've really cleaned this place up," Marty said, whistling softly. "It looks brand-new."

"Maybe your generation didn't take very good care of it," Doc Brown remarked acidly.

Marty shrugged, recalling the times he had written on walls and desks.

"Remember now," Brown said as they walked toward the main entrance. "According to my theory, all you have to do is introduce them to each other and nature will take its course . . . I hope."

"I don't think that's gonna be enough now," Marty replied. "Lorraine's father's hitting him with the car gave them a special relationship. She felt sorry for him, brought him into the house."

"You're probably right. Maybe you'd better push, make it seem like you think he's a great guy."

"That might not be so easy," Marty sighed. "He's a real prototype nerd."

"Don't do it for him. Do it for yourself."

"Yeah . . ."

They entered the school that was familiar and yet so different in Marty's eyes. The halls and classrooms looked basically the same but the atmosphere was totally different—it resembled something from an old movie, except that it was in color. As they walked, they spotted Lorraine rushing into a classroom. Marty started to move after her but Doc Brown grabbed his arm.

"That's your mother?" he asked.

"Yeah."

"It's better if you don't go in the same class," Doc Brown suggested. "The teacher won't know who the hell you are. My first notion of having you really go back to school isn't practical, I guess. Better we just hang around and see what we can accomplish."

"Sure. Let's see if we can spot Dad. Then at the end of the period, we can arrange to bring them together."

"Good idea."

They spent the next twenty minutes wandering the halls, systematically peering into classrooms in order to locate George McFly. Finally he could be seen in the back row of a class only a couple rooms away from Lorraine's.

"We have about ten minutes to wait," Marty said, looking at the hall clock.

"Ten seconds slow," Brown muttered, comparing it with his pocket watch. "You'd think a public school would at least have the correct time."

They strolled back to Lorraine's class and peered inside again. She was seated in the second row, writing. The class was obviously taking a test.

"I see the resemblance now," Doc Brown said. "She has your eyes . . ." Then, with a little chuckle, he added: "And eyes for someone else's paper, too."

"My God!" Marty whispered. "She's cheating."

It indeed seemed so. With her hand in writing position

and head tilted downward, Lorraine's eyes were pointed directly at the paper of the young man next to her.

"I can't believe Mom would do that," Marty whispered.

"Why not?" Doc Brown countered. "She's an ordinary human being, isn't she?"

"Not to hear her tell it. She always talked about what a straight-shooter she was in school, how moral and nice she was—and practically everyone else, too."

"She has a selective memory like the rest of us," Doc said philosophically. "Still, I can understand your feelings. It's kind of a shock to see our parents show their dishonest or seedy side."

"Maybe we better go get my father," Marty suggested.

They arrived back at George McFly's class just as the bell rang. As his father got up, Marty was doubly impressed with his nerdish qualities. His shirt tail was out, his hair poorly combed and his papers practically fell out of the three-leaf binder.

"That's the old man, eh?" Doc Brown said, displaying a notable lack of enthusiasm.

"Yeah."

They noted that several boys walked behind George McFly, barely suppressing giggles as he moved out of the classroom into the hall. When he neared them, another boy walked up behind George and very deliberately kicked his behind.

George turned, looked at the fellow with downcast eyes. A sign reading KICK ME was hooked onto the back of his collar. He was, of course, completely aware of it.

"Maybe you're adopted," Marty heard Doc Brown say softly.

Fat chance, Marty thought.

Just as George McFly was about to be kicked by another student, a familiar figure suddenly appeared on the scene, snatching the sign from his shirt and showing it to him.

"Good God!" Marty gasped. "It's Mr. Strickland."

It was true. Hill Valley High's avenging angel, still wearing a bow tie, was there in the form of Gerald Strickland. He looked younger, a bit tauter, but basically the same. His presence caused the other students to go quickly about their business.

"McFly! Shape up, man!" Strickland shouted.

George regarded him like a prisoner about to be sentenced.

"You're a slacker!" Strickland charged. "These things happen because you're not paying attention. Your head must be off on Mars or something. Do you want to be a slacker for the rest of your life?"

George shook his head unconvincingly.

"Then wake up and join the human race," Strickland continued. "That's all."

Thrusting the sign into George's hands, he stalked down the corridor toward his office.

"You're sure your Mom fell in love with that guy?" Doc Brown asked.

"Yeah."

"Looks like a match made in heaven."

"My Mom always said it was meant to be," Marty sighed, "I sure hope she's right . . ."

"Hey, she's coming now," Brown said. "Better get ready to make the introductions."

Marty nodded, took a deep breath and started toward George.

"George!" he cried. "Hey, buddy! How are you?"

George nodded weakly. "Fine . . ."

"You're just the guy I wanted to see," Marty continued. Then, noting George's nearly blank expression, he said: "You remember me, don't you? Saturday when you fell outa the tree . . . I probably saved your life."

"Oh, yeah . . ." George muttered.

"The binoculars didn't break, did they?" Marty asked, unable to help himself.

His father reddened. "No," he replied.

"Good! Listen, there's somebody I want you to meet. C'mere..."

Grabbing his arm, Marty led George down the hall in the direction of Lorraine. As his father's gaze fell on her, his expression whitened, his eyes filling with panic. Marty saw his body stiffen and for a moment he thought poor George was going to try making a break for it. Then he relaxed somewhat as the meeting became unavoidable.

"Excuse me, Lorraine," Marty began.

Lorraine's eyes caught his. For a split second, they were confused, but as soon as she stripped away the changes in Marty's clothes and hair style, she brightened considerably.

"Calvin!" she nearly shouted. "I mean, Marty!"

So delighted was she to see him, she dropped her books.

"Oh, let me get those," Marty offered.

He felt a hand on his elbow. It was Doc Brown.

"Let him do it, jerk!" Brown whispered.

But Marty was already bent over and George was just standing there, slack-jawed, looking as if he wanted to be anyplace but here.

Retrieving the books, Marty handed them to Lorraine, whose eyes shone with gratitude and infatuation.

"Oh, thank you," she gushed.

Marty smiled, cleared his throat, and then thrust his hand out at the pathetic figure of George McFly.

"Lorraine," he said. "I want to introduce you to someone. This is my good friend, George McFly. George, this is Lorraine."

"Hi, it's really a pleasure to meet you," George managed to say.

Lorraine's eyes moved toward him and then turned back

to Marty, bequeathing barely a flicker of recognition at her future husband.

"Build him up," Doc Brown whispered.

"How?" Marty demanded, sotto voce.

"I don't know. Fake it."

Bringing about a meaningful introduction being the purpose of his visit, Marty sallied forth. "George here is a terrific guy," he stammered. "Really great...He's smart ...and a good athlete..."

"No—" George interjected.

"He's got a great sense of humor, too."

"No—" George repeated.

Marty might as well have been speaking to Lorraine in Sanskrit or Choctaw. Her eyes never moved from his during the entire eulogy.

"Marty," she said, her voice dripping with sincerity. "I was so worried about you running off like that the other night with that bruise on your head. Is it better now? It looked so sore..."

She reached out to touch his forehead.

"Yeah, it's fine," Marty nodded.

"It could use something to take down the swelling," Lorraine suggested. "I'm sure we have something at home in the medicine closet."

"Uh...I believe in letting things get well by themselves," Marty replied. "That way, your body builds up certain types of immunities..."

"You're so smart," she smiled.

"Yeah. But George here—"

The bell rang.

"George here is even smarter than—" Marty continued.

"Never mind," he heard Doc Brown whisper.

Marty looked around. George McFly was nowhere to be seen.

"Where is he?" Marty asked Doc.

"He went thataway."

"Why didn't you stop him?"

"What did you expect me to do, tackle the guy? Anyway, he did it kind of sneaky-like ... Just sort of sidled a few steps away and then bolted."

"Damn," Marty murmured.

Lorraine was still smiling at him, obviously perfectly content to stare at him during the brief interruption.

The bell rang again, snapping her out of her romantic trance.

"I'm late," she said. "I'll see you later."

"Yeah ..." Marty said.

As she turned away, her girlfriend, who had been waiting patiently to one side, joined her.

"Isn't he a dreamboat?" Lorraine rhapsodized. "I'll tell you a secret. I'm gonna marry *him*."

•Chapter Nine•

As they watched the two girls walk away, Marty and Doc Brown issued perfectly synchronous sighs.

"She didn't even look at him," Marty said.

"You're right."

"On the other hand," Marty continued. "Why should she? He's a nerd."

"I understand perfectly what it means, but is that a 1985 word?"

"Yeah."

"That's interesting, and you're probably right. This is a lot more serious than I thought. Apparently your mother is amorously infatuated with you instead of your father."

"Are you trying to tell me Mom's got the hots for me?" Marty asked.

"At the risk of sounding crude, yes. If we let it happen, an Oedipal situation could develop..."

147

"Oedipal?"

"Yes. A very undesirable attraction between mother and son. Of course, this is probably the most bizarre condition under which it's ever occurred. Still, the psychological implications—"

"Jeez, Doc, that's pretty heavy..." Marty said.

"There's that word again," Doc Brown replied with a shake of his head. "Heavy. Why are things so 'heavy' in the future? Is there a problem with the world's gravitational pull?"

"Huh?" Marty said.

Doc smiled. He enjoyed confusing his young friend occasionally. But rather than explain the remark or try to add to Marty's confusion, he leaped ahead to another aspect of the Lorraine-George dilemma.

"New theory," he continued. "The only way those two are going to successfully mate is if they're alone together. So you've got to arrange to get your father and mother to interact in some sort of social encounter, some mutually acceptable and stimulating premating ritual."

"You mean a date?"

"Excellent, my boy. I think you've put your finger on it."

"But what kind of date?" Marty asked. "I don't know what kids do in the '50s."

"Kids are always kids, aren't they? It's the background that changes."

Marty shrugged. "She did talk some about the kids in her day going to the Essex Theatre and necking in the balcony. How's that sound?"

"It sounds plausible, but perhaps that might be pushing them a little. I think it would be better if we started them out on something a tad less erotic."

"I agree, but what?"

"Well, they're your parents. You must know them. What

are their common interests? What do they like to do together?"

"Just the two of them?"

"Yes."

"Nothing."

"Hmmm."

The school hallways were nearly deserted now, the vast majority of the students having gone into their next period classrooms. Doc Brown paused before a large bulletin board, hoping he would see something that would stimulate his imagination.

"Aha!" he said finally.

"What?" Marty asked.

"There seems to be a rhythmic ceremonial ritual coming up. Have him take her to that."

"A rhythmic ceremonial—"

"Dance, to you." Doc Brown smiled, pointing to a hand-painted banner which read: ENCHANTMENT UNDER THE SEA . . . THIS SATURDAY NIGHT . . . ADMISSION $1.

Marty grinned and slapped his hands. "That's right!" he cried. "They're supposed to go to that dance—'Enchantment Under the Sea.' That's where they kiss for the first time. It's perfect."

"All right, then. Make it happen."

Marty frowned. "That's the problem," he murmured. "How can we get that yo-yo to summon up enough courage to ask her?"

"And how can we get her over the hots for you so she'll accept?" Doc Brown added dourly.

"I think we got our work cut out for us."

They were still considering the problem an hour or so later when George McFly entered the cafeteria, found himself a table in the corner, and began eating his lunch. For a few minutes, he just read; then he took out a pad and pencil and started writing as he finished his sandwich.

Marty and Doc Brown sauntered over to him. He barely noticed them as they pulled up chairs and sat at the same table.

"Hi, George," Marty said after a while. "What are you writing?"

"Stories."

"Any particular kind?"

"Yeah."

"What kind?"

"Science fiction."

"That's interesting. I didn't know you were into that. What's it about, people visiting strange and faraway planets?"

"No. As a matter of fact, it's about visitors from other planets coming to Earth."

"I never knew you did anything creative."

"What do you mean, you never knew?" George asked in a rare display of any emotion other than resignation or despair. "You've only known me for a couple of days."

"That's right. I keep forgetting. Anyway, how about letting me read one of 'em?"

"Oh, no," George replied, shaking his head decisively.

"Hey, you said no," Marty smiled.

George looked at him blankly. Doc Brown also directed a blank stare at him.

"It's the first time I've ever heard George McFly say no," Marty said. "I guess it's a joke between me and myself. Forget it."

George looked as if he was getting ready to bolt.

"Wait a second," Marty said gently. "I'm just interested in you, that's all. It isn't often you meet a writer who's so young. I should think you'd like to have somebody read your stories."

"Oh, no," George muttered. "I mean, what if they didn't like 'em? What if they told me they were no good, that *I* was no good?"

Marty had the feeling he had heard these words before—himself complaining to Jennifer after he'd been turned down by the YMCA dance committee.

"This must be pretty hard for you to understand, huh?" George asked, obviously having noticed the slight smile on Marty's face.

"No, George," Marty replied sincerely. "It's not that hard at all."

It was a breakthrough moment. Something in his father's vulnerability and desire to create touched Marty; for the first time in a long time, he found himself not only liking the man but understanding some of his anxieties. Suddenly he wanted to help George McFly not only because it would be beneficial to himself but to George as well.

"Listen, George," he said. "You know that girl I introduced you to—"

"Lorraine."

"Yeah. She really likes you."

George shook his head.

"It's true," Marty persisted. Doc Brown added his nod as well.

"I don't believe it. She didn't even look at me. I felt invisible."

As they were discussing her, Lorraine and some girl friends walked into the cafeteria. She did not see either of the young men.

George spotted her first. After a brief expression of adulation, his face melted into a mask of terror. He lifted the writing tablet above the lower part of his face as if he wanted to hide.

"I'm telling you she likes you," Marty continued. "Now why would I say that if it wasn't true?"

"To embarrass me," George replied quickly. "Like Biff when he plays tricks on me or those guys who put 'kick me' signs on my back."

"Well, I'm different," Marty said. "I'm the one who saved your life, remember? Would Biff or those other guys have jumped in front of a car for you?"

George shook his head, partially convinced that Marty was on the level. Nevertheless, years of being used as a punching bag had taught him to be super-cautious. This guy Marty acted sincere enough, but he was decidedly a strange type. He seemed to know a lot more than most kids his age ... He also seemed to show up out of nowhere, wearing strange clothes (like a sinister visitor from out of space who got his time periods mixed up, George thought). And why was he hanging around with the man some people derided as the "village idiot"? No, he thought warily, it would not be a good idea to trust this newfound friend completely.

"I appreciate your saving my life," he said finally. "But that doesn't mean you're right about Lorraine. You saw yourself how she looked right through me."

"Yeah," Marty nodded. There was, after all, no sense trying to deny the obvious. "But she's shy..."

"She overcompensates," Doc Brown added.

"She's very shy," Marty continued. "That's why she asked me to come over here and tell you she'd like nothing better than to go with you to the Enchantment Under the Sea Dance."

"Really?" George asked.

"Yep. All you gotta do is go right over there and ask her."

"Now? Right here, in the cafeteria?"

"No time like the present."

"But she's with friends. There are lots of other people around! What if she bursts out laughing? Or just says no? I'd hate to be rejected in front of all those..."

He trailed off, a nervous mess.

"George, I'm telling you, if you don't ask Lorraine to the dance, you're gonna regret it for the rest of your life

. . . and I'm gonna regret it for the rest of mine."

"Why you?" George asked.

"Uh . . . Let's just say I have a rooting interest in you and Lorraine getting together."

"You mean, like a bet?"

"Something like that, only more important."

"I don't know," George temporized. "I've got a feeling she'd rather go out with somebody else."

"Anyone in particular?"

George nodded.

"Who?"

"Biff," he replied miserably.

Marty blanched. Was George's assertion a product of his overdeveloped paranoia or a fact? The very thought of his mother going out with a first-degree creep such as Biff Tannen made his flesh crawl. He had never considered her a mental heavyweight, but she did have a certain amount of common sense and taste. Even allowing for youthful ignorance, Marty simply could not imagine Lorraine at any age being attracted to an insensitive clod like Biff.

"I don't think so," he said simply.

"He's with her now," George replied.

Marty looked across at Lorraine's table. Standing behind her with his hands on her shoulders was Biff. His mother did not look happy, however. Turning sideways to avoid him, she wrestled his fingers loose. Smiling roguishly, Biff replaced them.

"He's there, but I don't think she wants him there," Marty said.

Getting up, he walked across the cafeteria until he was close to Lorraine's table.

"Quit pawing me, Biff!" he heard Lorraine say. "Leave me alone." And once again she pried his fingers loose.

She spoke in a rasping whisper, as if trying not to attract the attention of others nearby. Biff made no effort to play down the scene. Putting his hands back on her shoulders, his voice was embarrassingly loud.

"Come on, Lorraine," he said. "You want it, you know you want it, and you know you want me to give it to you."

Still the same old subtle swine, Marty thought.

"Shut your filthy mouth," Lorraine replied. "I'm not that kind of girl."

"Maybe you are and just don't know it yet," Biff leered.

"Get your meathooks off me!"

"Come on, you love these meathooks."

Marty took several steps forward until he was standing right next to Biff, close enough to tell that the greasy hair tonic he wore was a different brand than his own . . . close enough to see the mottled complexion and couch his warning in a firm but intelligible whisper.

"She said to get your hands off her."

Biff turned, his jaw slack and eyes full of anger.

"What's it to you, butthead?" he said.

"Never mind. Just clear out."

"Says you and what army?"

"Just me."

"You know, you've been looking for—" Biff began, his body coiled as if to strike. In midsentence, however, he paused; his eyes avoided Marty's, instead looking over his shoulder. In fact, they were focused on the domineering figure of Gerald Strickland, who had entered the cafeteria and, having sniffed out a trouble spot, was walking inexorably in their direction. Biff's expression softened from hostility to abject terror.

"Since you're new here, twerp," he muttered, "I'm cutting you a break today. So why don't you make like a tree and get outa here."

Marty, not seeing Mr. Strickland approaching, simply stared at Biff. Lorraine, also unaware of the despot's entry on the scene, looked at her hero with wide love-filled eyes.

Biff turned and walked off.

"Oh, Marty!" Lorraine cried. "That was so wonderful! Thank you!"

Marty shrugged.

"What did you say your name was?"

The voice was the familiar rasp of Mr. Strickland, who was now at Marty's side. Marty coughed, looked into the eyes which resembled a pair of slit trenches.

"Marty," he said.

"*Last* name."

"Uh . . . Brown."

"Well, here's some friendly advice for you, Mr. Uh-Brown. Don't slack off in my school."

"Slack off, sir?" Marty murmured, his tone questioning.

"In the vernacular, that means don't screw around," Strickland said. "Understand?"

"Yessir. And thank you, sir."

Strickland turned and marched away just as the bell rang. Lorraine hopped up, collected her books, and ran over to Marty.

"Thanks again, Marty," she smiled. "Maybe I'll see you later?"

It sounded more like a prayer than a suggestion. Marty nodded and pretended he was late for class.

Returning to Doc Brown, he noted that once again George McFly had flown the coop.

"He said he had a class," Doc Brown explained. "But he looked like he was getting ready to have a good cry, if you ask me."

"This is getting ridiculous," Marty murmured.

"That's the way life is, my boy. Try to be a hero or impress somebody and everything goes wrong. But when you're not trying, you can fall down the toilet and come up with gold."

"Yeah."

"So what's next?"

"I guess I just have to keep after George. He's the key. Until we can get him to ask for the date, nothing'll happen."

"Maybe we can get your mother to ask him," Doc Brown suggested.

"No. That won't work."

"How do you know?"

"Because girls in 1955 never asked guys for dates. At least that's what Mom says. They never called them on the phone, asked them out, or did anything that was fun until the boy thought of it."

"Hmmm."

"I'll grab him again after school," Marty said. "It's the only thing we can do."

Doc Brown nodded. "You know, it might be better if you took a shot at him alone," he suggested. "It could be he feels cramped with both of us around, particularly since I'm an old guy of thirty-five."

"Maybe you're right," Marty shrugged.

"I'm gonna go back and study those tapes you made," Doc said. "They may tell me something I need to know about how the time machine runs. If we're gonna blast you back to '85 Saturday night, I'll have to know everything possible about that boat and how she operates."

He waved and started for the door, his steps light. Marty knew Doc was happy now, anticipating tinkering with the machine he would invent someday.

The afternoon went slowly. Marty wandered around the halls, did some reading in the library, and spent the last period looking in classrooms for George McFly. When he finally located him, he leaned against the wall until his father came out.

When their eyes again made contact, George looked as if he wanted to run. Who is this person, he thought, and why has he been put on earth just to harass me?

Turning away, he tried to make it to the door by walking briskly and pretending he hadn't seen Marty. But his guardian angel soon caught up with him.

"Hiya," Marty said. "I'm sorry that thing in the cafeteria turned out the way it did."

"Me too," George replied. "That Biff Tannen is a real jerk. I hated to see him paw Lorraine that way. If only I'd had the—"

He paused, sighed.

The words ending the sentence rushed through Marty's mind. Nerve? Courage? Guts? Whatever, they all meant the same. George McFly simply had no stomach for conflict, mental or physical. He wanted a soft warm cocoon to crawl into and spend the rest of his life, preferably asleep. Much as he disliked him for having that attitude, Marty was now dedicated to helping George dispel his fears and anxieties. Until he summoned up the courage to ask Lorraine for a date he was doomed to a life of self-loathing and unhappiness. And unless the two fell in love, Marty had no future at all.

As they walked, Marty tried to think of a new and exciting approach. Nothing came. The best he could manage was suggesting that he ask Lorraine for George, a la Cyrano, but he knew that wouldn't wash. Even George McFly had some pride.

"This is gonna be a tough day for me all around," George said finally.

"How so?"

"Well, first there was my chickening out with Lorraine—"

"I wouldn't say you chickened out," Marty soothed. "It was more a matter of—"

"No, I chickened out," George retorted, a hint of real anger in his voice. "I really wanted to rush over and ask Lorraine for a date. And then when Biff was pawing her,

I wanted to run over and sock him on the jaw. But I chickened out in both cases. I couldn't move."

Marty didn't answer. In fact, he couldn't think of a comforting thing to say.

"And now I gotta talk to Dad about college," George continued.

"What's so awful about that?"

"He'll say it's no good. You know, give me all the reasons why I shouldn't go. And I'll believe him and end up not going."

"Sounds like a self-fulfilling prophecy to me," Marty observed.

"What?"

"You oughta stand up for what you believe in. What do you want to major in at college?"

George's eyes shone as he spoke. "I'd kind of like to study writing or journalism. Writing those stories is about the most fun I have. If I could learn to make a living doing something like that..."

"Then tell your father that."

"Oh, no. He'd laugh if I mentioned the stories. The idea of college is terrible enough."

"Well, anyway," Marty urged, "you gotta fight. Stand up to him."

"I will," George replied. "This is important to my future so I'll do it."

They soon arrived at the house with a placard hanging from the porch. It read THE MCFLYS. A bit tacky for 1985 but probably chic for 1955, Marty thought.

Arthur McFly was outside waxing the car. He waved his rag as the boys approached.

"Go and talk to him right away," Marty urged.

"About what?"

"About college."

"I'll get to that. I've gotta introduce you first."

"No," Marty said, stopping at the edge of the sidewalk. "I'm not moving until you talk to him about college."

"Sure . . ." George said hesitantly.

He walked over to his father, looked back over his shoulder at Marty. In order to make him feel more secure, Marty meandered toward the porch of the house so that he was out of George's line of vision. He was actually closer around the corner of the house, however, and could hear the conversation quite clearly.

"Who's your friend?" Arthur McFly asked.

"A new guy from school," George replied. "Listen, Dad, I have an important decision to make and, well, I really need some advice."

Only a C-plus beginning, Marty thought, although the bit about needing advice was probably good psychologically.

"Gee, son, I'm kinda busy here," George's father said. "Couldn't it wait a few days?"

"Not really," George replied. "You see, I've filled out an application for college and the deadline for sending it in is midnight tonight. I can't decide whether I should send it in."

Wrong, Marty thought, that makes it sound so wishy-washy.

"Well, if you want my advice," George's father said, "I'd say no. College is hard, son. And there's a lot of competition to get in. You'd be competing with the smartest kids in the state. Why would you want to put yourself through that kind of aggravation?"

"Well, I might get in," George responded. The tone of his voice, however, was not brimming with confidence.

"Son, you're a longshot," Arthur McFly said. "And most of the time longshots don't work out. The chances of you getting into college are mighty slim."

"Why?" George asked.

What a miserable counterpuncher you are, Marty fumed. Tell him you can do it.

"Why, son? Because you've never done anything like that before. You're just kinda average. Now if you send this application in and get all excited about it, what's gonna happen when they turn you down? I'll tell you what: you'll mope around the house, feeling rejected, and maybe your marks at school will suffer. If you want to know what I think, I suggest you go about your business and forget this whole thing."

Instead of fighting back, George waited a long moment and then nodded. "Yeah, Dad, that makes sense," Marty heard him say. "Thanks."

It was too much for Marty. He sighed, put his head in his hands.

Meanwhile, Arthur McFly put the finishing touches to George's ambitions with a rationale for failure disguised as homespun philosophy. "When you get to be my age, son," he said, "you'll realize that certain things just aren't meant to be."

"Yeah, I guess that's right," George murmured.

Marty started to walk away.

"What do you think of the car, son?" he heard Arthur McFly say. "Looks pretty good, eh?"

"Looks real good, Dad . . ."

Simultaneously, a crack of thunder split the afternoon quiet and rain began to pour down. Marty broke into a fast trot.

"Good," he said as he ran. "I hope the rain spoils his wax job."

He was soaked by the time he arrived at Doc Brown's garage laboratory but, underneath, Marty was still seething at the thought of George's weakness. Doc had the Twin Pines Mall videotape running and was working on modifications to the DeLorean as Marty entered.

"How'd it go?" he asked, not looking up from his work.

"Terrible," Marty sighed. "He's just the same as when I knew him. A Milquetoast. He makes up his mind to do one thing and then gets talked out of it. But at least I'm starting to find out why."

"Why the kid's got no self-confidence?"

"Yeah. No wonder he won't ask my mom out, or any girl for that matter. All he ever hears from my grandfather is that he's going to fail. No one ever tells him he can succeed at anything..."

"A familiar tale," Doc Brown philosophized.

"Jeez," Marty said, "if he got that kind of support from Grandpa, no wonder Dad gave me such rotten advice."

Doc Brown looked up for the first time. "In my own vast years of experience," he remarked, "I've made it a principle never to take advice from anyone—particularly if that someone is older than I am."

"Hey, Doc, that's good advice," Marty smiled.

"Thank you. Now take my advice and don't take it," he laughed.

"Not even from you, huh?"

"Actually, I may be the exception in your case. In the future—or in the past—if you ever need anything, need to talk to anybody, I'll always be there for you."

"Yeah, Doc. That's great."

The words were barely out when a sudden look of panic crossed Marty's face. Glancing at the TV monitor, he realized that the dramatic climax of the Twin Pines episode was about to unfold. Already the black van was in the picture.

"It's them," Doc Brown was saying on the tape.

"Who?" Marty's off-camera voice yelled back.

"They found me," Doc Brown continued. "I don't know how but they found me."

The tape ended abruptly. Marty, remembering what happened after that on that dark night in 1985, felt his body shiver with pain.

He looked at the Doc Brown of 1955, who had poked his head back into the DeLorean. "Doc," he said haltingly, "there's something I haven't told you about what happens . . . on the night we make that tape . . ."

Doc Brown looked up. "Fascinating device, that camera," he said matter-of-factly. "I can't believe it's made in Japan."

"Doc," Marty continued. "There's something I haven't told you about what happens . . . on the night we made that tape . . ."

He didn't know why, but he felt that he ought to warn his friend about the terrorists. Perhaps it was the violent way he died; no one should be forced to go that way if it's possible to prevent it.

But Doc Brown was already holding up his hand.

"Please, Marty," he said, "don't tell me anything. I don't want to take any more chances of screwing up the space-time continuum. No man should know too much about his own destiny. If I know too much about the future, I could endanger my own existence, just like you've endangered yours."

"Yeah," Marty said. "Maybe you're right."

There was certainly a great deal of logic to what the man said. This way, if Marty said nothing, Doc Brown at least had thirty years to live. Being told that, however, might make him so careless he would endanger himself and possibly even die earlier. So Doc's rule about not screwing around with the space-time continuum seemed to make a lot of sense. Pondering it and his own situation, Marty withdrew his wallet and again took out the family picture.

"Good God," he whispered.

The image of his brother Dave was almost completely gone. Only his feet could be seen in the photo.

Doc Brown was studying him. "Bad, huh?" he said.

Marty nodded.

"That's nature's way of saying, get your ass moving," Doc said. "I guess seeing your brother fade away like that must be pretty scary."

"Tell me about it," Marty grimaced. "I feel like I'm in an episode of the *Twilight Zone*."

"Twilight Zone?" Brown repeated. "That's an interesting phraseology. It's a perfect description of where you are, as a matter of fact... in a zone of twilight, neither here nor there... a middle ground, between light and shadow, between things and ideas..."

"Yeah, I know," Marty said. "'There's the signpost up ahead... You've just crossed over—'"

"If you get back, maybe you could make a movie out of this," Doc Brown smiled.

"Good idea. But what do you mean, if?"

"Things happen. I might mess up the time machine so that the lightning doesn't work. You might not be able to get your parents together before the end of the week. By that time, maybe your head will be missing from the family portrait..."

"Oh, God..." Marty moaned.

He sat down heavily on the lumpy old sofa Doc kept in his garage. It was half-filled now with old magazines, mail, and circulars. On the top of the pile was a newspaper, dated November 7, 1955. An article on the back page leaped out at Marty. It read: LOCAL FARMER CLAIMS 'SPACE ZOMBIE' WRECKED HIS BARN, and below that, in smaller type: "Otis Peabody Under Observation at County Asylum."

"Eureka!" Marty suddenly shouted, snapping his fingers.

Doc Brown's head popped out of the DeLorean.

"You thought of something?"

"You said it! I know how to get my old man to ask Mom to that dance."

"How?"

"I'm gonna scare the shit out of him."

164   George Gipe

"You thought of something?"

You find it's know-how to my my old men to stay Mary
so that time ...

Here

I'm gonna scare the out of him.

•Chapter
Ten•

George McFly went to bed early, yielding to an overall mood of depression generated by events in school and his father's lack of enthusiasm for a college career. Although the phrase "positive thinking" was not popular as such in 1955, he had read books that promoted a variation of the same philosophy. A year earlier, he had pinned his hopes on the prewar best-seller, *How To Win Friends and Influence People,* had memorized whole sections of it and tried to carve out a new life based on this sunny-side-up attitude. The first time he encountered Biff Tannen had negated all his efforts. According to Dale Carnegie, the book's author, a man cannot remain hostile to you if you show him you're sincerely interested in him. Biff Tannen had not only remained hostile, he had rubbed a hero sandwich in George's face after George spent nearly a quarter hour testing his new philosophy on him.

Girls proved no more malleable. Approaching them with a new positive attitude caused them to regard George McFly not only as a creep, but also as an insincere creep. Even his parents avoided George during the time he was under the sway of Mr. Carnegie, instinctively distrusting his strangely outgoing disposition.

And so George had retreated into himself again. "The hell with it," he said. "Let those who like me like me for what I am." It sounded good to say this, except that he couldn't say for sure who it was that liked him.

Retiring to his room at nine o'clock, he had written several more pages of his earth invasion story, fooled with his homework for an hour or so and then turned out the light. He did not fall asleep easily, but by one o'clock had drifted into a semiconscious state that led, a half hour later, to deep slumber.

He did not see the large form move to the side of his bed, nor did he feel the featherweight headphones being placed on his ears by the gloved hands. The same hands inserted a cassette tape into the Walkman tape player, a cassette labeled VAN HALEN. The dial of the Walkman was moved to "10" and the "play" button pushed.

George passed from peaceful sleep to a state of pulse-pounding agitation in less than a second. What was that sound? It was the worst noise he had ever heard—the torturing of humans, perhaps, mixed with background sounds from hell. Yet it had a terrifying throb that elevated it from the realm of noise to semi-intelligent creation. But it was the creation of mad people, the synchronized babble of idiots screaming, lemminglike, at the top of their lungs. What was going on? Had he died and was now approaching the gates of hell?

Then, suddenly, the sound was gone.

"Silence, earthling!" a voice intoned.

George, who was sufficiently frightened to be incapable

of any sound, could only stare at the creature near the foot of his bed. It was yellow, featureless, with only a square mouth through which it spoke to him in an eerie filtered voice.

He had no doubt it was a creature from another planet.

"Who..." George managed to squeak.

"My name is Darth Vader," the being intoned. "I am an extraterrestrial from the planet Vulcan."

George shook his head. "I must...be...dreaming..." he stammered.

"This is no dream!" the alien shot back. "You are having a close encounter of the third kind. You have taken one step beyond into the outer limits of the twilight zone."

"No..."

"Silence! I have instructions for you."

"I...don't want...instructions..." George moaned. "Mom...Dad..."

The creature reached into his belt and withdrew something that looked extremely lethal. It was made of one solid piece of hard shiny material with a round hole, about two inches in diameter at the end. From a distance of six feet, George could plainly hear its low hum and feel heat radiating from its nozzle.

"Don't speak or get out of bed!" the alien ordered. "My heat ray will vaporize you if you do not obey me!"

George raised his hands above his head.

"All right," he whined. "I surrender."

A strange beeping sound came from the alien. Lowering the heat ray, the creature lifted its right arm to listen to the sounds.

"What's—" George began.

"Silence! I am receiving a transmission from the Battlestar Galactica!"

After emitting several more beeps, the object on the alien's arm lapsed into silence.

"You, George McFly, have created a rift in the space-time continuum—" the creature said.

"I'm sorry," George whispered. "I'll repair any damage I did—"

"I said, silence! The Supreme Klingon hereby commands you to take the female earth person called 'Baines, Lorraine' to the—"

"You mean Lorraine Baines?"

"Of course, earthling! You are hereby ordered to take this Baines female person to the location known as Hill Valley High School exactly four earth cycles from now—"

"Earth cycles?"

"Days, stupid!"

"That's Saturday. School's closed on Saturday."

"There is an event at school Saturday!"

"Oh, you mean the dance?"

"Exactly!"

"I'm ordered to take Lorraine to the dance?"

"Affirmative!"

"Does she know about this?"

"No. It is not necessary."

"But I don't know if I'll be able to—"

The creature made a movement with his hands, causing the avalanche of sound to start again in George's ears. He screamed.

"Stop! Please stop it!"

The noise was stopped.

"You must not protest our decisions or you will be made to hear the brain-paralyzing sound all the time," the alien threatened. "It will melt your brain."

"No," George moaned. "I'm sorry. It's just that I don't know how to approach Lorraine."

"You will know at the time. We will give you the necessary confidence."

"You will?"

"Yes."

"You mean I'll be able to do magic?" George asked, brightening.

"No. Our power will be behind you, to guide you. That is all, but it will make a difference."

"Thanks. I'm sure I can do it with your help."

"Very good, earthling," the creature said. "You will close your eyes now and sleep. When you awaken, you will tell no one of this visit."

"O.K.," George murmured.

He closed his eyes, lay back against the pillow. The creature moved closer to him, reached out to hold something under his nose. In less than a minute, young George McFly was snoring like a truck driver. Gently removing the featherweight earphones from his head, the alien figure walked to the window, paused to take a long look back at the sleeping figure, then disappeared into the night.

Doc Brown, waiting in his Packard convertible near the McFly house, opened the door as Marty approached and helped him into the car. The hood of the radiation suit was down and Marty was smiling.

"I guess it went all right," Doc Brown said, starting the engine and pulling away.

"Yeah. It was great. He swallowed everything like a ton of bricks."

"You mix metaphors beautifully, my friend. How did the chloroform work?"

"Fine. He's out like a light."

"Good. I've had it a while. I don't know whether chloroform gets weaker or stronger the longer it's kept."

"Well, it did the job," Marty smiled. "Let's hope he remembers everything when he wakes up."

"That's our only danger," Doc Brown nodded. "Sometimes things which are vivid and frightening at night lose their strength when the sun comes up. Your father-to-be,

I'm afraid, is the perfect candidate for doing a mental flip-flop."

"God," Marty said. "You mean after all that trouble he's liable to chicken out?"

"Even with supernatural or extraterrestrial help, some people screw up. My knowledge of human psychology tells me that with George McFly it will be touch-and-go all the way."

Marty sighed.

Nearly twelve hours later, he was still sighing—and alternately cursing George. Marty got to school bright and early, despite his loss of sleep from the night before, but George McFly was nowhere to be seen. Unfortunately, Marty had no copy of his schedule, so he was forced to waste a great deal of time looking into classrooms before he found out that George hadn't shown up at all. By that time, it was midday and Marty hoped he would show up for afternoon classes. Part of him—the more sanguine part—reasoned that George had spent the morning planning strategy for his meeting with Lorraine; another part of him knew that George had just plain chickened out. He was presently surprised to discover that both parts of him had been mistaken.

School was over and Marty was loitering around the town square when he suddenly spotted George running toward him. He looked even more disheveled than usual and his eyes were wild and a little glassy.

"George!" Marty cried. "Are you all right?"

George stopped, nodded.

"You weren't at school. Where've you been all day?"

"I just woke up. I overslept."

Marty's jaw dropped. Had the chloroform been that powerful? If so, was there a possibility he could have killed George? The thought sent a shiver of terror racing through his system.

"What time did you go to bed last night?" he asked,

forcing his voice to sound calm.

"About ten or eleven o'clock," George said. "I don't know what happened. My folks slept a little late, so when they got up, they assumed I'd already left. I had some strange dreams. Maybe that did it."

"What kind of dreams?"

"Never mind. Just fantastic stuff."

It would not do to have George dismiss the careful scenario he had executed as "fantastic stuff," of course. The wimp's talking himself out of it already, Marty thought, but even as he began to despair, a new plan of action crossed his mind.

"By the way," he said, "did you happen to see the flying saucer last night?"

"What?" George cried, his eyes wide.

"It was about one o'clock," Marty continued. "After everybody was in bed. I guess that's why there wasn't much talk about it at school. Although a dozen kids did see it. They all agreed it was in your neighborhood."

"Really?"

Marty nodded. "Nothing much happened. The saucer just hovered in the air over one house for about ten minutes and then took off like a shot. I guess maybe a space man had to go to the bathroom."

"Holy cow..." George whispered.

"Too bad you weren't awake," Marty said. "You could have gotten some great material for those science fiction stories you write."

George nodded. A glint of energy seemed to come into his eyes.

"Look, you've gotta help me," he said suddenly. "I want to ask Lorraine out, but I don't know how to do it."

"All right," Marty nodded. "She's over there in the soda shop."

As they turned and headed toward the local teen hangout,

two kids on homemade scooters—roller skates nailed to a two-by-four with an orange crate on top—rattled past them. Marty smiled at the crude prototypes of the sleeker and speedier skateboards that would come later.

"There she is . . ." he said a moment later.

Lorraine, seated with girlfriends Betty and Babs, was seated in a booth sipping an ice cream soda and talking.

The moment of truth at hand, George felt his resolve beginning to slip away. Where was the help the alien had promised him? He thought it would be a lot easier than this. In fact, he was every bit as tongue-tied and nervous as before last night's apparition assured him everything would be all right. Was it possible space people were even more sophisticated bullshitters than his fellow earthlings? If not, where was the magic phrase or surge of power that would carry him through this ordeal?

Marty sensed George's indecisiveness. "It's simple," he said. "You just go in there and invite her. I promise you, she won't throw anything at you. The worst that can happen is she'll say no."

"No. The worst than can happen is she throws up or laughs when I ask for the date."

"She won't. Believe me."

"Maybe I'd better wait until she's alone. You know how girls are when they're together."

"George," Marty said softly. "There are only a few days until the dance. Lorraine will probably be snapped up by tomorrow morning. This may be your last chance."

The threat had its effect. George swallowed, nodded slowly, and took several steps toward the entrance of the store. "What should I say to her?" he asked.

"Say whatever feels natural, whatever comes to your mind."

George took a deep breath and closed his eyes. "Nothing's coming to my mind," he said.

"Christ, it's a miracle I was even born," Marty muttered acidly.

"Huh?"

"Nothing."

"If I had just one clever thing to say, it would help a lot."

"All right," Marty replied. "Just tell her destiny has brought you to her and you think she's the most beautiful girl you've ever seen. Girls like to hear that—What the hell are you doing, putting me on?"

George had taken a pencil and pad from his pocket and was meticulously writing down Marty's words.

"Yeah," he nodded. "I'm putting it down. I mean, this is good stuff."

"Well, don't recite it like a speech, for God's sake," Marty cautioned. "At least memorize it."

George nodded briskly, looked the words over, his lips moving softly. "O.K.," he said finally.

"Good. Relax. Just go and ask her. It'll all be over in a minute. Unless she invites you to spend tonight at her house."

George blushed. "No chance of that," he smiled.

A moment later, he was in the store. He took nearly a dozen steps directly toward Lorraine, then suddenly veered off to the counter. The counterman appeared, waiting for his order.

"Gimme a milk," George said. "Chocolate."

He hoped it would take a long time, but the milk arrived with disappointing speed. He took a slurp to fortify himself, then literally hurled himself toward the booth where the three girls sat.

"Uh, Lorraine," he began in a rapid, strident voice. "My density has brought me to you."

Lorraine looked up, heard the words almost before she realized who had delivered them. She recognized the young man whom she'd been introduced to yesterday by Marty.

He looked approximately the same, except that now he was wearing a brown mustache of chocolate milk. She did her best not to giggle.

"I beg your pardon?" she managed to say with feminine dignity.

"Oh," George muttered. "What I mean to say id—"

"Id?"

"Is . . ."

His mind a blank, George reached into his pocket for the notepad.

Lorraine filled the conversational void. "Haven't I seen you somewhere?" she asked.

George smiled broadly. So far, she had neither thrown up nor laughed and he was optimistic. If he could just remember those words!

"Yes," he replied. "I'm George. George McFly. I'm your density. I mean, destiny."

Now Lorraine did giggle. Babs and Betty joined her. But to George, the sound wasn't as demoralizing as he thought it would be. The errant notion even crossed his mind that they might think his goofing up was part of his normal routine, that he actually intended to amuse them. Their laughter was, after all, relatively noncommittal. Those seated in nearby booths probably thought he had said something quite amusing to the girls and admired him for it. For the first time since he had awakened in a cold sweat an hour earlier, George actually believed he had the help promised by the creature who had appeared to him last night either in a dream or in the extraterrestrial flesh. A surge of confidence took hold of him. Say it, his mind urged. Just tell her you want to take her to the dance and it'll all be over in a second.

"Lorraine," he began, the word emerging with a tonal strength that surprised even George. "I want—"

"McFly, I thought I told you never to come in here!" a

familiar voice bellowed, interrupting George's speech as effectively as someone yelling "Fire."

Biff Tannen and his henchmen were at the door, leering at George, their hands on their hips. Slowly, deliberately, like gunfighters taking over a small Western town, they strode into the store toward George McFly.

Marty had seen them arrive just at the worst possible time—when George actually seemed on the verge of popping the question to Lorraine.

"Damn!" he muttered.

He then did the only thing he could—walked in behind them so that he could help if necessary.

George, his resolute and happy expression melting into his usual mask of misery, stared slack-jawed at the approaching Biff.

"Well, your showing up here after I told you to stay out is gonna cost you, McFly," Biff grated, making no attempt to keep his voice down. "How much money you got on you?"

It was blatant bullying and outright extortion but no one in the soda shop made a move to come to George's assistance. After a long moment, he reached into his pocket and withdrew his wallet.

His beefy hand outstretched, Biff took several long strides toward George, a look of malicious greed on his face.

Then, suddenly, his face had disappeared from view and was resting against the tile floor.

Marty withdrew his foot, inwardly congratulating himself on the best-timed trip he had ever executed.

Biff looked up from the floor.

"You!" he thundered, getting up quickly as a titter of derision circulated throughout the shop.

"All right, wiseass," he spat, taking a step toward Marty. "It's fat-lip time."

Marty moved his body into position, preparing for action.

Lumbering toward him, Biff threw a roundhouse right which he was able to avoid easily, countering with a hard left to Biff's gut and a right to the temple. Staggering drunkenly, Biff fell backwards into a table.

Seeing that their leader was in trouble, Match, 3-D and Skinhead started toward Marty.

Oh-oh, he thought, these aren't good odds unless you happen to be Superman. In midstride as he moved forward to finish off Biff, Marty suddenly spun on his toe and headed out the front door. Biff's lackies pulled him to his feet and rushed after him.

"That's Calvin Klein!" Lorraine shouted to her girl-friends, "I mean, Marty! Oh, God, he's a dream!"

George McFly stood to one side, transfixed with fear and awe as the scene unfolded. Fortunately, no one was looking at him or they would have seen his eyes mist as if he was about to burst into tears.

Damn, he thought, it's gone wrong again. Even with help from outer space. I'm a dud.

Marty raced out of the soda shop, hesitated a moment at the corner of 2nd and Main, then turned to his left and started running as fast as his legs would carry him. Biff and his three lieutenants followed. Biff was slow but two of the others were faster than Marty and were rapidly closing the distance between pursued and pursuers.

Damn these new shoes, Marty thought, wincing with nearly every step as the backs chewed into his heels. Whirl-ing to his right, he doubled back toward the town square. The maneuver gained him a step or two but he knew it was only a matter of time before the two fast boys caught him. Passing again in front of the soda shop, he saw that most of the kids had come outside on the sidewalk and were yelling encouragement to him. He would gladly have traded all that moral support for a couple of tough friends, but none seemed in the offing.

He had almost resigned himself to being caught when one of the youngsters on scooters turned off Hill Street in a path that paralleled his.

"Eureka!" Marty shouted.

Grabbing the scooter and literally yanking it out from under the kid, Marty lashed out with his feet, kicking the orange crate loose so that what remained was a crude home-made skateboard.

"Sorry, kid!" he yelled over his shoulder as he hopped onto it. "I'll make it up to you later."

He gave himself a kick just as hostile hands grabbed for his neck and missed. A second later, he was free, moving down the sidewalk at twice the speed of his pursuers.

"Wow! Look at him go!" yelled the kid whose scooter had been appropriated and instantly transformed into a lighter, faster vehicle.

"What is that thing?" another kid shouted, watching Marty speed away.

After a half block of falling rapidly behind their prey, Biff's pals turned and shrugged, looking to Biff for a new tack.

"Get the car!" Biff ordered.

The four hotfooted it over to Biff's convertible, which was parked nearby. A few seconds later, they roared off after Marty, burning rubber on the town square and disappearing in a cloud of black smoke.

Two blocks away, Marty looked back over his shoulder. The convertible was closing in on him. Indeed, it was just about to hit him when he suddenly cut a sharp turn directly in front of it and started heading in the opposite direction.

"Goddamn!" Biff shouted, hitting the brakes and twisting the car into a U-turn.

"Look at that!" Skinhead yelled.

Behind them, Marty had grabbed on to the back of a passing car and was now moving away from them at better than forty miles an hour. The driver of the car, who didn't see the crouching Marty, shook his head with puzzlement as he passed the corner soda shop. There, at least twenty kids were standing on the sidewalk, applauding wildly and cheering as he passed.

"You'd think I just won a race or something," the driver muttered.

Lorraine, who had seen all the action except that at the far end of the street, leaped up and down as Marty zoomed past, the skates sending sparks behind him.

"He's an absolute dream!" she shouted to her two girl-friends.

Ten seconds later, Biff's convertible roared past. Most of the kids booed and hissed the four tight-lipped villains who stared ahead with deadly intent.

The chase made a right turn as the driver of the host car headed toward the courthouse. Biff gained ground swiftly on the unwary driver, closing the distance until the bumper of his car was nearly touching Marty's buttocks. As the host car passed the courthouse near Statler's Studebaker dealership, Marty released his grip and hung a sharp right. Biff, going too fast, overshot the intersection. Cursing, he jammed on the brakes, backed up, and then roared down the sidewalk in front of the courthouse after Marty. Bewildered and terrified pedestrians spun or dived out of the way, scurrying for the safety of the concrete steps or trying to hide behind the World War I cannons. Oblivious to all objects in his path except Marty, Biff roared forward, bringing terror even to the eyes of his own passengers.

Marty found too late that he had underestimated Biff's maniacal determination. At the end of the intersection, he had time only to see that Biff was right behind him, do a quick 180 on his board and—

Suddenly, thrown off balance and about to fall, he reached out—and found himself holding on to the front end of Biff's car.

"Now we got the son of a bitch!" Biff shouted. "If he holds on, he's dead, and if he lets go, he's dead!"

Smiling sadistically, he pushed Marty down Hill Street, past Gaynor's Hideaway, where customers had come outside, some still holding their drinks, to view the action. Dead ahead was the T of the intersection and Main Street, with the display window of Hal's Bike Shop directly in their path. Biff decided to drive Marty right through the glass rather than fool with him any longer. If worse came to worst, he would simply tell the judge that his brakes had failed.

Looking back through the windshield at the malevolent Biff, Marty could only gulp. Their speed was such that he couldn't veer to one side without being hit by Biff's fender as he did so. Weaving back and forth on his skateboard, Marty maintained his grip while searching for a way out. Usually there was at least one cop car hanging around Town Square but as luck would have it, this was the day when the men in blue were totally absent. A quick vision of his tombstone flashed before his eyes as Biff drove him inexorably backward. It read: MARTIN MCFLY—BORN 1968—DIED 1955.

Now, as they were about to pass a large manure truck in the same traffic lane, new devilment was added. Match had picked up a beer bottle and was about to throw it at Marty's head.

"Got to get outa here!" he cried.

With that, he leaped up, sending the skateboard forward, under the car, and landed on Biff's hood. With no loss of motion, he bounded over the heads of the four open-mouthed boys, onto the rear deck and off the car, just in time to catch the skateboard as it passed underneath.

"Holy—" Biff wheezed.

So stunned were the four pursuers that all turned in their seats to stare at Marty.

A split second later, they felt a crash and were hurled upward as the car roared into the back of the manure truck. Hanging in the air a moment, the convertible tilted forward, pitching Biff and his cohorts head first into the icky brown mass.

Across the square, from the corner soda shop, cheers and applause could be heard. To the rear also, from the newly involved customers from Gaynor's, shouts and hand-clapping added to the furor. Like a Fourth of July demonstration, the chase had brought all activity in beautiful downtown Hill Valley to an utter standstill.

"He's wonderful!" Lorraine shouted hysterically. "Isn't he just the most terrific thing you ever laid eyes on?"

Her friends, impressed, nodded agreement.

George McFly, also watching, viewed the proceedings with mixed emotions. He was glad to see Biff and his pals end up in the manure pile, but he'd have given ten years of his life to have engineered the trick himself.

Marty, smiling in acknowledgment of the victory, looked around for the youngster whose scooter he had used.

"Thanks a lot, kid," he said, returning the skateboard with a flourish. "I'm sorry I messed it up for you."

"Are you kidding?" the youngster laughed. "Thanks a lot!"

He immediately hopped on his new vehicle and began trying it out. As the crowd slowly started to disperse, it could be seen that the other youngster was in the process of removing the orange crate from his scooter so that he could have a skateboard like that of his friend.

•Chapter Eleven•

Lorraine, her eyes fixed on Marty as he walked down Main Street away from the scene of the accident, had made up her mind.

If he won't ask me, she thought, then I'll just have to ask him.

Turning to Babs, she said: "Can I borrow your car?"

Babs hesitated. "You know it's not mine," she replied. "It belongs to my sister."

"Well, it doesn't matter. I'll be careful."

"What do you want it for?"

"Promise not to tell?"

Babs nodded.

"I want to trail Marty and see where he lives. He's so secretive about himself."

Babs giggled. Here was a mission she could understand. "I'll drive you," she said.

"All right. Let's go before he gets out of sight."

The two girls were headed for Babs' car when Lorraine suddenly found herself face to face with George McFly once again.

"Hi," he muttered.

The chocolate mustache was still there. Looking away, Lorraine said brusquely: "Hi. Sorry I have to go now, but I'm really busy."

He fell in step beside her. "This'll only take a second," he began. "I was wondering if you'd like to go to the dance with me Saturday night."

"The dance? Oh, yes—"

"Yes, you'll go?" George leaped in.

"No. What I meant to say was . . . yes, that's right, the dance is this Saturday. Time sure flies, doesn't it?"

"Yeah . . . Well?"

"I'm sorry. I sort of made a prior commitment but I haven't found out about it yet."

"How can you do that?" George asked.

"It's very complicated. But if I didn't have this thing that may be coming up, maybe I'd go with you."

George took her reply as a positive one, despite the network of disclaimers.

"Maybe if I . . . that is, we waited a day or two—"

"Oh, no," Lorraine smiled. "That wouldn't be fair to you."

"Well, you're the only girl I want to take," he said, hating himself all the while for wearing his heart on his sleeve.

"Thank you," Lorraine said. "Maybe next time."

"The next dance isn't until spring."

"Well, if winter comes, can spring be far behind?" Lorraine cooed, having just learned the line in English class.

"Yeah, but it's not even winter yet," George protested weakly.

"Thanks very much for asking," Lorraine said, leaping into Babs' car. "I'll see you later."

"Yeah . . ."

"And wipe off your mouth."

She drove off, leaving him standing on the sidewalk, his fingers exploring his upper lip.

The candles masquerading as lamp posts were the nicest touch, Doc Brown thought, moving several steps backwards to admire his work.

"Very good," he murmured, smiling. "Maybe I'll keep it up until Christmas and use it as a garden."

He had spent most of the afternoon planning and constructing his own replica of Hill Valley's Town Square. Set up on a large piece of plywood, it consisted primarily of a piece of wood with a watch strapped around it (the clock tower of the courthouse) with a "lightning rod" (a nail) attached to the top. A wire ran from the lightning rod down across the square and between two lamp posts across the street. Near the lamp posts sat a windup toy car with a small wire sticking straight up from the back. To the wire was attached a hook.

Consulting his worksheet which contained lines of statistics and computations, Doc Brown nodded. He was sure it would work.

"Good," he said as Marty entered. "Now I can explain this to you. How did you make out with the continuing saga of George and Lorraine?"

Marty sighed. "We got closer. That's all I can say. Except that I had a little run-in with Biff Tannen and four of his goons. I came within an inch or two of being squashed to death."

"Is that all?" Doc smiled. "So what was the final outcome of the run-in?"

"The four guys ended up in a pile of shit. I have to admit, I handled myself and them pretty well."

"Of course, you have thirty years of advanced technology

to draw from," Doc Brown rejoined.

Marty snorted.

"Just pulling your leg," Doc smiled. "Step over here and take a look at this."

"Sure. What the hell is it?"

"It's my own clever-as-hell method of getting you back to 1985."

"Good. Tell me about it."

Doc Brown explained the nomenclature of the setup and then launched into a description of how it was supposed to work. "You see, we put a lightning rod on the courthouse clock tower," he said. "Then we run some industrial strength electrical cable from the lightning rod, across the street . . . Meanwhile, we've outfitted your car with a big hook directly connected with the flux capacitor . . ."

He took the toy car and wound it up.

"You'll be in this," he said. "Now, on a signal, you'll take off down the street toward the cable, accelerating until you hit eighty-eight miles an hour . . ."

He released the toy car from one end of the model. It raced toward the strung wire. Picking up a stripped wire that was plugged into an AC outlet, he brought it toward the "lightning rod" nail.

"Then," he continued, "lightning strikes, electrifying the cable, just in time to . . ."

With that, he touched the live wire to the nail. As the toy car's antenna snagged the cable, sparks flew, the car caught fire and sailed off the table top. Striking the drapes nearby, it rolled down them, spreading flames as it went. In a split second, the cheap curtains were a mass of fire and smoke.

Doc Brown rushed to the far end of the room, grabbed a fire extinguisher and had the blaze under control in less than a minute.

"Well," Marty said when it was all over, "I'm glad to know you figured it all out. Why don't we just set fire to me now instead of going to all that trouble?"

"This is theoretical," Doc Brown shrugged. "It'll be different with a car you can control and a flux capacitor that directs the lightning into energy instead of letting it go loose, as this did. At least I hope that's the way it turns out."

"You're instilling me with a lot of confidence, Doc," Marty smiled grimly.

"Believe me, it should work."

"The operative word there is 'should.'"

"Well, how can I guarantee you this *will* work? It's a scientific experiment, my boy—something that's being tried for the first time. Nothing is one hundred percent foolproof. Take the simplest part of the plan here—your driving eighty-eight miles an hour through Town Square at just the right moment. Even that's not guaranteed. Suppose an old lady steps off the curb at the wrong moment? Suppose there's a cop car that decides to cut you off? Suppose that beautifully engineered car breaks down during the run? Suppose you miss the hook or the lightning strikes early or late? Suppose the newspapers got the time wrong? Suppose—"

"O.K., Doc," Marty interrupted. "I get the point. It's a big gamble, no matter what."

"Don't worry. I'll take care of the lightning. You just take care of your old man."

Marty sighed. Once again he took out the family snapshot and looked at it. His brother Dave was completely gone and Linda's head was partially obscured.

"Jeez," he gulped. "I'm next."

There was a knock at the door. Doc Brown and Marty exchanged anxious glances.

"Biff," Marty said. "Somehow he got out of the shit and followed me."

He looked around for a crowbar or some other heavy object as Doc Brown raced to the window and peered outside. Marty heard him grunt.

"It's worse," Doc Brown said, rushing back toward him. "Quick, let's cover the time machine."

As they threw a heavy tarpaulin over the DeLorean, Doc continued. "It's your mother," he said. "Did you tell her where you live?"

"No. I'd be crazy to do that."

"Then she must have tracked you down by herself. Boy, this dame really has the hots."

The knock at the door was repeated.

"Should we let her in?" Marty asked.

"We better," Doc Brown said. "I think she saw me when I looked out. Anyway, if she followed you here, she probably knows you're inside."

Marty went to the door and let Lorraine in.

"Hi," she smiled.

"Mom—I mean, Lorraine. How did you find me?"

"I followed you."

"Why?"

"I wanted to know where you lived."

"That makes sense, I guess."

Lorraine looked around him, smiled tightly.

"Oh," Marty said, moving aside. "Uh, this is my Uncle Brown."

"Uncle Brown?" she repeated.

"Emmett," Doc said.

"Hi."

Returning her glance to Marty, Lorraine took a deep breath and launched into a brief speech which was obviously rehearsed.

"Marty," she said, "this may seem a little forward, but I was hoping you might take me to the Enchantment Under the Sea Dance Saturday."

Marty should have been prepared for the proposal but somehow was not. Clearing his throat nervously, he glanced down at his right foot. "I don't think I can make it," he replied. "You see, all that running around this afternoon— I think I twisted my ankle so bad—"

"You walked home without any trouble," Lorraine interjected.

"Yeah, but I've done this before. I know it'll really be bad tomorrow morning and probably keep me in bed a week or so."

"I don't believe you," Lorraine murmured. Her eyes started to mist over. "I think that's just an excuse to get out of going with me."

"No," Marty cried. "It's not that. It's just that . . . well, I'm a lousy dancer. I've got two left feet. Make that three left feet. I get so embarrassed . . ." He trailed off, trying to appear inept.

"We don't have to dance," Lorraine suggested. "If you're shy about your dancing, all right, but I think you're just being modest. Anybody who could move around on skates the way you did this afternoon has got to have something."

It was a good point but Marty decided not to deal with it. Instead he said: "You know who really wants to take you, and I really think you'd hit it off with him—George McFly."

"I knew you were gonna say that."

"Because I happen to think it's true. I think there's some chemistry there between you two. Maybe you don't feel it yet, but it's coming."

"Maybe, but why should it?" Lorraine asked. "I feel more chemistry with you. Anyway, George already asked me and I turned him down."

"You did *what?*" Marty demanded. "Don't you realize what courage it took for him to ask? It was like sky-diving or getting into the ring with Muhammad Ali—"

"With who?"

"Rocky Marciano," Doc Brown interjected.

"Oh, well, I can't worry about that," Lorraine said. "George just isn't my type. He's sort of cute and all, but he's . . . well . . ." She moved closer to Marty so that her head was nearly touching his chin. "I think a man should be strong . . . so he can stand up for himself and protect the woman he loves. Don't you?"

"Don't I what?" Marty asked nervously.

Sensing he was procrastinating, Lorraine tossed her head angrily. "Just tell me yes or no," she demanded. "And it better be yes, because if you don't take me to the dance, nobody will."

Marty sighed. Something in her eyes told him she wasn't bluffing. He looked at Doc Brown miserably.

"It sounds like she really wants to go with you, boy," he said. "You better say yes."

"Yes," Marty said.

"Oh, thank you," Lorraine smiled, reaching out to kiss his cheek. "You won't be sorry."

Then she turned and rushed out of the house, gave him a little wave at the door, and was gone.

"A fine mess," Marty said.

"It does complicate the situation," Doc Brown admitted. "But at least if she goes to the dance with you, she'll be there. Now we gotta figure out a way to get George there so they can discover love and enchantment under the sea, whatever that means."

"Oh, God," Marty sighed. "That means I have to convince my father to go stag."

"Either that or get him another date."

"Doc, you may be a genius with flux capacitors and electricity and space-time continuums, but when you say I have to find another gal for that nerd at this late date, you're really asking the impossible."

* * *

He caught up with George the next day shortly after lunchtime.

"Hi," George said, "and congratulations."

"Congratulations about what?"

"Going to the dance with Lorraine. I checked with her this morning and she said you were the lucky guy."

Marty exhaled wearily. "Let me explain something," he said. "She only agreed to go to the dance with me because she knew you'd be there."

"How can that be?" George asked. "She could have gone to the dance with me if she wanted."

"She's really screwed up," Marty said. "And that gets her in hot water. You know how it is when a person wants to buy something but he wants to keep the price down? So he pretends to find a lot of things wrong with it and maybe even says he doesn't want it—but all the while he wants it like crazy?"

George nodded.

"Well, that's the way it is with Lorraine. Deep down she wants you, only she doesn't want you to know. And maybe a part of *her* doesn't know it yet. But take it from me— she wants you to be at the dance so that the two of you can get together..."

"Get together?" George mumbled. "I'm for that. Why didn't she ask? Or say yes when I asked?"

"Some women will accept wonderful things only if they seem like accidents," Marty replied sagely. "It ties in with what I just said. They don't want to admit they want them. That's why she asked me. She doesn't really want me. She wants you, George. Now all we gotta do is make her realize you're what she wants."

"Well, how can we do that?"

"I think we begin by making her see that you're not a chicken."

"But . . . I think I am a chicken."

"No, George," Marty said. "Every guy has one thing he'll stand up and fight for, and I think with you it's Lorraine."

"Yeah . . . but when Biff comes at me . . ."

"Well, we're just gonna have to teach you how to handle that," Marty said. "We'll start this afternoon, right after school's over."

George took a deep breath and nodded. A faint hope seemed to appear in his eyes.

Four hours later, the two young men got together again in George's back yard. Marty brought along a homemade body bag which consisted of clothes stuffed into a duffel bag until it was solid as a rock. After spending several minutes trying to teach George how to throw hooks and jabs, he offered himself as the target.

"I want you to hit me in the stomach," Marty said. "Right there. Go ahead."

He dropped both hands to his sides.

"But I don't want to hit you in the stomach," George protested.

"You're not gonna hurt me. Just give me a punch."

"Look, I'm not a fighter."

"How many times do I have to explain it to you?" Marty demanded. "We know you're not a fighter. You know it. I know it . . ."

"And Biff knows it."

"Forget Biff. The important thing is Lorraine doesn't know it. That's why we've gotta make you at least look like a fighter, somebody who'll stand up for himself, who'll protect her."

"But I've never picked a fight in my life!" George cried.

"You're not picking a fight, Dad—" Marty said. "I mean, George. You're coming to her rescue."

"It sounds so corny . . ."

"Girls like corn. Now maybe we'd better go over the plan again. Where are you gonna be at 8:55?"

George sighed. "At the dance."

"And where am I gonna be?"

"In the parking lot with her."

"O.K. So right around nine o'clock, she's gonna get very angry with me—"

"Why?"

"Why what?"

"Why will she get angry with you?"

"Because I'm gonna get pushy. And nice girls get angry at guys who try to take advantage of them."

"You mean you're gonna—"

Marty nodded.

A strange sad look crossed George's face. "Suppose she lets you?" he asked.

"How can you say that?" Marty shot back. "She's not only a nice girl but she's my—"

"Yeah?"

"She's my friend. I couldn't lay a hand on her."

"Are you sure?" George asked through narrowed eyes. "I mean, she's pretty. A guy'd have to be made of stone to say no to Lorraine."

"Not this guy," Marty retorted. "Now let's get back to the plan, O.K.? It's all gonna be an act, so don't worry about it. Just remember that at nine o'clock you'll be strolling through the parking lot and you'll see us . . ." He gulped, went on. "You'll see us struggling in the car. As soon as that happens, you run over, grab the door, yank it open, and say what?"

George opened his lips but no words emerged.

"You're gonna have to be more forceful than that, George," Marty murmured.

"I can't think—"

"Damn it, you shouldn't even have to think. Here you

are face to face with a guy who's pawing the girl you love. It should be automatic."

"Yeah . . . You're right."

"Deliver the line, George."

His jaw working fiercely, exaggeratedly, rather like an old-time vaudeville villain, George spat the line: "Uh . . . Hey you! Get your damn hands off her!" Then, his expression reverting to type, he asked in a soft voice: "You really think I should swear?"

"Yes, definitely," Marty nodded. "Then you hit me in the stomach, I go down for the count and you and Lorraine live happily ever after."

"You make it sound so easy," George smiled. "I wish I wasn't so scared."

"Scared of what?"

"I don't know. Maybe I'll hit you hard and it'll hurt. And that'll make you so angry, you'll slug me back."

Marty laughed. "Believe me, George, you can hit me as hard as you want and I won't hit back."

"Maybe she'll think it's a put-up job."

"That's why you have to make it look convincing. You have to really hit me. Now give it a shot."

"O.K."

As Marty stood still, George took a deep breath and threw a punch at Marty's gut. It looked like someone swatting a fly.

"No, George," Marty corrected. "Put some confidence behind that punch. Some emotion. Some anger. Come on. You can do it."

George threw another punch, slightly better than the first but only marginally so. He seemed satisfied with it, though, particularly with the solid sound it made.

"How was that?" he said. "Pretty good, huh?"

"Well, I guess it'll have to do," Marty shrugged. "I'll tell you what—practice on this."

He hung the duffel bag on the clothesline T-bar, stepped back and blasted it with a powerful uppercut. The bag recoiled nearly a foot.

"Work on something like that," he said.

"Sure," George nodded.

He heaved a punch at the bag, then another. They weren't championship punches but Marty noted with some satisfaction that at least he was learning to enjoy it.

"Anger," he prodded. "Anger."

"Right!" George growled. "Anger!"

Lashing out with all his strength, George mistimed the sway of the bag and missed it completely. Whizzing past its intended target, his fist smashed solidly into the tree behind it.

"Yeeeowww! Goddammit!" he yelled.

"Good," Marty said. "That's real anger." He waved as he walked off. "See you later."

George watched him go, fuming at his own ineptness. His right hand continued to throb but the frustration in him was stronger than the pain. Balling his left hand into a fist, he took two steps forward and uncorked a mighty punch at the slowly swaying bag. The shock of solid contact raced up his arm and he knew instinctively that he had finally done something right. He was not prepared, however, for the sight of the bag flying loose from the rope, sailing toward and shattering the window of his own home. Realizing the possible repercussions of the broken window, George did what he always did in similar situations—ran away.

"The weather forecast for this evening, Hill Valley and vicinity . . . lots of cold wind out of the southwest, generally clear and brisk . . . Down at the airport, they're predicting a bit of a thundershower, although it seems awfully late in the year for that . . . Consensus with the United States Weather Service seems to be that it'll be getting colder with temperatures dropping to about forty-five tonight but nothing worse . . . So have a nice evening. Now back to Bill Sharp, who's gonna give us fifty-five minutes of Eddie Fisher and Patti Page . . ."

The sounds emanating from the radio of Doc Brown's Packard were heard only by the few Hill Valley residents who passed by his car early Saturday evening. Doc Brown himself was standing on a ladder at the corner of 2nd and Main Streets, connecting the paddle plug end of a cable to an extension cord tied to a lamp post.

The Packard was parked several feet away from the lamp posts; behind it, covered with a tarpaulin, was the DeLorean.

Whistling softly, Doc Brown completed the connection and looked across at the courthouse. Swaying softly in the light breeze was the cable he had just finished installing— a very expensive 500 feet of triple-strength wire from the lightning rod atop the courthouse to the connection he had just made.

"There," he said, looking down at Marty, who was waiting at the bottom of the ladder. "We're all set up and ready to go. But it doesn't look much like a thunderstorm's brewing and the weather forecast I just heard said cold and clear. You sure about this storm?"

Marty nodded. "Doc," he said. "Since when can a weatherman predict the weather—let alone the future?"

"You're right," Brown smiled. Testing the cables once again to make sure the connection was tight, he grunted with satisfaction and came down the ladder.

"You know, Marty," he said when he had descended. "I . . . well . . . I'm gonna be sad to see you go. You've really made a difference in my life. You've given me something to shoot for. Just knowing that I'm going to live to see 1985 . . . that I'll succeed in this . . . that I'll get a chance to travel through time . . . well, it's gonna be hard for me to wait thirty years before we can talk about everything that's happened in the past few days. I'm gonna really miss you . . ."

"I'll miss you, too, Doc," Marty replied. "But it could be you won't see me, you know. If something goes wrong with this . . ." He indicated the cable connection. ". . . I might not be around in 1985, or any year for that matter."

Brown nodded grimly. "It's not too late to change your mind, you know," he said. "Why not just stay here? We can work on projects together—"

"No, thanks, Doc," Marty said. "If I don't get all this straightened out with Mom and Dad and get back to 1985, it'll mess up too many lives. I've gotta take the chance that your experiment will work." He smiled. "After all, everything else you've done has turned out all right. Except the brain-wave analyzer."

"Don't remind me."

Once again Marty's mind projected the image of Doc Brown being killed by terrorist bullets, and once again he yearned to warn him. Could it really hurt that much? After all, by the time the terrorists arrived on the scene, Doc Brown's time machine was already a success. Thus history would not be affected if he escaped their vengeance; he would merely be given a few years of extra time to enjoy the fruits of his labor, perhaps travel back and forth in time a bit. Was that so bad?

He concluded that it was not. "Doc," he said. "About the future and you . . ."

Again the upraised hand.

"No, Marty, my boy. Say no more. We've already agreed that having knowledge of the future can be extremely dangerous. Even if your intentions are good, it could backfire drastically. Whatever it is you want to tell me, I'll find out through the natural course of time."

Marty could see that there was no use arguing with him. Nevertheless, the desire was still in him to convey the warning.

"Yeah, Doc . . . I see," he nodded. "Listen, I'm gonna get a candy bar. You want anything?"

"No, thanks."

Marty turned and went into the cafe nearby. He purchased an Almond Joy bar from the perennially scowling counterman and also bummed a piece of paper and envelope. Then he sat at a booth and composed a brief note to Doc. It read:

Doc Brown—On October 26, 1985, at about 1:30 a.m., you will be shot by terrorists at the Twin Pines shopping mall parking lot. Please take whatever precautions are necessary to prevent this terrible disaster. Your friend, Marty. November 12, 1955

He read it over a couple times, folded the paper and put it in the envelope, which he sealed. On the outside he wrote: "Do Not Open Until October 1, 1985."

Meanwhile, Doc Brown was in the process of stringing one final strand of cable between the two lamp posts. As he went merrily about his work on municipal property, a cop meandered over from the Bank of America to watch.

"Oh-oh," Marty whispered as he came out of the cafe. "That's all we need now, is some meddling flatfoot."

He started toward the two men, then thought better of it. Doc Brown would be able to handle it better alone. And Marty would also have time to finish his errand of mercy.

He walked over to the tarped DeLorean and picked up Doc Brown's trenchcoat, which was laying atop the hood. An inside pocket will be best, he thought, one that he might not stick his hand in for a day or two. Placing the envelope in the left side, he tossed the coat back on the car. Even as he did so, however, another thought entered his mind. Suppose he never uses that pocket and *never* finds it? Wouldn't it be better to put the note in the glove compartment of his Packard? He took a step back toward the Delorean.

"No," he said. "Stop trying to outthink fate. If he gets it, he gets it. If he's not meant to, he won't find it no matter what you do."

That matter resolved, he moved closer to the two men so that he could at least hear the conversation.

The cop spent a great deal of time just looking. Then, finally, he spoke. "Evening, Dr. Brown," he said. "What's with the wire?"

"Oh, I'm just doing a little weather experiment. Something that'll benefit the city a lot if it works."

"Is that so?"

"Yessir. That's so."

"And what's under here?" the cop asked, pointing to the DeLorean.

Doc Brown never flinched, the consummate verbal escape artist. "Some new specialized weather-sensing equipment," he replied.

"Looks like a car," the cop said.

"Well, it has wheels," Doc answered. "It has to have wheels so I can move it. Anyway, officer, why do you ask? Does it make a difference if it's a car or a portable laboratory?"

"If it's a car, it's parked illegally," the cop pointed out. "There's a red line."

"Yessir. I won't do that again, even though it's not really a car. But if you don't mind, I need to leave it there temporarily."

He came down from the ladder, his work completed, and smiled genially at the officer.

"You got a permit for this?" the cop asked, not returning the smile.

"Of course I do," Doc Brown replied. Reaching into his pocket, he took out his wallet and withdrew a fifty-dollar bill. "A permit straight from Washington," he added.

"You're not gonna set anything on fire this time, are you,

Dr. Brown?" the cop asked, looking around nervously as he allowed the bill to slide from Brown's palm to his.

"No, sir," Doc Brown replied. "This experiment is child's play."

"In that case," the cop said, "good luck."

"Thank you, officer."

The cop nodded, crossed back over the street and continued testing the doors of the shops along 2nd Street.

"Well done," Marty said. "I thought for a minute there one of your many variables was gonna screw us up."

"I had a twinge myself," Doc Brown said. He looked at his watch. "Say, kid, you'd better pick up your mom and get going."

"Yeah, I guess I'd better," Marty mumbled.

"You look a little pale. Are you O.K.?"

In fact, Marty didn't feel so good. There was so much to do! And nothing could go wrong. First he had to get his mom and dad together, then time his run just right, attain the fastest speed anybody had ever done on Main Street, and hope that Doc's calculations were correct. For the first time, he felt that he was truly balancing a tightrope between three separate worlds—1985, 1955 and ... death. If the lightning bolt did not function in exactly the same manner as plutonium, Marty would end up buried in the back wall of the Bank of America. Or perhaps he and the DeLorean would be hurled in some sort of imperfect time-space orbit that would deposit them in Kansas, Afghanistan, or Irkutsk. Strangely, however, he knew that he could face those tests. What bothered him more than anything was having to deal with his parents, particularly Mom.

"What is it?" Doc Brown asked, sensing his mental turmoil.

"I don't know, Doc," he replied. "I guess it's this whole thing with my mother. I don't know if I can go through with it."

"Why not? What's the problem?"

"Hitting on her is the problem."

"Hitting on her?" Brown repeated, frowning. "You didn't mention beating her up. I thought George was supposed to beat you up."

"It's an expression," Marty explained. "Hitting on a girl means trying to make her, you know . . ."

"Yes. Take liberties. What's so terrible about that?"

"She's my mother!"

"Not yet, she isn't."

"That doesn't make any difference."

"All right. I see your point. But if you consider it from a strictly practical standpoint, you'll be a lot closer to her than whatever you do tonight."

"Yeah, but as a baby. Don't you see, Doc? This is the kinda thing that could permanently screw me up!"

"How?" Doc Brown asked. "Pardon my denseness."

"What if I get back to the future and end up being gay? It sounds like a little thing, but copping a feel from your mother could change a guy's whole life."

"I see," Doc nodded. "But there's a difference. Copping a feel for pleasure is one thing. Copping a feel to accomplish a serious and moral purpose is another. Therefore, I don't think you have to worry about a damaged psyche. Especially if you put the feel in the same category as setting her leg after an accident . . ."

Marty brightened a bit. "Or performing mouth-to-mouth resuscitation," he added.

"Sure," Doc replied. "Whatever that is. Now you better get going."

Marty nodded, took a step and then paused. Once again, with morbid fascination, he took out his wallet and looked at the family snapshot.

Every bit of his sister Linda was gone except her feet.

"Doc," Marty said slowly. "I just had another thought.

Suppose I start fading out on this picture sometime before we're finished? Do you think when the head goes in the photo my brain will cease to function?"

Doc Brown looked Marty directly in the eyes and responded without the slightest hesitation.

"Beats the hell outa me," he said.

Suppose I start fading out on his picture sometime before
we're finished? Do you think when the head dies in the
photo my brain will cease to function?" . . .

Doc Brown leaned Marty directly in the area and reappeared without the slightest hesitation.

"This is the future," he . . . "It's real.

•Chapter
Twelve•

"Enchantment Under the Sea" was well underway. The Hill
Valley High School gymnasium still looked basically like a
gymnasium, but there were enough displays and artifacts to
create a pleasant illusion. The lighting was blue with silver
sparkles created by glass mobiles cut in the shape of fish.
Against the walls were various papier-mâché attractions—
a sunken ship, undersea caverns, a treasure chest, masses
of seaweed, and a diver suspended by a long cable stretching
to the ceiling. As an example of contemporary humor, a
single school locker labeled "Davey Jones" occupied one
corner of the huge room.

Onstage was the band, Marvin Berry and the Starlighters.
All five men were black, consisting of drummer, piano
player, sax and bass, with Marvin himself playing guitar
and singing. Now he was rendering the popular melody
from the motion picture *Three Coins in the Fountain*. On
the dance floor, several hundred young men and women,

elegantly dressed, leaned against one another and moved in torpid time to the music.

Watching them, wearing artificial smiles of enjoyment, were three chaperones appointed by the school—the inevitable Gerald Strickland, standing stiff as a ramrod with his eyes darting quickly back and forth; a chubby algebra-geometry teacher named Dexter Gore; and Miss Deborah Chambers from the library. Strickland's chief occupation seemed to be looking out for trouble or hands that moved suggestively; Gore seemed most interested in glomming refreshments while no one was looking; Miss Chambers took it upon herself to get the wallflowers up and circulating.

"Walk around and at least talk, ladies," she said at frequent intervals. "Remember, a body in motion is more exciting and enticing than a body just sitting there."

One of the male wallflowers was George McFly, looking distinctly uncomfortable in a tight collar, white tux, and bow tie. Most of the time, George just stood and watched the other dancers, but every once in a while he bopped out of time to the music. He tried not to think too much about Lorraine, who looked more beautiful than he had ever seen her. He also tried not to think too much about the scenario that was supposed to take place at nine o'clock.

"How the heck did I get involved in this?" he sighed. "I wish I was home."

Of course, he could have left, but Marty had already seen him and winked knowingly. To have walked out after that actually required more courage than staying, so George hung around. Over and over he thought: it'll be done with soon. Maybe it'll work and maybe it won't but it won't be any more embarrassing than some of the problems you've had with Biff.

The selection ended and was immediately followed by a faster number. On the dance floor, Marty looked at his watch. It was 8:45, time to start the ball rolling.

"Let's sit this one out, O.K.?" he said to Lorraine.

She nodded, a seductive smile illuminating her features. She headed for the row of chairs along the side of the floor but Marty deftly steered her toward the door.

"Outside is better," he suggested.

"I'm with you," she said.

Going out to the parking lot was not as easy as it sounded. Mr. Strickland kept a sharp watch for who left the dance area and how long they stayed away. He seemed to have a computer in his head which told him exactly who was missing and how long they'd been gone. As a result, Marty and Lorraine had to hang around the entrance, waiting for Strickland to look away before they were able to leave. It was ten of nine when they slipped into Doc Brown's Packard.

"Uh, you don't mind if we . . . uh . . . sit here a few minutes, do you?" Marty asked.

"Why do you think I'd mind?" Lorraine replied.

"Well, I don't know. Some girls just . . . don't like . . . you know . . ."

"Marty, I'm almost eighteen years old," his mother said. "It's not like I've never parked before."

With that, she scooted over, very close to him, and put her hand on his leg. Marty felt his face turn crimson and very hot.

"You seem nervous, Marty," Lorraine said. "Is anything wrong?"

"Uh, no . . ."

"Usually you're so cool, like when you took care of Biff and his friends. But I hear that's the way it is with a lot of strong, silent men. They get a little nervous with women."

"No. It's all right."

"Well, just in case," Lorraine smiled. "Why don't you have some of this? It'll help you relax."

She opened her purse and took out a pint bottle of gin. Marty gasped. His mother? Not even his mother as a grown woman, but as a teenager! It was a bit more than he could accept.

"What are you doing with that?" he whispered.

"I'm opening it."

"But . . . where did you get it?"

Lorraine giggled. "Oh, I swiped it from the old lady's liquor cabinet."

She put the top on the dashboard, tossed her head back and took a nip.

"Lorraine," Marty muttered. "Is this the first time you've done this?"

"Done what?" she asked. "Sat in a car with a boy, had a slug of gin, or sat in a car with a boy and drank?"

"Drink," he replied. "Are you doing this just . . . to show off or something?"

"No," she said, looking insulted. "Certainly not. I do it because I like it."

"But you shouldn't drink," Marty scolded, realizing even as he said the words how much he sounded like an old-fashioned parent.

"Why not?"

"Well, it's just not healthy."

"Don't be so square, Marty," she laughed. "Everybody who's anybody does it."

Marty sighed. He looked at his watch, saw that it was almost time to make his move.

Lorraine passed the bottle to him. He decided to take a swig to humor her.

As he was doing so, his mother pulled out a pack of cigarettes and lit one. Marty gagged on the gin, he was so shocked.

"Jesus!" he cried, his voice sounding terribly strident. "You smoke, too?"

Lorraine looked at him and rolled her eyes to the top of her head.

"I'm serious," he said. "You shouldn't do it. Cigarette smoking is danger—"

"Come on," she said. "I sort of understand that it's not exactly ladylike to drink, but smoking is nice. There's nothing wrong with it."

"Are you kidding? Everything's wrong with it."

"Like what?" she countered.

"It's unhealthy."

"Then why do doctors advertise it on TV?"

"Because the cigarette lobby's too powerful—"

"Oh, bull," she replied. "Everybody knows smoking's good for your circulation. It also calms your nerves and soothes the heart."

"Soothes the heart! My God, it'll give you all sorts of heart problems. And lung cancer. Look! It says right here on the pack—"

He took the cigarette pack from her and looked for the Surgeon General's warning. It was not there. Instead, there was a line, obviously written by the cigarette manufacturer, which read: "This fine blend of Turkish and domestic tobaccos calms the nerves, improves the circulation, gives you a sense of well-being."

"Good God!" Marty whistled.

He handed the pack back. Somehow he'd avoided smoking all his life and he wasn't about to start now.

Lorraine regarded him with an irritated glare. "You know, you sound just like my mother," she said. "It's really stupid the way parents don't understand their kids and try to run their lives for them. When I have kids, I'm gonna let them do anything they want. Anything. And I'm not gonna lecture them or say how it was different back in the good old days when I was young. No, sir, they're not gonna get any of that crap from me."

"I'd sure like to have that promise in writing," Marty smiled.

The remark went over Lorraine's head.

They sat silently for a few moments, Lorraine occasionally sucking on the gin bottle while Marty continued to look at his watch or out the rear-view mirror. It was already past the appointed time. Where the hell was George?

"Are you looking for somebody?" Lorraine asked.

"Uh . . . yeah. Strickland. Just wanted to make sure he's not out on patrol."

"He's got enough to worry about inside," Lorraine smiled. Putting the bottle back in her purse, she slid closer to him. "So tell me what your parents are like? Are they as square as mine?"

"Lately," Marty said softly. "I've come to the conclusion that I don't know anything about them."

"That's a shame."

George felt weak and cold and on the verge of fainting, like the time he'd stuck his finger in the gears of a portable cement mixer his father had rented and nearly severed the end of it. Fifteen minutes before the time he was due outside, his abdomen had been wracked with serious pain, causing him to rush to the men's room twice. Now, as the hour of nine rapidly approached, he experienced a new wave of spasms too powerfully unrelenting to ignore. He knew it was a bad case of nerves, that his cowardly body and mind were collaborating to keep him inside, away from possible embarrassment or failure. Knowing this, however, did not lessen the pain. If anything, it intensified it. Bent nearly double, he stumbled toward the men's room for the third time.

Inside, class prankster Mark Dixon and several other boys were sneaking a smoke and talking. Suddenly, the bathroom door slammed open so hard it seemed as if a raid were in progress.

"Jesus!" Dixon shouted, dropping his cigarette into the urinal.

Instead of Gerald Strickland, they saw only a white-faced George McFly. He grimaced at them and moved quickly to a stall.

The terror in Dixon's eyes changed to annoyance and then amusement.

"That son of a bitch made me lose my last weed," he said. "Look at that."

He pointed to the cigarette floating and slowly disintegrating in the urinal. "He's gonna have to pay for that," Dixon said. "Comin' in here like the riot squad."

Motioning with his head, he ambled toward the stall in which George sat.

Acutely aware that there is a fine line during which a woman can be romanced successfully, Marty sat nervously in Doc Brown's Packard, Lorraine's hip firmly pressed against his. She was ready to be kissed and then touched, hopefully just enough to insult her, create fear and anger and the need for a new champion to rescue her. Marty's dilemma was one of timing. If he went after her too soon, he would be forced to continue the assault until George came—and perhaps it would be over too soon. If, on the other hand, he continued sitting here like a genial lump, Lorraine might conclude that he was either retarded or that she had no appeal. In either case, her next logical move would be out of the car, back to the dance and out of his life, probably forever.

Where the hell is that chickenshit father of mine, Marty thought.

Lorraine noticed the veins in his neck standing out and his jaw twitching. "Marty, why are you so nervous?" she asked.

He took a deep breath. "Well, have you ever been in a

situation," he began, "where . . . well, you know you have to act a certain way, but when you get there, you don't know if you can go through with it?"

"You mean like how you're supposed to act with someone on the first date?"

"Uh . . . yeah."

"Very polite and sweet and like that?"

Marty nodded.

"I don't worry about that!" Lorraine gushed.

With that, she threw her arms around his neck, reached up and kissed him passionately.

"Come on, guys, let me outa here."

George pushed as hard as he could against the door of the stall, but it was just too heavy to budge with three guys leaning against it.

"You're gonna stay there and stew in your own stink," Dixon said.

"Why? What did I do?"

"You made me lose a very valuable cigarette."

"I'll buy you a whole pack," George promised. "Let me out."

"Maybe," Dixon smiled. "When can I have the pack?"

"Tomorrow."

"No. I want them tonight."

"But there's no place at school I can buy them and most of the stores are closed."

"Then the hell with you," Dixon said. "You can stay in there all night."

"Look, it's silly for you to keep me prisoner like this," George pleaded. "You got dates. They're probably wondering where you are."

"True," Dixon conceded. "So two of us will hold you in while one goes out and gets reinforcements. We'll set up a system of watches, ten-minute shifts, so that we can enjoy the dance and still keep you in here until it's time to leave."

"Why are you doing this to me?" George whined. "Come on, guys..."

"No," Dixon vowed. "You're a pain in the ass, McFly, and pains in the ass should stay just where you are."

His pals hooted. George sighed, sat down, and looked at his watch. It was ten after nine.

Lorraine continued her passionate assault on Marty for perhaps a minute before realizing that something was wrong. Moving away from him, she looked at him closely.

"This isn't right," she said.

"Doing this?" he murmured.

"No. What's wrong is we're not doing it right. I don't know what it is...but when I kiss you, something's wrong..."

"With you or me?"

"I'm not sure. Something's missing. It's like...I'm kissing my father."

Marty looked at her, his eyes wide.

"I guess that doesn't make much sense, does it?" she said.

"Believe me. It makes perfect sense. Maybe you got it reversed, but the picture is right."

"What do you think it is?"

"Uh...I don't know."

She dropped her hands into her lap. "Damn," she muttered. "It seemed too good to be true."

"Yeah..."

The sound of footsteps alarmed both of them, each for a different reason. Lorraine was afraid some faculty member had spotted the gin bottle and would tell her parents; Marty now had no idea what to do when George arrived. Should he make a quick grab at Lorraine now in a desperate attempt to give George a chance to rescue her? Somehow it didn't seem appropriate. As Lorraine moved farther away from him on the seat, it didn't even seem possible. Hoping to avoid the person who was approaching, she was practically out the passenger's door.

Marty decided to make a lunge for her. As he did so, the driver's door was opened and a hand reached in to grab his shoulder.

Marty turned to look and was surprised to hear himself gasp.

The face looking into his was not that of George, but Biff Tannen. Behind him stood 3-D, Skinhead, and Match, their faces wreathed in menacing smiles.

"You caused $300 damage to my car, you son of a bitch," Biff rasped. "And I'm gonna take it outa your ass . . . Hold him, guys . . ."

Lifting Marty bodily out of the car, Biff spun him roughly into the arms of Skinhead, who grabbed one of Marty's arms just as 3-D grabbed the other.

"Good work, guys," Biff said. "Skinhead thought that was you, sneaking out to the parking lot. We might never have got you alone otherwise."

He drew back his fist.

"Let go of him!" Lorraine yelled from inside the car, sliding over to the driver's side. "Leave him alone, Biff! You're drunk!"

Biff regarded her with a smile that was very close to a leer. "Well, lookee what we have here," he said. "Maybe I'll take part of it outa your ass."

Marty slammed his foot down on Skinhead's toe, causing him to shout with pain. Then, jack-knifing forward, he threw his elbow up and back, striking 3-D's jaw solidly. Both boys released their holds but only briefly. Although struggling mightily, Marty was soon helpless in their grasp.

Biff, meanwhile, had leaped into the Packard and grabbed Lorraine.

"Let go of me!" she screamed.

"Oh, no, baby, you're staying right here with me," Biff laughed.

Marty pulled his tormentors nearly a foot forward as he tried to get at Biff. "Take your filthy hands off her, you bastard!" he ordered.

Biff smiled coolly at Marty, confident that he could make no trouble. "I'll take care of you after I take care of her," he said.

"You want us to start?" Skinhead asked.

"No, not yet," Biff answered. "That's one party I don't want to start without me. Take him around back. I'll be there in a minute."

When 3-D and Skinhead pulled Marty only to the edge of the rear bumper, Biff whirled around and shouted at them. "This ain't no peepshow! Get the hell outa sight while I . . . romance this lady."

As they dragged Marty farther behind the car, Biff slammed the door and reached forward to kiss Lorraine. A moment later, all Marty could see and hear through the rear window was the struggling form of his mother accompanied by her muffled screams.

Inwardly, he cursed himself nearly as much as he cursed Biff and his friends. If it hadn't been for Marty, Lorraine would be enjoying the dance instead of having to fight to avoid being raped.

There was also enough anger left over to direct at George. If that simpering chicken hadn't reverted to form at the last moment—

But the time for recriminations was short. Dragging Marty bodily, 3-D and Skinhead noticed a Cadillac parked with its trunk open near the side of the school.

"Hey!" Skinhead suggested. "This guy's more trouble than he's worth. Let's lock him in that trunk."

"Good idea!" 3-D replied.

As he spoke, he reached down to grab Marty's legs. It took the two young men nearly a minute to wrestle him to the side of the car, but finally they were able to push him into the trunk. Before he could start to scramble out, Skinhead slammed the lid shut.

The sound and jolt brought Bob Jordan back to earth with a bang. Seated behind the wheel of the Cadillac, the young black man was enjoying a marijuana cigarette while awaiting the rest of the band. As the drummer of the group, he had moved his gear out early while Marvin Berry did his familiar solo guitar closing. Halfway into the joint, he had grown sleepy and contented, so much so that he hadn't heard the scuffling feet and voices until they were accompanied by the trunk lid slamming.

Leaping out of the car, he walked quickly over to the two white boys.

"Say, what you messin' with my car for?" he demanded.

"Beat it, spook," 3-D shot back. "This don't concern you."

"It sure does if you're screwin' around with my car trunk," Jordan said in a firm, slightly raised voice. "And who you callin' spook, peckerwood?"

Despite being outnumbered, he advanced toward 3-D and Skinhead, who took a step backwards. A moment later, Marvin Berry and the other three band members appeared from the back entrance of the gymnasium.

"What's goin' on?" Berry asked.

Skinhead and 3-D looked fearfully at the five black men.

"They called me spook," Jordan said. "And I was about to ask them if they wanted a couple of new breathin' holes in their faces."

"Hey, I don't want to mess with no reefer addicts," Skinhead muttered.

"Reefer addicts, huh?" Berry said, taking a step toward them.

By that time, Skinhead and 3-D were ten feet away and running as fast as they could.

"Lemme out!"

The black men exchanged glances. The muffled voice and beating sounds were definitely coming from inside the Cadillac's trunk.

"They musta dumped somebody in there," Jordan said.

"Hey, Reginald, where's your keys?" Marvin Berry asked, looking at one of the others.

Reginald checked his pockets, frowned, and shook his head.

"Can't find 'em," he said.

"They're in here!" the faraway voice cried. "The keys are in here."

Marvin Berry glared at Reginald. "Dammit, boy," he yelled. "You did it again! That's the third time you left them suckers in the trunk!"

"All right! What's going on here?"

To George McFly, the grating sound of tyrannical Gerald Strickland's voice was simultaneously welcome and infuriating. Having been kept prisoner in the High Valley High gymnasium men's room for close to twenty minutes, he had no desire to continue in his present state; on the other hand, the perverse action of his tormentors did provide him with a built-in excuse not to carry out Marty's plan. Even more important was that the excuse was acceptable to George himself. When he had entered the men's room, there was still time to play his part; now it was unlikely he would have to do so.

"Nothing, sir," one of George's captors replied fearfully.

"I smell cigarette smoke. Does anybody here have cigarettes?"

"No . . . sir."

"I'll give you one chance to hand over the packs now.

If I search you and find cigarettes, it'll be a lot harder on you."

In his cubicle, George heard the sound of material being torn and thrown in the trash can.

"That's better," Strickland said. "Now clear out of here."

George gently pushed open the door of the stall and stepped out. Strickland eyed him coldly.

"What's been going on here, McFly?" he asked.

"Nothing, sir."

"Bull droppings. I saw you go in here twenty minutes ago. Why were you here that long?"

"Nothing important, sir. We were just fooling around. You know . . ."

"Well, never mind. The dance is just about over. You'd better get back to your—never mind, I don't suppose you have a date."

He made a motion toward the door. George took the cue and darted out of the men's room. As he moved through the hallway outside of the gymnasium, he saw that the dance floor was almost completely crowded and the lights very low, indicating that the final number was about to begin. Although he doubted that Marty was still manhandling Lorraine in the parking lot, George decided to make a dutiful appearance and explain the reason for his delay.

Walking briskly onto the parking lot, he headed for the spot where Marty had parked the Packard. At first, his eyes caught no sign of a struggle but just as he sighed with relief he realized he was in the wrong lane. Doubling back, he walked toward the correct area, approaching the Packard from the rear.

"Damn," he whispered.

The scenario was still in progress, just as if time had stopped for more than twenty minutes so that he could accomplish his mission.

Taking a deep breath, he began to run toward the car.

Through the windows he could see arms and even what he judged to be legs flailing. Lorraine was screaming as the male figure pressed his body against hers and groped wildly with his hands.

"Holy cow," George muttered. "It looks like Marty is going all out."

Arriving at the car, he adjusted his pants and took a couple of steps, John Wayne–style. Then, reaching out to grab the door handle, he jerked it open as roughly as possible, thrust his head into the car and said in a loud, forceful voice: "Hey, you! Get your damn hands off—"

The face of the attacker twisted in his direction and George immediately recognized it.

"I think you got the wrong car, McFly," Biff said.

"George! Help me!" Lorraine cried.

For a moment, George stared in dumbfounded amazement. A hurricane of partially formed thoughts rushed through his mind. Was Marty behind this? Was there a slim possibility Biff was in on it, too? Should he run? Or was it too late to back out now? He stared into the angry eyes of Biff Tannen, searching for clues, but saw only hostility. And—yes!—there was a flicker of fear there, too. He had been caught in a potentially damaging situation that cried out for immediate action. George McFly must be frightened away and later intimidated into silence. If he ran and brought help—

"Just close the door and walk away, McFly," Biff said evenly.

George didn't move. A part of him had already reached the verge of panic, but another part of him simply would not allow his feet to move. He saw a quick flash of that scene in grade school five years ago when he had been unable to come to the aid of his friend Billy Stockhausen. Since that moment, he had feared physical combat, had learned to anticipate it and avoid it. But there was no avoiding this crisis unless he just turned and ran. The look of utter fear on Lorraine's face prevented that.

"Are you deaf, McFly?" Biff demanded, his voice losing all restraint. "I told you to close the door and beat it! Now do it!"

George took a deep breath.

"No!" he said. "You let her alone."

Lorraine sighed. At last someone had come to her assistance. He wasn't Marty, but in some ways he was even better. Her lips started to form the words "Thank you" even as Biff removed his hands from her body and started to get out of the car.

"All right, McFly," he snarled. "You had your chance. Now I'm gonna teach you a lesson."

He moved toward George, one large hand reaching out to grab any part of the interloper's body. It brought back a large section of sleeve with George's arm enclosed. Twisting, Biff had the satisfaction of hearing George groan and saw fear register in his eyes. As he applied even greater pressure, a flailing fist moved slowly toward his head. It struck Biff on the shoulder, causing no damage or pain at all.

"Help!" Lorraine shouted.

George wanted to yell the same thing, but managed to grit his teeth and choke off the cowardly word. Twisting his body back and forth, he attempted vainly to get out of Biff's clutches. One arm of the bully encircled George's neck; the other forced his arm up his back so hard George was sure he would hear the snap of bone at any moment.

"Stop it, Biff!" Lorraine shouted. "You'll break his arm!"

"That's right, baby!" Biff shot back. "That's just what I'm going for."

He applied more pressure. Then, far on the periphery of his circle of awareness, he heard a sound . . . like faraway riveting . . . or was it running footsteps? Partly distracted, he allowed his grip to relax.

Desperate with pain, George reacted to the split second respite with blind instinct. Pulling himself from Biff's grasp, he turned and, with both eyes firmly closed, threw the hardest punch of his life.

To his—and Biff's—surprise, it landed flush on the jaw of his attacker, driving his entire head up and backwards like it had suddenly been struck by a flying two-by-four. Biff's moan immediately followed the sharp crack of bone meeting bone.

Delightfully reminiscent of the duffel bag, Biff Tannen dropped to the asphalt like an inanimate object. A referee could have counted to at least a hundred before there was the slightest movement of his body.

"Oh, George! You were wonderful!"

Lorraine's sparkling eyes stared at George's, projecting a message of total adoration. George shook his head, looked down at his fist and then at the crumpled form of Biff Tannen near his feet. He couldn't believe it!

Nor could Marty, who, followed by the five black musicians, had just arrived on the scene. But the picture was clear and perfect, with every detail in place—Lorraine's torn dress, the prostrate form of the bully and nervously grinning face of the unlikely hero. Others arriving on the scene immediately grasped the significance of the scene and were touched by it.

"Who is that kid?" one male voice asked. "Does he go to our school?"

"It's George McFly," another answered. "He's been in our homeroom for two years."

"Never noticed him before . . ."

"Look at that guy out cold, will you? What a punch that little guy must have!"

"Way to go, Georgie!"

Reaching out to his father, Marty grasped his hand and shook it.

"Great work, Dad," he said. "I mean, George."

"Thanks."

A disquieting thought rushed through Marty's mind—his work wasn't done yet. Not only had he to make his getaway; he still had to get his mother and father together, have them kiss romantically on the dance floor. But the final number had been played and a few couples already left, although the vast majority of the young people were still hanging around, talking.

"It's not too late," Marty breathed. Then, in a louder voice, he said: "Hey, everybody! I think we should have one more dance just so this nice couple can celebrate!"

A shout of approbation mingled with the sound of distant thunder.

Marty looked at the sky, grabbed Lorraine with one hand and George with the other. "Come on, gang!" he shouted. "We're going back in for one more number."

The group rushed back to the gymnasium, passing the Starlighters on the way.

"Hey, you guys!" Marty said. "How about giving us one more number?"

"Dance is over," one of them said.

"Forget it," mumbled another.

Marty reached into his pocket, pulled out his wallet. "Here," he said, taking out all his money. "It's yours for just one dance."

The musicians looked at each other indecisively.

"It's O.K. with me," said Reginald, "except that Marvin cut his hand opening the car trunk."

"Yeah," Jordan added. "He can't play with it like that. And we can't play without Marvin. He plays lead guitar, man. You can't do anything without that."

"But you've gotta play!" Marty urged. "That's where they kiss for the first time—on the dance floor! If there's no music, they won't kiss and fall in love! And if they don't fall in love, I'm a goner!"

The black men looked at each other. "What the hell's this guy talking about?" one of them asked.

"Hey, man," said Reginald, handing the money back. "The dance is over . . . unless you know somebody who can play guitar."

Marty smiled.

"Of course!" he said. "I can do it."

"Come on . . ."

"Trust me," Marty said.

Reginald smiled. "Why not?" he suggested. "It might be worth it just for the laughs."

Grabbing their equipment, the musicians followed Marty and his friends back into the gymnasium. The surge created a ripple of interest among the other students which soon became a tidal wave. Within two minutes, the entire gymnasium was again filled with bodies.

"What's going on here?" Gerald Strickland shouted over and over. Grabbing arms, he tried to force the students out of the hall but his efforts were ineffectual.

Meanwhile, Marty had set himself up with the band in the far corner, plugged in the equipment and shouted into the microphone. "One more dance," he said. "A special number for my parents."

He and the Starlighters launched into "Earth Angel" and the students paired off to dance. Lorraine slipped into George's arms, put her cheek against his.

At first following the band and then confidently taking the lead, Marty looked around. The musicians were casting quick glances his way, glances that told him they admired the job he was doing. He could see his parents dancing just a few feet away, their heads together. Now it was just a matter of time . . . All was going well.

During a brief sax solo, he put down his guitar and looked at the family snapshot in his wallet. Sister Linda and Dave were gone but his own image was intact. Then . . . as George and Lorraine's lips moved toward each other, Marty thought he could see Linda beginning to reappear.

"Great . . ." he breathed.

His moment of exultation was short-lived. No sooner had the positive transformation taken place than it reversed itself. Linda faded and Marty's right hand disappeared from the photo.

"What the hell—" he began.

Looking toward his parents, he saw the cause of the reversal. Just as the couple were about to kiss, a rough hand had been placed on George's shoulder. It was Dixon, wearing his usual malevolent expression.

"Beat it, McFly," he ordered. "I'm cuttin' in."

On the bandstand, the sax solo had ended and the full orchestration started again. Marty joined in, but his right hand couldn't seem to follow. Instead, fishlike, it flopped along the strings like a numb or completely dead object.

"Hey, man," Bob Jordan whispered. "What's wrong?"

"I can't play," Marty murmured. "I don't know how to play the guitar!"

He lifted the offending right hand and gasped with horror. He could see through it!

Bob Jordan, losing the beat himself, stared at Marty's wide eyes and open-mouthed expression.

"What kinda drugs is that cat on?" he whispered.

Marty closed his eyes, struggled to his feet. "I . . . don't feel so good . . ." he mumbled.

On the dance floor, many of the young people were so wrapped up in the magical moment they failed to notice the band's disintegrating sound. George McFly in particular was totally oblivious to mere music. Having been shunted aside, he saw Dixon encircle Lorraine's waist with one arm as he prepared to take her hand.

Lorraine looked helplessly at George.

George's hesitation was brief. Taking a long stride toward Dixon, he said simply: "Excuse me."

It came out in the best Clint Eastwood tradition, a soft phrase with underlying tones of businesslike, very confident menace. Reaching out with one hand to shove Dixon ten feet away, he took Lorraine with the other and folded her to his chest. Turning her chin upward, he kissed her gently on the lips.

Marty felt a surge of new energy race through his entire body. Jolted upright as if struck by an electrical shock, he looked at his right hand and arm again. No longer were they transparent!

"Thank God!" he smiled.

Whipping the family photograph from his pocket, he laughed, did a little pirouette on the bandstand, and grabbed the guitar again. Linda, Dave and himself were all back in the picture, completely intact, and the feeling in his hand told him his musical powers had been restored.

"All right!" he shouted. "Let's do it!"

Picking up the beat again, he led the group in a snappy windup to "Earth Angel." The crowd applauded.

"Say, you're good, man," Marvin Berry said. "Do another one."

Marty looked at his watch. Through the far doorway at the end of the gymnasium, he could see a flash of lightning.

"No, I've gotta go," he said.

But Bob Jordan had grabbed him gently but firmly by the arm. "Come on, let's do something that cooks," he smiled.

Marty decided there was time.

"Well, all right," he said. "You guys will just have to follow me on this one . . ." Stepping to the microphone, he said: "We're gonna do one more. Where I come from, they call this *rock 'n' roll!*"

He hit a guitar riff, took a beat and then looked at Jordan. "Gimme a blues beat, like this," he said, picking out the rhythm. Jordan, smiling, grabbed it immediately and sent the pulse moving.

"Good!" Marty said. Turning to the bass player, he hummed a two-bar line. "Do this and then pick it up when I change," he said.

The bass player nodded, getting it.

"Piano, take the bass line and play it up three octaves," Marty continued. "And sax—improvise on the three chord progression."

It was ragged at first, but a moment later, the team started functioning—and the music sounded like vintage rock 'n' roll. On the dance floor, heads turned and the kids started dancing faster. A few minutes later, pandemonium started to spread—they had never heard music like this before. Getting caught up himself, Marty whipped off his sport jacket and threw it into the crowd. His movements became more and more like that of Mick Jagger...then Michael Jackson...then he drifted into pure Heavy Metal, putting his guitar next to the amp so as to generate feedback. Laughing and shouting encouragement, the band members improvised wildly, following every progression Marty made with amazement and then professional dexterity. Within the walls of the gymnasium, only one face remained cold and unaffected by the new sound—that of Gerald Strickland.

"Just when you think they can't get any worse," he muttered to himself, "they turn around and find a way to get worse."

George, dancing breathlessly with Lorraine, felt a new spirit moving through him. He'd finally done something right and the evening seemed magical! Lorraine, the music, the congratulations of those around him, everything meshed into a pattern that said *Happily ever after*. He wanted the night to continue forever.

That, of course, was impossible. All too soon, Marty wrapped up the song with a final riff and stepped back, smiling, to acknowledge the thunderous applause.

Everyone started to talk at once—about the music and George McFly's exploits. As he and Lorraine walked toward the bandstand, George felt a dozen hands reach out to touch him.

"Hey, George!" one voice said. "I hear you laid out Biff! Nice going!"

"George, did you ever think about running for class president?" an attractive girl asked.

"We sure could use you on the team, George," another boy said.

Not knowing what team he represented, George could only hedge pleasantly. "Well, I'll have to think about it," he smiled.

Lorraine, basking in his notoriety and newfound respect, grasped his arm tightly and smiled up at him.

A smiling, perspiring Marty came up to them, stuck out his hand for George to shake.

"Congratulations," he said. "And just in case you're worried about it, Biff was dead serious."

"Good," George said. The one tiny fear in his paranoia— that somehow Biff Tannen had faked being knocked out— was now laid to rest and George was completely happy. "Congratulations yourself," he said. "You're terrific."

"Thanks."

They stood smiling and chatting about small things until Lorraine finally put her hand on Marty's arm.

"Marty," she said. "I hope you don't mind, but George asked if he could take me home."

"That's fine, Lorraine," Marty nodded. "In fact, that's great. I'd like nothing better. You know, I had a feeling about you two."

"I know," she said. "I sort of have a feeling, too. I think George could really make me happy."

"Yeah. Listen, I've gotta be leaving town."

"Oh, I'm sorry. When? At the end of the semester?"

"No. Tonight. And I just wanted to say that it's been . . . educational."

"Will we ever see you again?" Lorraine asked.

"Oh, yeah. I guarantee it."

George stepped forward to shake his hand again.

"Good night and good-bye then," he said. "Thanks for your help . . . and all your good advice. I hope I can do the same for you someday."

Marty laughed. "You'll probably give me more advice than I can possibly handle."

He turned to go, then paused. "Uh, listen," he said, "if you guys ever have kids, and one of them when he's eight years old accidentally sets fire to the living room rug . . . please go easy on him."

"Er . . . sure," George replied, thinking it one of the strangest requests he had ever heard.

A moment later, he was gone. George and Lorraine stood looking at each other, their hands tightly clasped.

"Marty," she breathed. "It's such a nice name. When I have kids, I'm going to name one of them Marty."

"Aren't you rushing things a little?" George laughed.

"Well, maybe a little. I was thinking I'd like to go to college next year."

"Me, too," George said. "In fact, I'm gonna go no matter what my father says."

• Chapter
Thirteen •

At 9:45, Doc Brown began to grow apprehensive. Five minutes later, he was definitely in a nervous state. By 9:55, he was pacing wildly back and forth.

"Damn!" he muttered. "Where is that kid?"

His trenchcoat was whipping loudly in the wind, like the spinnaker of a sailboat caught in a storm. The distant thunder now rumbled sullenly all about him, punctuated by sharp flashes of lightning illuminating the outline of his tower-to-lamp-post cable network. Town Square was deserted except for a small pack of dogs and he was ready to go. But no Marty.

Doc reached into his pocket and pulled out a small round watch, circa 1890. It read: 9:56. The same time was also showing on watches worn on either wrist. There was no doubt in his mind that only eight minutes remained before the appearance of the lightning bolt that could send Marty back to 1985.

"Damn!" he repeated, this time in a loud and clear voice.

Moving away from the curb into the center of the street, he grunted as he saw a car moving toward him with precipitous speed.

"Good," he grunted finally, satisfied that the vehicle was his Packard. "But why drive like that, dummy? Why crack up in the wrong car?"

A moment later, Marty was available for the answer. Dressed in his 1985 clothes, he pulled Doc's car to the curb, leaped out, took a deep breath and smiled a bit sheepishly.

"You're late!" Doc Brown scolded. "Do you have no concept of time?"

"Sorry, Doc."

"And why were you driving my car like a maniac?"

"It was a test. I wanted to see how fast I could go on that stretch. And I'm glad I did. There's a rise in the road down near Cherry Street that's almost like a speed bump. If I'd hit that at a higher speed, it could have sent me into a store window. But if I use the left side of the road it'll be O.K."

"Hmmph," Doc Brown replied. "That's all very well, but what if you'd been spotted by some cop?"

"What if I'm spotted by a cop when I'm in the time machine?" Marty countered.

"If that happens, you keep going, dummy. You'll either end up in 1985 or in the lobby of that movie theater."

"Yeah," Marty gulped. "I see your point."

Grumbling to himself, Doc Brown began to pull the tarpaulin from the DeLorean and raise the trolley hook on back to its full height.

"Rush, rush, rush," he muttered. "You couldn't have cut it much closer."

"Look, I'm sorry," Marty replied, feeling guilty now because he spent so much time jamming with the Starlighters. "I had to change my clothes and getting Mom and Dad together took longer than I thought."

Most of the anger was starting to leave Doc Brown now that he'd had the opportunity to whine and complain a little. Brightening, he said: "Well, I can understand that, knowing George McFly. So the plan worked?"

"To a *T,*" Marty smiled. "They're all lovey-dovey and will stay that way to the bitter end. And here's proof that it's true."

Pulling out his wallet, he showed Doc Brown the family picture with all members restored.

"Good," Doc said.

"I think Dad may even go to college," Marty added. "He's got extra confidence now."

Doc Brown frowned as he made the last of his preflight checks on the DeLorean. "Then that's something else you'll be able to worry about between now and the time you get back to 1985," he said.

"What?"

"Well, if he does go to college, thanks to you, it'll change his life."

"For the better, I hope," Marty countered.

"Maybe, but suppose while he's there, he meets some coed who's more attractive to him than your mother? That could cause you to do a quick fade out. Or suppose because of college expenses, your mom and dad decide to hold off having kids for a couple years? If that happens, you may find that you're twelve or fourteen years old in 1985 instead of seventeen? How do you like them apples?"

Marty shook his head with awe. What his friend and mentor said definitely made sense. All he could do was hope the future existence of his parents was approximately the same as the first time around.

"Good thinking, Doc," he said. "But I guess it's too late to worry about that. I'm just glad Dad finally came through. He really laid out Biff Tannen with one punch . . . just plain coldcocked him . . . I never knew he had it in him. Hell, my old man's never stood up to Biff in his life. And to think I actually saw it when it happened."

"Fine," Doc Brown nodded. "Now get in there and set your destination time. We're rushed as hell."

Marty leaped into the DeLorean and watched as Doc punched the keypads so that both LAST TIME DEPARTED and DESTINATION TIME read 10-26-1985, 1:31 A.M.

"There," he said. "If it works, it'll be the same as if you never left."

"Thanks, Doc . . ." Marty began. "I'd really like to thank you—"

Brown held up his hand. "No time," he said. "Listen. I've painted a white line way down the street there. That's where you start from. I did some calculations so that your run will be as short and efficient as possible. If you floor it from that point and never lift your foot, you'll hit exactly eighty-eight miles an hour when you have to."

"Great."

"Now I've calculated the precise distance, taking into account the acceleration speed and wind resistance retroactive from the moment the lightning will strike . . ." He handed Marty a wind-up alarm clock which seemed quaintly old-fashioned compared to the digital readouts and flashing dials of the DeLorean's dash. "When the alarm goes off, hit the gas from the white line. That's all you have to do, except guide this baby to the right spot."

Marty nodded.

"Well, I guess that's everything," Doc Brown said. "Good luck."

Marty extended his hand. "Doc, I'd like to thank you for everything. Even if something goes wrong—"

"Don't even think about that," Doc interrupted. "It'll go fine. And I'd like to thank you for everything. It's been a pleasure."

The two men shook hands.

"I'll see you in about thirty years," Doc said.

"I hope so."

Once again Marty thought of Doc Brown's date with the terrorists and hoped that the letter he had planted would help bring about a happier ending to his friend's life.

"Don't worry," Doc Brown continued, mistaking Marty's expression for concern about the upcoming race forward into time. "As long as you hit that wire with this hook, everything'll be fine."

"Right," Marty nodded.

Making sure that everything had been taken care of, Doc Brown patted himself down, checking bits of paper and pads for something he might have forgotten. While doing so, he did the one thing Marty didn't want him to do—discovered the unfamiliar envelope in his inside coat pocket. Withdrawing it, he looked at it curiously.

"What's this?" he asked.

"Just a note, from me to you," Marty stammered.

"It's about something in the future, isn't it?" Doc Brown said.

"No. It's just a thank-you note," Marty lied. "It's kind of gushy."

Doc shook his head skeptically. "People don't write thank-you notes to be opened thirty years later," he said. "I warned you about fooling with the future, kid. The consequences could be dangerous. Now I know this is something about the future, and I've told you a million times we shouldn't mess with that."

"I've gotta take that risk, Doc," Marty replied firmly. "Your life depends on it."

"Well, I'm not going to accept the responsibility," Brown muttered.

With that, he tore up the letter and tossed the pieces into the ashtray of his Packard.

Marty was furious. Why wouldn't the guy take a warning for his own good? "All right, Doc," he shot back. "In that case I'm just gonna have to tell you straight out—"

Before he could get the words out, a tremendous gust of wind shook the car and nearly blew Doc Brown away from his spot next to the open door. At the same time, a loud cracking sound was heard, followed by a succession of lesser crashing noises.

"Good Lord!" Doc Brown yelled.

Marty leaped from the car and both men rushed toward the lamp posts. A huge tree limb from one of the giant oaks in the square was now resting atop the cable between the clock tower and the first lamp post. A paddle plug attached to the lightning rod had come loose and the cable from the clock tower was now swinging free.

"Great Scott!" Doc Brown shouted as they ran. "Kid— find the end of that cable. I'll throw the rope down to you!"

With that, Brown grabbed a large coil of rope and dashed into the courthouse.

Marty gulped once and then set to work. In the semi-darkness, it wasn't easy to locate the end of the cable amidst the tangle of limbs and leaves, but he leaped into the pileup of debris and started searching. As he did so, he could feel the wind pick up even more. Long rolls of thunder warned him that time was running out; the storm was increasing in ferocity; only a few minutes separated them from 1985 and the blast of lightning that would carry him there.

"Damn!" he yelled. "Where the hell are you?"

Oblivious to the branches tearing his skin, he continued to tear into the pile. Doc Brown, meanwhile, raced up the courthouse stairs like a madman, taking the rough-hewn steps of the ancient belfry three at a time. Arriving at the clock tower room which opened to the ledge directly below the clock, he saw pigeons scatter as he invaded their inner sanctum of safety. His hair blowing wildly in the wind and his rough features illuminated by flashes of lightning, Doc Brown truly resembled the stereotypical mad scientist on a mission that would shake the world.

He looked up, saw that the connecting socket was dangling on its cable between the *1* and *2* of the huge clock face. The other end was still attached to the lightning rod on the tower above.

Looking down, he saw Marty, five stories below, waving the paddle plug which he had just located.

"Good!" Doc Brown shouted.

He tossed down the rope, which uncoiled to land a few feet in front of Marty. The young man grabbed it, tied the end to the paddle plug, then waved to Doc Brown.

Doc nodded and began hauling the rope with the cable attached back into the tower. As he continued the hand-over-hand operation, he saw Marty's mouth working and heard partial words.

"What?" he yelled down.

Marty cupped his hands around his mouth and shouted as loudly as he could. "I gotta tell you about the future, Doc! Please listen to me!"

The words were lost amid a new rush of wind which nearly tore the rope from Doc's grasp.

"Can't hear you!" Doc shouted back.

"The future!" Marty yelled. "On the night I travel back in time, the terrorists show up and get you—"

"Terror-what?"

"Terrorists! They—"

Bong! Bong!!

The clock began to toll ten o'clock. Kicking angrily at the ground, Marty waited, knowing he hadn't a prayer of being heard.

With the huge bells tolling so close, Doc Brown nearly lost his balance. He quickly regained his footing, however, and was able to haul the rope the rest of the way. Grabbing the paddle plug, he looked down at Marty and gestured that he should get in the car and go.

On the ground, Marty hesitated. He knew what Doc Brown meant and understood the urgency of the situation. Still, he wanted one more shot at telling his friend what was in store for him if he wasn't careful. He looked up. Doc Brown gestured wildly toward the DeLorean, then at his watch.

Marty sighed, turned and raced back toward the car.

"Run, boy, run!" Doc Brown shouted from the clock tower. Seeing Marty do so, he untied the rope from the end of the paddle plug and looked at its socket mate dangling against the face of the clock. It was a good stretch away. Reaching for it, he realized he'd have to go out on the ledge to make the connection.

As he lifted himself cautiously onto the narrow ledge, Doc saw the DeLorean start up and move down the street.

"Good," he whispered. "Now all I have to do is make sure he's not barreling down the street for nothing."

Creeping along the ledge, his hands flat against the wall with the nails gripping as tightly as possible, Doc tried to think of anything but the wind and distinct possibility of falling. Blasts of lightning cast weird shadows and outlines on the clock tower wall and each roll of thunder caused the building to shudder.

"I'll be alive in 1985," he said, realizing even as he said it that he was whistling past the graveyard. "I'll be alive in '85—so I'm safe now."

The words came out but he knew they were fallacious. His being alive in 1985 was predicated on his *not* climbing clock towers in 1955.

"Well," he gasped. "Let's just get it done."

Leaning into the wind, he reached for the dangling cable, felt it slip through his fingers, took a deep breath and reached out again.

* * *

Marty pulled up to the "starting line" Doc Brown had arranged for him, made a U-turn and sat in the idling DeLorean, his eyes fixed hypnotically on the alarm clock next to him.

"Dammit, Doc," he murmured. "Why'd you have to tear up that letter? If only there was a little more time for me to explain..."

As he considered the problem, he withdrew his gaze from the alarm clock and looked at the DESTINATION TIME and LAST TIME DEPARTED readouts, both of which were set for 1:31 A.M.

"That's it," he said finally. "There's no way I can have more time at this end, but why can't I make time at the other end?"

With that, he began pushing the appropriate buttons on the DESTINATION TIME keypad so that it moved from 1:30 to 1:29 and even earlier. "Sure," he murmured. "I'll just show up in 1985 a few minutes before the terrorists shoot Doc and warn him then."

He watched as the DESTINATION TIME readout changed from 1:26 to 1:24 and then paused, wondering if seven minutes was enough.

A moment later, the engine of the DeLorean shook twice and then died. Marty turned the key in the ignition but the car wouldn't start.

"Come on, come on," he growled. "Don't tell me I came this far to run out of gas!"

Doc Brown, holding the loose cable in his left hand, took a small step along the ledge of the clock tower and had his foot poised to take another when he heard the sound. It was the crunch of rapidly disintegrating stone and he heard it a split second before he felt his body start to fall. Dropping the cable, he leaped forward to grab the only object between himself and the ground—the minute hand of the courthouse tower clock.

"Goddamn!" he yelled.

Even as he spoke, he felt something strike his left foot. Looking down, he saw that the cable was still hanging in midair, its end balanced precariously on the instep of his foot. For a long moment, Brown just hung there, the wind blowing his hair and lightning illuminating his terrorized features. Then, carefully moving his right foot toward the intact section of ledge, he moved his body toward safety, all the while trying to keep the cable balanced and ultimately reachable. When his right foot gained the ledge, he took a deep breath, hopped across and, at the same time, kicked the cable into the air so he could catch it with his left hand.

He thought the next part of his job—plugging the cable plug into the socket—would be easy. But when he tried putting them together, he discovered they were about a foot apart.

"How the hell did that happen?" he groaned.

Shaking his head, he peered downward into the alternating gloom and garishly-lit scene below. The cause of his dilemma soon became apparent—a tree limb was caught on the cable, eliminating the slack necessary to get the two ends together. Jerking and whipping the end of the cable, he struggled to free it but was unsuccessful. In desperation, he increased the violence of his tugs, finally giving the cable a tremendous yank that pulled it free from the tree.

"Good!" he yelled, and then: "Damn it!"

The plug at the other end of the connection was now loose, leaving Brown with a useless plug in his hand.

Considering the utter despair he felt, Doc Brown's reaction was comparatively mild. Clutching the side of the tower, he merely closed his eyes and tried not to think of anything for a moment. But even with his eyes closed, he could see the lightning crashing about him with increased ferocity and feel the thunder shake the courthouse. Forcing his mind to think, he asked himself: Is there any way I can get everything connected?

"Yes," he whispered finally. "I'll probably kill myself but what the hell?"

Tying the two loose cable ends together, he plugged them in, tested them to make sure they were tight, took a deep breath and jumped.

As he slid down the cable toward the ground, he felt his hands burn but held tight until his feet struck the solid earth. Then he was running with the cable toward the lamp post.

"Shit!"

Continuing to grind away at the ignition, Marty winced as he heard the alarm clock go off.

"Come on! Come on!" he shouted.

The ignition sputtered, coughed, and then—miraculously—caught.

Jamming his foot against the accelerator, Marty was thrown back in the seat as the DeLorean peeled out. Burning rubber, it hit forty within a half block and was approaching sixty-five as Town Square came into view. Staring straight ahead, Marty caught sight of the wire strung across the street and locked his vision on it. So intent was he that he failed to see the figure of Doc Brown as he raced toward the lamp post, cable in hand. Less than a second before a spectacular bolt of lightning struck, Doc plugged the cable in, spun around and fell backward. Glancing at his speedometer, Marty saw that the car was moving at eighty-eight miles an hour.

Then there was a terrific crash of simultaneous lightning and thunder. The landscape and buildings all around Marty went completely white, like the homes in the film about atomic bomb testing. My God, he thought, I've neen nuked. A slight bump told him the trolley hook on the rear of the

DeLorean had made contact with the cable. On the dash, dials flashed as the flux capacitor glowed and discharged. A dissonant rushing noise followed, the DeLorean kicked forward as if it had been thrust into orbit, and blackness descended.

From his prone position next to the lamp post, Doc Brown watched as the time machine made contact with the electrified cable. Rain continued to pour down but he didn't notice it. Instead, he saw a montage of quick images—the glowing cable, lightning bolt striking the tower clock, the DeLorean seemingly enveloped by a yellow mist—which made him leap to his feet and let out an Indian war whoop.

"We did it!" he shouted. "It was impossible but we did it!"

It was true. As if swallowed up by the earth or a giant hand from above, the DeLorean was gone. All that remained was the trolley pole, which had been wrenched free when the car passed under the cable. Now it dangled limply, buffeted by the rain and wind, the only souvenir of young Marty McFly's sixty-year round trip backward and forward in time.

"Good luck," Doc Brown breathed. "I'll see you soon enough . . . I hope."

•Chapter Fourteen•

The journey into the black tunnel slowed and finally ended. The car came to rest but the darkness continued to surround Marty, broken only by the glowing dials and readouts. Glancing down at them, he saw that LAST TIME DEPARTED read 11-5-1955, 10:04 P.M. PRESENT TIME and DESTINATION TIME, which were the same, read 10-26-1985, 1:24 A.M. That being the case, why the darkness? Marty thought of the scene in a movie he had seen about a time travel machine where the vehicle is enclosed in a mountain. Could that possibly have happened to him?

Gradually, as his eyes became used to the darkness, he realized that he was inside a building. Behind him was a circle of dim light.

"Well," he murmured. "Looks like there's no place to go but backwards."

Slamming the car into reverse, he moved toward the light source. When he emerged into the night, he saw that his point of arrival had been the interior of the boarded-up Town Theatre. Everything else was as it became in 1985—the Studebaker dealership was now the Toyota place, the soda shop was gone, and the courthouse had thirty years of additional age on it.

"All right!" Marty shouted.

He reached down to turn on the car radio. A contemporary rock tune was playing.

"All right!" he repeated.

Then he thought of Doc Brown. There would be time enough to celebrate later. Now he had to concentrate on saving his friend from a bloody and violent death.

He slammed the car into forward gear, felt the engine shudder and then die.

"Shit!" he yelled.

This time it was really dead. After grinding for a minute, Marty was unable to generate the slightest hint of renewed power. And as he continued to grind, he looked up and saw the familiar terrorist van cruising down the street and around a corner.

Horrified, he leaped from the car.

"The terrorists!" he yelled.

Then he was running, through Town Square and all the way down 2nd Street toward the mall. Arriving at the entrance, he noticed that it was called Lone Pine Mall and was decorated with the image of a single pine tree instead of two. Otherwise everything was the same. But the stalled DeLorean had cost him valuable time; the terrorist van was already on the parking lot, chasing Doc Brown while the lone figure of Marty McFly watched in horror.

Marty stood frozen, horrified and amazed.

"Oh, no!" he gasped. "I'm too late!"

The scene blew his mind. There was Doc dying again while he looked on. Then, as the hail of bullets sent Brown falling to the ground, Marty saw himself leap into the

DeLorean and race off. He had already experienced the scene once in the flesh but he watched again, fascinated by the replay seen from a different point of view.

Just as before, the terrorist van turned and pursued the DeLorean, which executed a neat U-turn and raced to the opposite end of the parking lot. It continued to accelerate even as it was shot at until being enveloped in a blinding white glow.

Losing control of their vehicle, the terrorist van driver was forced to swerve into a Fox Photo stand on the edge of the parking lot. The vehicle fell over and landed door-side down, trapping the terrorists inside. In the distance a police siren wailed.

"Jeez," Marty whispered.

Suddenly remembering Doc Brown, he turned and ran toward the sprawled figure, still lying face down on the asphalt. There were tears in Marty's eyes as he turned his friend over.

"Doc . . ." he said softly. "Doc . . . please don't be dead, Doc . . ."

"Well, all right, if you insist," the apparently dead man replied, opening his eyes and smiling.

"You're alive!" Marty shouted.

"Of course I'm alive."

"But you were shot—I saw it!" Marty cried. "I saw it twice!"

"On instant replay, as it were?" Doc smiled again.

Marty nodded.

"The explanation is simple," Brown said.

He ripped open his radiation suit to reveal a bulletproof vest.

"It's the latest fashion in personal protection," he explained. "Guaranteed to stop a slug from an elephant rifle at thirty yards."

"Were you wearing that all along?" Marty asked.

"Sadly, no," Doc Brown replied. "The first time around, I must have been taken by surprise. No, my boy, it was your warning that saved me."

With that, he reached into his pocket and pulled out the letter that Marty had written in 1955. It was yellow and brittle, the scotch tape holding it together withered and ready to fall apart.

Marty smiled and shook his head. "What a hypocrite," he said. "After all that lecturing about screwing up the space-time continuum . . ."

"Yeah, well, I figured what the hell . . ."

Nearby, the police had poured out of their cars and were busily rounding up the terrorists.

"Let's get out of here," Doc Brown said. "This is going to be impossible to explain."

"I'm with you," Marty said.

Together, they ran toward the mall core and disappeared in the shadows just as even more police cruisers turned the corner into the mall.

As they sped away in the step-van, the two men discussed their adventures. "I guess I did screw things up a little," Marty said at the entranceway to the mall.

"How so?"

"Well, this used to be Twin Pines Mall in the 1985 I knew first time around. But when I went back, I accidentally ran over one of the farmer's pines. I guess that's why they call it Lone Pine now."

Doc Brown smiled. "You'll probably notice a lot of things like that," he said. "It'll be your own private joke with Hill Valley for the rest of your life."

"Yeah . . ."

A few minutes later, they reached the DeLorean and Doc got inside.

"Won't start, eh?" he said.

Marty nodded.

Doc reached under the ignition, flipped a hidden switch and smiled as the engine roared to life.

"What are your plans now?" Marty asked.

"Well, first, I'm gonna wait until the cops clean up that mess at the parking lot and then I'll drive my step-van outa there," he said. "I got a few more plutonium pellets that I can use to travel, so I think that's what I'll do. After all, time's a-wasting."

"How far ahead are you going?"

Doc shrugged. "I figure I'll take it slow at first," he replied. "Maybe I'll go about thirty years, just to get my feet wet. Then maybe I'll take a look-see at the 22nd or 23rd centuries..."

"Well, good luck," Marty said. "If you get a chance, look me up in 2015. I'll be ... let's see ... forty-seven years old. Wow. That's ancient."

Doc Brown snorted. "That's just a kid. Anyway, I sure will look you up, my boy. It's funny, isn't it? I had to wait thirty years to catch up to you. Now you've gotta wait thirty years to catch up to me. Ain't life weird..."

He winked. Marty closed the door and watched him drive off.

When he awakened, he was still in his clothes and morning sunlight was streaming through the window of his bedroom. Opening his eyes slowly, Marty looked around at the room which he knew so well and yet seemed so foreign to him now. Everything was still there, from the SR5 posters to the audio equipment. A calendar on the wall with *X*'s through the first twenty-five days of October 1985 informed him that today was the 26th.

Could it have all been a dream?

Getting out of bed, he looked at himself in the mirror, pinching himself several times to make sure the flesh staring back at him was real.

Next to the full-length mirror was a waste can with a familiar object projecting from it—the submission form to the record company. He had tossed it there in despair the night—or was it thirty years?—before. Now this act seemed as juvenile as the George McFly of 1955. Pulling a demo tape from his top drawer, he put it and the form into a mailing envelope.

"Why not?" he said. "My music has been wowing them for three decades. I'm a cinch to win."

A few minutes later, after cleaning up, he went downstairs to breakfast. Linda and Dave were seated at the dining room table. They appeared the same facially but nearly everything surrounding them, from their clothing to the furniture, was different. Dave wore an expensive business suit and was reading *Forbes* magazine; sister Linda was dressed casually but elegantly as she ate what appeared to be eggs Benedict. The dining room was equipped with much more expensive furniture than he remembered, the table set with delicate linen.

At the door, he stopped, shook his head.

"Say, are we having company or something?" he asked.

Linda and Dave looked at him and smiled.

"Not that I know of," Linda smiled.

"Then why is everything so ritzy-looking?" Marty murmured. "Isn't today Saturday?"

"That's right," Dave replied. Marty noticed that he was reading the business section of the morning paper.

"Aren't you working this morning, Dave?"

"Sure. I always work on Saturdays."

"At Burger King?"

Dave laughed.

"What, are you hungover or something?" he asked.

"No. I just don't understand the fancy suit."

Dave looked at him, obviously confused. "Are you all right, Marty?" he asked.

"Yeah. Are *you* guys all right?"

"Sure. Never better." Noticing Marty's envelope, he reached out his hand. "Here," he said. "Let me take that— I'll mail it from the office."

Marty released the envelope and sat at the table. A bowl of fresh strawberries was waiting for him.

"I still don't get it," he muttered. "Strawberries . . . eggs Benedict. We never used to eat that kind of stuff. It was just cereal and toast with a paper towel for napkins. What's going on?"

Halfway through his strawberries, he heard his parents' voices from the hallway. Their conversation was light and happy-sounding, the two of them just having come in from outside.

"Where were they, anyway?" Marty asked.

"Same as always," Dave replied. "Tennis at the club."

"Tennis? Dad and Mom don't play tennis."

"Then that explains why they've been club doubles champions for six years," Linda said archly.

"I can't believe it."

"Where *have* you been?" Linda demanded.

Marty was seriously considering telling her when his folks walked in the room. Their appearance was quite a shock to Marty. Both looked tanned and healthy in their tennis outfits, but the transformation was far deeper than that. George McFly radiated confidence and self-esteem while Lorraine was thin and dynamic-looking.

Marty's jaw fell.

"What's the matter, son?" George McFly asked.

"Mom! Dad!" he said. "You look—great!"

"Why, thank you, Marty," Lorraine smiled.

"What can he want?" Linda said. "He's already got everything."

His parents eyed him quizzically.

"I don't want anything," Marty said. "It's a great present,

just seeing how terrific you look."

"Wow," Dave laughed.

His mother put her hand on Marty's shoulder. "Well," she said. "Tonight's the big night, isn't it?"

Marty looked at her blankly.

"Isn't tonight your big date with Jennifer Parker?" Lorraine asked. "She's such a nice girl. I really like her a lot."

Marty could hardly believe this was his mother talking, even taking the physical transformation into account. Could this be the same woman who continually bad-mouthed Jennifer? Obviously not.

"Pardon me, Ma?" he muttered.

"You're going up to the lake tonight, aren't you? Just the two of you. Haven't you been planning it for two weeks?"

"Mom, we went through this last night," Marty replied. "How can I go if Dad's car is wrecked?"

"Wrecked?" Dad said.

"He's been like this all morning," Dave explained. "It's like he went to bed and woke up in a different house with strange people."

That indeed was the case but Marty didn't say so. Instead he murmured: "I'm sorry. I . . . thought the car . . . was wrecked. You lent it to Biff Tannen and he ran into somebody with it."

Dad chuckled. "Well, there's nothing wrong with the car that I can see. In fact, Biff is out there waxing it right now."

Marty got up, walked to the kitchen window and looked out. There in the driveway was a sparkling new BMW. Next to it stood Biff Tannen, polishing diligently. His expression also seemed subtly altered, devoid of the usual arrogance and belligerence. As he worked, he whistled a happy tune.

"Jeez," Marty murmured. To himself he said: "What a difference a belt in the chops can make."

His father opened the kitchen window and called out to Biff. His tone was pleasant but firm. "Hey, Biff," he said.

"Don't forget—two coats of wax this time. Your job last week was a little sloppy."

"Yessir!" Biff replied in a voice that was friendly and eager to please. "You're the boss, sir!"

"Don't be dictatorial, George," Lorraine cautioned, smiling at her husband. Despite the warning, it was obvious she adored him.

George shrugged. "Sorry," he said. "I don't mean to sound that way. It's just that some employees will try to get away with murder if you don't stay on 'em. I've had to keep Biff in line ever since high school." Then he added with a smile: "Although if it hadn't been for Biff, your mother and I never would have met."

"Yeah, Dad," Linda interrupted. "You've told us a million times already. You beat him up when he was bothering Mom and that's how the two of you fell in love."

"It was more than that," Lorraine added. "Your father literally came to my rescue." She sighed. "It was so romantic..."

"Cornball city," Linda said, rolling her eyes.

"Whatever happened to the other guy?" Marty asked.

"What other guy?" his father asked.

"The guy I was named after."

"Oh," Lorraine murmured. "We never saw him again. He vanished into thin air." Then, looking at Marty closely, she said: "I don't remember ever telling you about him."

"Well, you must have. Otherwise I wouldn't have known, would I?"

"No..."

Biff entered a moment later and handed George a hardcover book.

"Oh, Mr. McFly," he said. "This just came in."

"Good," George nodded.

He held up the book, which was entitled *A Match Made In Space*. The art work showed a bedroom with a space alien very reminiscent of Marty's Darth Vader speaking to a young man cowering beneath the covers. The author's name, in large letters, was George McFly.

"Holy cow," Marty said. "You wrote that, Dad?"

George nodded proudly. "My first novel," he said. "I sure hope it sells."

"Of course it'll sell," Lorraine gushed. "After all, it's not like you're a nobody. You've been selling stories ever since college."

"That's right, Dad," Dave added. "You're the one who's always telling us to have confidence and a positive attitude. Where's yours now?"

"You're right," George said. "I'm sure this book is going to do just fine."

Then, turning to Marty, he put a strong hand on his shoulder and said: "And that tape of yours is going to do just fine, too."

"I hope you're right," Marty muttered, suddenly thrust back to his 1985 cares and aspirations.

"Marty," George said, "haven't I always told you that all it takes is a little self-confidence? If you put your mind to it, you can do anything."

Biff, standing with a deferential smile during the previous conversation, took advantage of the silence to thrust a hand toward Marty. "Oh, Marty," he said. "Here's your keys. You're all waxed and ready for tonight."

"My keys?" Marty stammered.

Biff nodded. "I put it in the garage," he said. "Just in case it rains."

Turning and racing to the garage, Marty gasped with amazement when he opened the door. There sat a tricked out black Toyota SR5 truck, as shining and beautiful as when it sat on the showroom floor. Only now it was his!

He ran to it, got inside and caressed the upholstery, gear shift, every switch and dial within reach. Opening the garage door, he was all ready to take a spin when he heard a familiar voice.

"How about a ride, mister?"

It was Jennifer, standing on the parking pad, looking as gorgeous as ever.

"Jen!" he cried. "Are you ever a sight for sore eyes! Let me look at you!"

Jennifer was somewhat taken aback by the unexpected display of emotion. It wasn't as if they had been separated for a long time, having seen each other only the evening before.

"Are you O.K.?" she asked. "You're acting like you haven't seen me in a year."

"I feel like I haven't seen you for thirty years," Marty smiled.

"That's a long time to be deprived," she smiled back.

He pulled her toward him and was about to kiss her when he suddenly felt a rush of electricity race through his body. Jennifer must have experienced it as well, for her hair crackled and literally stood on end for a few seconds.

"Holy—" Marty began.

A sonic boom drowned out the rest of his thought.

The source was Doc Brown's DeLorean, which roared up to the front of the house and came to a squealing stop. Inside sat Doc Brown, wearing a cowboy hat. When he got out of the car, it was possible to see that he was dressed in a bizarre mixture of clothing types that included striped plastic pants, a cape and strange variation on a Roman tunic.

His features agitated, Doc got right to the point.

"Marty," he said. "You've gotta come with me—back to the future!"

"Why?"

"It's important."

"But I've got Jennifer here," Marty said. "I was just gonna try out my new wheels."

"That can wait," Doc replied. "Anyway, you can bring her along. This concerns her, too."

Marty felt a strong surge of apprehension. "What do you mean?" he demanded. "Does something happen to her? To us? Do we turn into assholes or something?"

Doc Brown smiled. "No, you and Jennifer turn out fine," he said. "But your kids! Marty, something's gotta be done about your kids."

"Our kids?" Jennifer asked, her head swiveling between Marty and Doc Brown. "What kids? We aren't even engaged yet . . ."

"We'll explain later," Marty said. "Would you like to come along?"

"Along to where?" she asked.

"The future," Marty replied. "The year 2015 or thereabouts. I think that's where Doc was headed—"

"We better hurry," Doc said.

The two men looked at Jennifer.

"Sure," she said. "Why not?"

"O.K. Let's go," Doc said.

He lifted the gull-wing door and Marty got in. Jennifer sat on his lap. When Doc Brown jumped behind the steering wheel, Marty reached over to touch his arm.

"You'd better back this thing up, Doc," he cautioned. "We haven't got enough road to get up to eighty-eight."

"Where we're going, we don't use roads," Brown smiled.

He pointed to a new switch on the dashboard labeled MR. FUSION HOME ENERGY CENTER, hit it, and grinned with satisfaction as the DeLorean rolled about a hundred yards down the street, blasted off into the sky trailing a thin flume of silver smoke, and then disappeared.

Bestsellers you've been hearing about—and want to read

___	**E.T. THE BOOK OF THE GREEN PLANET**	07642-3-$3.50
	William Kotzwinkle	
___	**GOD EMPEROR OF DUNE**	08003-X-$3.95
	Frank Herbert	
___	**HERS THE KINGDOM**	08109-5-$3.95
	Shirley Streshinsky	
___	**FOR SPECIAL SERVICES**	05860-3-$3.50
	John Gardner	
___	**THE CASE OF LUCY BENDING**	07640-7-$3.95
	Lawrence Sanders	
___	**THE NEW ROGET'S THESAURUS**	07269-X-$2.95
	IN DICTIONARY FORM	
	ed. by Norman Lewis	
___	**FLOATING DRAGON**	06285-6-$3.95
	Peter Straub	
___	**STEPHEN KING'S DANSE MACABRE**	08110-9-$4.50
	Stephen King	
___	**SAVANNAH**	06829-3-$3.95
	Eugenia Price	
___	**ICEBREAKER**	06764-5-$3.50
	John Gardner	
___	**DANCEHALL**	08173-7-$3.95
	Bernard F. Connors	
___	**THE SEDUCTION OF PETER S.**	07019-0-$3.95
	Lawrence Sanders	
___	**A SHIELD OF ROSES**	07020-4-$3.95
	Mary Pershall	
___	**THE AUERBACH WILL**	07101-4-$3.95
	Stephen Birmingham	
___	**RED SQUARE**	08158-3-$3.95
	Edward Topol and Fridrikh Neznansky	
___	**DARKFALL**	07187-1-$3.95
	Dean R. Koontz	

Prices may be slightly higher in Canada.

Available at your local bookstore or return this form to:

B **BERKLEY**
Book Mailing Service
P.O. Box 690, Rockville Centre, NY 11571

Please send me the titles checked above. I enclose _____. Include 75¢ for postage and handling if one book is ordered; 25¢ per book for two or more not to exceed $1.75. California, Illinois, New York and Tennessee residents please add sales tax.

NAME_____

ADDRESS_____

CITY_____STATE/ZIP_____

(allow six weeks for delivery)   1D

49

The greatest space epic ever!

BattlestaR GALACTICA

___ **BATTLESTAR GALACTICA #1**
by Glen A. Larson and Robert Thurston   (07472-2) @ $2.50

___ **BATTLESTAR GALACTICA #2: THE CYLON DEATH MACHINE**
by Glen A. Larson and Robert Thurston   (07473-0) @ $2.50

___ **BATTLESTAR GALACTICA #3: THE TOMBS OF KOBOL**
by Glen A. Larson and Robert Thurston   (05523-X) @ $2.50

___ **BATTLESTAR GALACTICA #4: THE YOUNG WARRIORS**
by Glen A. Larson and Robert Thurston   (05353-9) @ $2.50

___ **BATTLESTAR GALACTICA #5: GALACTICA DISCOVERS EARTH**
by Glen A. Larson and Michael Resnick   (07476-5) @ $2.50

___ **BATTLESTAR GALACTICA #6: THE LIVING LEGEND**
by Glen A. Larson and Robert Thurston   (05249-4) @ $2.50

___ **BATTLESTAR GALACTICA #7: WAR OF THE GODS**
by Glen A. Larson and Michael Resnick   (05660-0) @ $2.50

___ **BATTLESTAR GALACTICA #8: GREETINGS FROM EARTH**
by Glen A. Larson and Ron Goulart   (07696-2) @ $2.75

___ **BATTLESTAR GALACTICA #9: EXPERIMENT IN TERRA**
by Glen A. Larson and Ron Goulart   (07574-5) @ $2.50

___ **BATTLESTAR GALACTICA #10: THE LONG PATROL**
by Glen A. Larson and Robert Thurston   (07105-7) @ $2.75

Prices may be slightly higher in Canada.

Available at your local bookstore or return this form to:

B **BERKLEY**
Ⓐ *Book Mailing Service*
P.O. Box 690, Rockville Centre, NY 11571

Please send me the titles checked above. I enclose _____ Include 75¢ for postage
and handling if one book is ordered; 25¢ per book for two or more not to exceed
$1.75. California, Illinois, New York and Tennessee residents please add sales tax.

NAME_____

ADDRESS_____

CITY_____STATE/ZIP_____

(Allow six weeks for delivery.)   **(BG) #14**

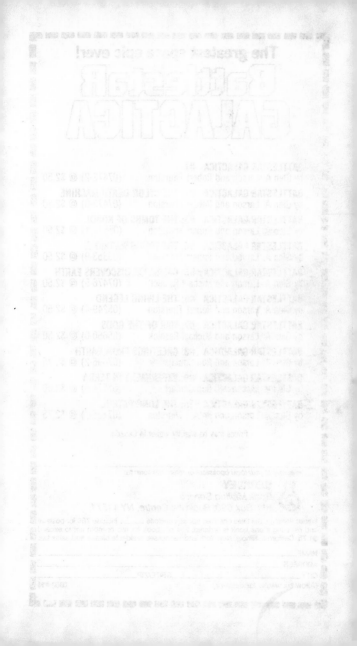

ATHENS REGIONAL LIBRARY SYSTEM

3 3207 00010 3350